Destined To Play

Indigo Bloome is married with two children. She has lived and worked in Sydney and the United Kingdom, with a successful career in the finance industry. Indigo recently traded city life with a move to regional Australia, which provided her with an opportunity to explore her previously undiscovered creative side. Her love of reading, deciphering dreams, stimulating conversation and the intrigue of the human mind led her to writing her first novel, *Destined to Play*.

Also by Indigo Bloome

Destined to Feel (*Second in the Avalon Series*)

Destined to Fly (*Third in the Avalon Series*)

Destined to
Play

Indigo Bloome

HARPER

Harper
An imprint of HarperCollins*Publishers*
77–85 Fulham Palace Road,
Hammersmith, London W6 8JB

www.harpercollins.co.uk

A Paperback Original 2012
4

A catalogue record for this book
is available from the British Library

ISBN: 978-0-00-749881-9

Set in Sabon

Find out more about HarperCollins and the environment at
www.harpercollins.co.uk/green

For my mum,
whose unconditional love,
support and nurturing since birth
has enabled me to live my dreams
many times over

Acknowledgements

THANK YOU...

To my mother, who encouraged me to continue when I wasn't sure if I should and who painstakingly edited material I know was shocking for her to read.

To my sister, without her bravery five years ago we wouldn't be living and sharing our dreams now.

To Melissa, whose door was thankfully left ajar enough for me to slip through in the knick of time.

To Rob, for pointing out that anyone who completes a manuscript, whether published or not, has achieved something very special.

To Adrienne, I can't wait to hug you and thank you in person for your inspiring and encourating words and for enabling me to move forward.

To Kate, who was going through so much and still found time to meet with me.

To my gorgeous, wonderful, special friends who bore the brunt of my first, raw version and didn't discard me as a friend.

To my boys, you know who you are and you know my life, or this novel, wouldn't be the same without you.

To my father, for his love, support, humour and storytelling.

To my husband, for being my rock for the past two decades and standing by me through thick and thin, when I know it hasn't always been the smoothest of rides.

To my family and my friends, my life would be meaningless without you...

Finally, it is just so important to thank my agent, Selwa Anthony and Shona Martyn from Harper Collins. This novel would never have been published had it not been for their miraculous and fateful meeting just a short time ago. Thank you, Selwa, for guiding me through a whirlwind introduction to the publishing industry. And a wholehearted thanks to the team at HarperCollins Australia, in particular Anna Valdinger, Rochelle Fernandez and Graeme Jones who worked around the clock to make this happen.

'Do you ever feel like you were destined to play?'

'Only in my dreams …'

Preface

If I had known then what I know now, would it be any different?

I'm not sure why or how my life changed so dramatically so fast, yet it continues as if nothing has changed at all. It began with one weekend that perhaps, in hindsight, should never have happened, but deep in my soul I have a vague nagging that it was always meant to be ...

This leaves me embroiled within a psychological and sexual tornado that landed without any advance warning or forecast — or maybe I just missed the signs? Either way, what has happened, has happened, what will be, will be. I just don't know how it will end, or whether I will survive the journey.

Part I

'No ordinary work done by a man is either as hard or as responsible as the work of a woman who is bringing up a family of small children; for upon her time and strength demands are made not only every hour of the day but often every hour of the night.'

— Theodore Roosevelt

I'm pretty sure I have everything organised for the family before I walk out the door.

Kids' bags packed.

Extra food prepared.

Outdoor gear organised.

Jordan and Elizabeth are going on their first wilderness expedition for a week with all the dads charged with helping out given the nature of outdoor activities they will be pursuing. Great idea from a mother's perspective, but we all know in our hearts we will miss them from the first night they are away. The kids were devastated when the expedition was almost cancelled due to a lack of funding and support for the Tasmanian Wilderness Foundation. Thankfully, some last-minute sponsorship from the Fathers4Kids program enabled the expedition to take place after all. The kids are so excited. Actually when I think about it Robert, my husband, seems more awakened and engaged by this adventure than I have seen him in years. Must have something to do with men and their exploring tendencies — the mysteriousness of the confounding thylacine providing the perfect avenue — or maybe he is just happy to be away from me. Either way, he's excited too and they haven't been able to sleep in anticipation of the great adventure traversing the west coast of Tasmania's wilderness in search of the elusive Tasmanian tiger.

I've decided to make the most of the children's absence from my life to complete a series of lectures I had been deferring for the last few months until the 'time felt right', so I'm preparing to fly to Sydney, Brisbane, Perth and Melbourne to deliver my latest findings to postgraduate students, academics and other professionals in their given field of expertise.

I now really need to focus on getting myself organised for the first lecture this afternoon in Sydney. Mentally, I go through my checklist — I have my notes, slides, discussion themes, workshop challenges, laptop and mobile phone, so all good. I am still fascinated by the research I have been conducting on visual stimulation and its impact on the development of perception and even now I find my mind wandering off and becoming lost in my work, considering a different spin on some of the provocative challenges I have developed for the lectures …

All of a sudden, I become intensely aware of butterflies in my stomach, so much so, I have to lean against the kitchen bench to steady myself. How strange; I never usually get nervous before giving lectures, quite the opposite, as I really enjoy it. The challenge of engaging new minds, intellects sparring with one another on a quest for deeper, broader knowledge — fantastic! But where on earth are these butterflies coming from?

I pause for a moment to investigate these feelings and attempt to locate their source, which might seem strange to some people, but it is something that has always intrigued me. They are more intense than usual, and it certainly isn't the lecture making me feel this way. Perhaps it is the trip away from family. No, it is not as if I haven't been away from them before, particularly for work purposes. I broaden my mindset to include the rest of the weekend when I stop suddenly — as my stomach flips again. I surprise myself as I instinctively inhale at the thought of my 5.00 p.m. meeting at the Hotel InterContinental with Jeremy.

Doctor Jeremy Quinn. My uni buddy, my best friend, the man who opened my eyes and my body to the world in ways I never considered possible. He knew me inside and out when we were younger and we shared an incredible array of experiences during our time together. It is hard to believe after all of our tomfoolery during many years at university, that Jeremy is now one of the most respected, pre-eminent medical research doctors in Australasia — I can't bring myself to say 'the world' because it's Jeremy, after all. He has just returned from presenting ground-breaking research at Harvard University with Emeritus Professor E. Applegate.

Jeremy always had a knack for pushing conventional boundaries and wisdom, continually searching for the unknown, the unexpected or unanticipated solutions to some of our most insurmountable medical problems. I even read in a newspaper article recently that he had been in meetings with none other than Melinda and Bill Gates in conjunction with his and Professor Applegate's research in New York. It seems as if he is certainly mixing it with the global movers and shakers. I suppose, on reflection, he always had the determination and potential to achieve mastery in his chosen field. It is amazing what he has achieved in less than forty years of life. He is an exceptionally gifted human being, intellectually and emotionally, and people just adore his company. No doubt all these traits, along with his hard work, have enabled the success he is now hopefully enjoying.

My career needs to fit in with my family life, well, the kids really; Jeremy's career is his life, more or less. He has always been tenacious about his quest for sourcing medical cures and has been involved in discoveries that the western world almost takes for granted these days. With that sort of personal motivation and drive, it's not surprising he hasn't had time to settle down or find anyone special to share his life with. At least I'm not aware of anyone. He has always attracted interest from the opposite sex, like a George Clooney of the medical world; he certainly doesn't suffer from lack of attention.

Anyway, that's what is making my stomach do flips, which is utterly ridiculous at my age. I allow myself a small smile as I find it mildly amusing I am still capable of that sort of fluttering teenage reaction. I am excited and a little nervous about seeing him after so long. The memories of our university days still flood my mind and haunt me whenever I'm alone and in a dark sensual mood, usually in the early hours of the morning ...

What is happening to me? I'm going to miss the plane if I don't get moving!

'Right, kids? Where are you? I need kisses and cuddles before I leave — I won't see you for ten whole days!' Big family hugs all round. I tell them I love them more than life itself and wish them a fabulous adventure in the wild west as they endeavour to track that elusive tiger; apparently legend has it there have been recent sightings. No doubt a camp of school kids is just what they need to be discovered again! However, the kids' excitement and optimism filters through regardless.

'And keep safe,' I declare, promising that I can't wait to hear every detail of their experience when I return.

I hear the honk of a horn indicating my taxi's arrival and do my last-minute check to ensure I have everything I need. I am thankful the butterflies have finally subsided. My lips barely touch my husband's cheek as I tell him to take excellent care of my children and ensure he keeps them safe. A fleeting thought passes through my brain wondering when our relationship became so plastic, so platonic ... I have too many things on my mind to delve further and quickly wish them all a wonderful adventure as he dutifully places my bag in the car and I wave goodbye, blowing kisses to the kids from my window as the taxi pulls out of the drive, airport bound.

* * *

Focus, focus, focus! I keep saying to myself to little avail. My mind is in a state of complete distraction today, which is highly unusual. I hear the captain speaking, good weather, clear flight path, not expecting any delays. Flight attendants are telling me to put my seat belt on and tray up for take-off as they do every flight. It's not like I don't know that for goodness' sake, I think, my irritation surprising me. But of course, I do what I'm told expeditiously as I don't want to cause a scene. I reluctantly put my notes away and close my eyes momentarily as the plane slowly manoeuvres toward the runway. I feel my chest rising and falling lightly with each breath. Jeremy's face flashes through my mind, his gorgeous cheeky smile and smoky green, seemingly bottomless eyes ... his lips gently kissing my neck ... his fingers lightly caressing my nipples ... then teasing them to life ...

What am I doing? I force my mind to a screeching stop. This is absurd. I force myself back to the here and now and suddenly notice we are in the air and the seat belt sign is off. I breathe a sigh of relief. Now, back to my lecture. I talk myself into believing I am disciplined enough not to let my mind wander off for another second.

I am good at being disciplined, I tell myself. I run an organised house, career and life overall. I love my family and my work and have studied long and hard to achieve what I have. Dr Alexandra Blake. I work between the business world and academia given my studies in both commerce and psychology. This combination has worked well for me financially and I am forever grateful that I am one of the lucky people in life who love their work and are passionate about what they do. Enough of self-talk and affirmations ... I need to think about the presentation today.

Once again, I ponder the topic of the lecture which I will be delivering to approximately 500 people in just a few hours' time. This fact finally snaps my mind to attention. I consider using some additional questions and challenges to open discussion and promote their thinking. I like the idea so I note down the following points on my notepad to use for the end of the session.

✤ How important is visual perception to your mindset?
✤ How much do you depend on visual stimulation to interpret your world?
✤ What senses do you believe would most compensate for a lack of visual perception? Why? How?

Given research shows that body language — a visual sense — accounts for more than 90 per cent of communication between people, the significance of these sorts of questions becomes exponential.

I'm feeling much calmer now that I am once again absorbed in my work. The rest of the flight goes smoothly and I arrive on time at the University of Sydney.

* * *

'Dr Blake, good morning, great to have you back.'

I look ahead and smile toward my PhD examiner, Samuel Webster. 'Well, good morning to you too, Professor; it's great to be back.'

'You know you are always welcome, Alexandra. It's been too long. It seems to be very difficult to draw you away from the south isle.'

'Hmm, on reflection, it's been a while. I guess time flies when you are having fun.'

'I'm glad to hear it. You have certainly been busy on the research front. We're looking forward to your lecture this afternoon.'

'And as ever, I'm looking forward to hearing your insights and expertise. Thank you so much for your support in bringing this together.'

'My pleasure, my dear, my pleasure. Do you have time for a quick lunch with some colleagues before you take centre stage?'

'For you, Samuel, always.' I smile again warmly as he leads me along the manicured lawns beside the beautiful, historic buildings. It feels good to be back.

At lunch with Samuel, I reflect on what an honour it was to have him oversee my PhD. He specialises in defensive (passive and aggressive) behaviours in the workforce and was instrumental in developing my thesis. His global connections both in the corporate world and academia are second to none and his knowledge is immense. He's recently been working hand in hand with the Brain and Mind Research Institute, which enables him to analyse many of his revolutionary hypotheses about behaviour and sexuality in the field of neuroscience. I find his work truly fascinating and being with him today allows me to see how passionate and absorbed he has become in this branch of his research.

I find myself reflecting just how much of an impact Samuel has had on my career. The support and the sage advice when it all became too hard, made me feel obliged to hang in there for both him and the future rewards. He drives his PhD students hard and wants no stone left unturned. I smile internally at those years of insanity and frustration, pleased I completed them and relieved they are behind me.

Samuel had offered me a senior lecturing position at Sydney University and was not happy when I turned it down for a similar role at the University of Tasmania. He taught me so much, I felt indebted to him, but he understood my reasons, that it was a lifestyle choice, particularly with a young family in tow. He promised he would stay in touch and support me both professionally and personally, and he has definitely been a man of his word. Samuel was instrumental in getting my research on visual perception off the ground and more recently became my chief academic sponsor, which is how I come to be presenting this lecture series today.

I'm touched that he has taken the time to introduce me to his team of, in his words, 'elite researchers', who appear to be hanging on his every word. I suppose I looked the same way when I was a new postgrad. Brad, Max, Denise and Elijah, all of whom are doing fascinating work within the world of psychology and neuroscience. It makes me feel alive, interacting with kindred folk again. It certainly isn't the type of discussion for the average dinner party. Very quickly the specifics of their research unfold and it would be remiss of me not to say I'm more than a little astounded by the path that follows. Given the calibre of people engaging in the impassioned discussion, the comments fly around the table almost too fast for me to assimilate.

'Even the source of the female orgasm is still to be scientifically determined, unlike the male orgasm which has been extensively funded, researched scientifically and agreed medically.'

'Basically, medical science continually refuses to acknowledge the physical reality of the female ejaculation and unfortunately it is not a priority. Lack of funding has impacted the ability to provide coherent education on the study of women's sexual behaviours. We are hoping to change that.'

'Even today, there is a notable disconnect between medicine and science in relation to the female orgasm, to the extent that the primary understanding of female ejaculation is still urinary stress incontinence.'

'Did you realise that no one has been able to medically agree on the source of the orgasm, whether it be uterine, clitoral, vaginal, vulval or a blend of any of these combinations? Even though this concept of the female orgasm has been recorded in literature throughout history?'

'The main problem being a distinct lack of participants able to generate orgasmic fluid in a clinical environment.'

'Nobody can agree on the most effective way to generate the female orgasm which in effect makes sourcing it extremely difficult.'

'The physical, emotional, hormonal and environmental states of the female all seem to play a significant role, but at this stage it is impossible to determine whether one plays a greater or lesser role than the other. The hypotheses are many and varied so we are now conducting more research on the neurological connections to help develop our theories further.'

My mind at this point envisions rows of women wearing white robes all lined up in hospital beds with legs spread open attempting to generate an orgasm to be captured in a test tube. I quickly shake my head to dislodge the disturbing image penetrating my brain. I notice I have barely touched my lunch; I'm so caught up in the flow of the discussion.

Samuel eventually concludes: 'As you can see, my dear Alexandra, there is much more to understand and discover regarding the intricacies of the female orgasm, including the impact of intellectual and emotional components. The research is still highly subjective, personal and seemingly dependent on each woman's individual experience of orgasm. We can only aspire to develop a more consistent approach regarding our research and conclusions.'

I can't help but be enthralled with the history and mystery that seemingly surrounds this subject. I had no idea the topic was still so contested medically and in some areas considered career and research 'taboo', for want of a better word. How it is possible that the female orgasm is so under-researched, when the male orgasm is considered scientifically and psychologically a fait accompli is frankly shocking to me, to say the least. I can't quite believe what I'm hearing, and indeed wouldn't have had it not come from the mouths of the people seated around the table. I manage to quickly swallow a few mouthfuls of food before Samuel and his crew wish me luck as we pack up and make our way toward the lecture theatre.

'Would you care to join us for a Friday night drink, for old times' sake? I'm sure the team would love to share some of the insights of their research so far.' Samuel has a twinkle in his eye as I feel my cheeks flush a pale pink.

'You know I'd love to, but unfortunately I have other plans for after the lecture.'

'Of course you have, my dear, one can only ask.'

For some reason, a nervous laugh escapes me, as if I've been caught off-guard.

'I'm actually meeting an old friend from my undergrad days; you may remember him. Jeremy Quinn?' I try very hard to keep my tone neutral — difficult when the mere mention of his name makes my heartbeat quicken.

'Yes, indeed I do. Dr Quinn is taking the medical world by storm I hear, causing all sorts of waves and excitement in the US in connection to his research on depression. He's working with Professor Applegate, is he not?'

I should have known Samuel would be more up to speed than I was in relation to what's hot in global academia.

'I believe so, albeit from an article, not from him personally.'

'Send him my best regards. A very talented man, that Dr Quinn. No doubt there will be many a pharmaceutical company keen for his research. He certainly won't have any of the funding concerns that constrain us, lucky chap.'

I'm not sure I fully comprehend this connection as my mind automatically shifts into gear for the lecture just moments away.

'Will do and thanks for everything, Samuel. It's been wonderful catching up with you again. I wish you and your team the very best. Let me know if I can be of any assistance.'

Suddenly, given the discussion at lunch, I wasn't one hundred per cent sure whether that was an appropriate comment or not!

'Indeed my dear. Go forth and conquer.' We hug farewell and I head to the lectern for my imminent presentation.

* * *

What a beautiful Friday afternoon in Sydney, everyone basking in glorious sunshine. This city can really turn it on when it needs to. The harbour is sparkling with yachts and ferries merrily bouncing along, the colours are sharp and bold and the city is bustling. Office workers are gearing up for the weekend with such a vibrant beginning, as they head off to drinks along the harbour foreshore. I see some 'beautiful people' bouncing along for cocktails, laughing and smiling with a buoyant swing in their step. They look like they have just stepped out of *Vogue* magazine. I remember when I was one of those girls, focusing on career but as carefree as the wind, with the luxury of time and whispers of what the future might hold caressing every interaction. The main priority occupying our minds then was wondering how the weekend would unfold from twilight onwards and which cocktail to choose first.

It was on one of those nights that my relationship with Jeremy transformed from best friends constantly mucking around with each other to a high-octane sexual one. As the taxi drives past the key visual triggers where it all started in the city, I can't help but remember the carnal lust and intensity we shared; the impact of such memories makes me squirm in my seat.

Back then, I had just started vacation work with one of the big four banks in the city. The job wasn't that exciting but the people were fun and it provided me with some much-needed cash during the summer holidays. It was great to be free from study for a few months and I was secretly thrilled to be wearing a suit and high heels, and mum had bought me a sensational new handbag, which I still have today ...

'Hi, Jeremy, I'm just going out to my first official corporate work function—'

'Yeah, I'm excited. I'll be at the Wentworth and will be meeting the girls at nine-ish for a drink and a boogie.'

'Sure, grab them and come along. We'll meet you there.'

'No worries. Cool. See you later then.'

I hang up the phone.

He seems really keen to catch up with us all. Hmm, I think secretly, I wonder if he likes Eloise, most guys do ... maybe I should mention something ... The girls think she is going through a phase of exploring the other side, i.e. chicks, but we haven't been able to confirm or deny the rumour ... I'm sure she'll tell us either way when she is ready. No, I confirm to myself, keep out of it, what will be, will be ...

These corporate functions are cool because you get free food and drinks. We stay for a while, then decide it is time for our real Friday night to begin. We pack up and head to the club, where it's straight to the ladies room to discard jackets, our pantyhose, undo a few buttons, plump up our cleavage, puff our hair, reapply mascara, eyeliner and lipstick. We reappear audacious and revamped, ready to embrace the evening.

The music is pumping and given we have already had a few sparkling wines, we hit the dance floor — as only a group of girls can do. I'm lost in the music, dancing with my eyes closed, when strong hands grasp my hips and pull me backward toward their body. Instinctively, I know Jeremy has arrived and happily gyrate into his swivelling hips in time to the music. For some reason, we are in complete sync on the dance floor, our bodies are moving as one. It's hard not to get lost in the feel of his body against mine, the pounding music creating a heady atmosphere around us. This is hot with a capital H! I almost feel as if I am magnetically drawn to him; some strange pent-up energy between us makes me unwilling to let him go … Something has shifted between us as I look into his darkened eyes, utterly mesmerised by the intensity of his being. What is wrong with me tonight? My hormones seem to be locked in lust overdrive.

The music is too loud to hear his words, so he grabs my hand and leads me in a determined path off the dance floor to one of the shadowed corners of the club where the music is slightly muffled. He pushes me gently back against the wall and places his hands either side of my shoulders, his presence pinioning me against the wall. In his fitted black shirt, his body looks toned and hot and his face is glistening, close to mine, due to our heroics on the dance floor. It takes me a moment to catch my breath as I allow myself to become lost in his seductive presence. It is as if my eyes have been opened for the first time as his sexual magnetism overwhelms and draws me in. I open my mouth slightly to ensure enough oxygen is getting to my brain.

'I don't think I can keep my hands off you any more, AB.'

He honestly looks like he is pushing his hands harder into the wall to keep them away from me.

'Then don't.' Emboldened by this swelling of lust and desire, I'm sure I must be producing alluring sexual pheromones.

I pull his right palm off the wall, bring it to my lips, give his middle finger a gentle kiss and slowly slide it over my breast. His eyes widen as I continue its journey lower until it finds the secret passage under my skirt. I part my legs slightly, never breaking eye contact, and slide his finger past my knickers and lead him directly to my sweet spot.

'Jesus, Alex, you are so wet.'

'Hmm. I am. Do you have a solution for my problem?'

The shock on Jeremy's face is truly priceless and I have to admit, I never expected those words to leave my mouth, but they're out now. We are both a little stunned as we continue to silently question each other to ascertain a true sense of this new reality.

Seemingly compelled to action, Jeremy immediately removes his hand leaving a draft in his wake, grabs my wrist and strides so fast back toward our friends, I am almost stumbling along behind him. I hope I haven't offended him … maybe I shouldn't have said that …

He stops suddenly and I slam into his body. Jeez!

He grabs my handbag, marches straight to the dance floor and shouts something in my friend's ear, so she waves and smiles at me. I raise my eyebrows at her and shrug my shoulders as I give her a wave before I am just as suddenly whisked away and out the front door of the club.

'What are we doing?'

No response. Jeremy is in action mode.

He readjusts his hand from my wrist to clasping his fingers through mine as we charge down the street. My ears are still ringing from the noise of the club.

'Are you not talking to me?' Maybe he is as mad as hell. Oh dear, what was I thinking? Maybe I've ruined our whole friendship.

We are striding uphill and I'm panting to keep up with him. We seem to be heading toward the botanical gardens. When we reach grass, he swoops down, lifts me over his shoulder and walks silently under the moonlight before depositing me in a standing position under a particularly large tree. He drops my handbag to the ground, immediately cupping my face with his hands and devouring my mouth with such ferocity I'm forced up against the tree. His body anchors me in position and I'm wild with lust for him. He pulls a condom out of his pocket, unbuttons his jeans in record time, slides it on ... this is the first time I have seen Jeremy's penis and even though it is dark, what a sight. His eyes have returned from their carnal state when he registers my look with a mischievous grin.

'Ready?'

I nod in greedy agreement.

He hitches my skirt up to my waist, lowers my knickers to my feet, bending my knees to free them from underneath my shoes and stuffs them in his pocket ... Interesting, I can't help but think, kinky but interesting!

He hoists my legs up to wrap around his waist and I curl my arms tight around his neck with my back against the enormous trunk of the tree. It's rough and bark pokes into my satin blouse. I briefly hope that it doesn't rip the fabric but realise at this point, I don't care either way. He pauses before I nod again, confirming that I am more than ready for this, beyond ready, as if we have been teasing and tantalising and playing with each other platonically for far too long. The sexual electricity between us needs to explode in order for it to begin — confirming that we both need this and we need it NOW.

He slams into me.

And it is glorious!

And he does it again ...

And it is more glorious ...

And again!

And again!

He impales me.

And I am loving it.

I stare up at the moon and release my howl in honour of its magnificence, of our magnificence. He explodes inside me as our carnal desire for each other is finally given physical recognition.

Could anyone see us? Did anyone see us? Do I care ...

We lay on the grass for hours with each other, wondering at each other, talking and playing and laughing and teasing. Until the night lightens and dawn breaks. It's as if we have been in a void of time. We stumble into a taxi together; I fall asleep on his shoulder and find myself tucked in my bed a few hours later. My first time with Jeremy is confirmed to be a reality and not a dream by the twigs in my hair and grass stains on my shirt. My knickers apparently never made it home ...

I let out a sigh. Wow! I'm sure I am flushing and I know I'm wriggling around in my seat. I'm glad the driver hasn't noticed. I smile to myself at the distant, delicious memory. I haven't felt like this for years, well, probably since the last time I saw Jeremy alone. The fun days and carefree nights, no responsibilities — although we thought we had them at the time — no kids, no house, no mortgage ... Would I honestly want life to be any different from what it is now? Not really, a bit more fun and carefree every now and then wouldn't go astray, but I am reasonably happy with my life as it is now. Not my sex life admittedly, which has been less than average since Jordan was born, or pretty well non-existent if I'm perfectly honest. That thought is a shock. How have I missed this? Have I been too busy in life to notice this key element has gone missing? Isn't it even more concerning that I haven't considered it an issue? No wonder I'm sitting in the back of a taxi in a state of latent, lustful desire. A vision enters my mind of sleeping beauty awaiting her sexual awakening after decades of sleep, which is quite sweet until I realise her face is mine and the prince is Jeremy. But the kids, remember the kids ... Would it be worth the risk? I resolutely block my mind from receiving any more of these unproductive thoughts.

It feels good having the first lecture successfully behind me. The feedback and questions have given me more food for thought in respect to further investigative and academic research. I think ahead to my weekend. Catching up with my old school friends over a glass of wine, their careers, their social lives and family news. Who's still with whom, who has moved on, and I'm sure there are a few more babies I have missed since being based in Tasmania. Then catching up with my siblings and nieces and nephews for a BBQ on Sunday. It's a shame

Jordan and Elizabeth won't be there, as they love catching up with their cousins, but next time perhaps.

With my trip down memory lane and thoughts about the weekend ahead, I'm a little surprised how quickly we have arrived at the destination. I quickly check my lipstick and hair and decide I will definitely need to refresh in the hotel lobby. As I pay the taxi driver, the butterflies previously asleep in my stomach announce their tumultuous arrival and my palms moisten as I gather my bags together.

That memory has certainly destabilised me more than I would have liked. Stay calm and composed, you are a professional, married woman, a mother of two ... Enough with the self-talk!

I head straight through the lobby of the five-star hotel to the ladies room in an attempt to stabilise my stomach. What is going on with me today? I shake my head and try to pull myself together. The tingle down below is certainly not helping to calm my nerves nor my ability to control my physiology. Quite frustrating to say the least. How is it that I felt perfectly comfortable lecturing to hundreds of people just hours ago, yet now my fingers are trembling so badly that I can barely unwind my lipstick?

I gaze into the mirror while both hands grip the basin. I notice the slight wrinkles around my eyes. Were they there last time I saw Jeremy? Maybe I should have taken my friend's advice and given Botox a try, in her words 'before it's too late!' I shudder at the thought of it. I can't stand anything around my eyes let alone the idea of an injection piercing through such sensitive skin. Oh well, I think to myself, I'll just have to put up with what I see in the mirror until they come up with something a little less invasive.

Distracted and flustered, I can't decide whether to leave my hair up or take it out. I'm grateful my hair is still dark and as yet I haven't managed to find a random grey strand, although I'm sure that day isn't far off. I figure I will stay with the more professional look and leave it up; I am in a suit after all. Right, all ready to go, or at least as ready as I will ever be. Not too bad for thirty-six. I take a final glance in the mirror, and think it could certainly be worse, as I desperately search for a positive spin. Deep down, I am very much looking forward to catching up with Jeremy. So I let myself run with that emotion as my mind takes me on another quick trip down memory lane …

Jeremy and I were at university together, although he was two years ahead of me. My cousin introduced us during my first year, as they were both in the same water polo team. I'm not absolutely sure how our acquaintance evolved but he was a lot of fun and as we spent more and more time together we eventually became best friends, almost by default. As time went by we explored drinking, drugs and sex — as many uni students do. Partners came and went throughout our years of study but we were always there for each other, first and foremost. It was difficult for people to describe, let alone determine, our relationship with each other, more than likely because it was also impossible for us. After a while, our friends didn't bother to try and label us and just accepted that Jeremy and I would be friends forever, whatever came our way. Funnily enough, over time, we eventually accepted it too …

Life took us in different directions post-university. Jeremy continued his studies before getting his pilot's licence and joining the flying doctor service for a truly Australian outback experience, which he loved and I was always a little jealous of (the pilot's licence anyway). I worked in London focusing on building strong financial foundations before further exploring psychology in the workplace.

22

We caught up in various locations around the globe over the next decade, particularly in Europe where his medical research brought him regularly to London. We had many short fun-filled flings that are treasured memories, before we embarked on the serious responsibilities of life. Although we knew our relationship was significant in our lives, we understood that it would never be long-term, or at least I knew that Jeremy was far from ready to settle down, unlike me. It was the 'unspoken word' between us, although, deep down, we knew it to be a fully acknowledged reality.

His career was of paramount importance to him and I desperately wanted to start a family and our differing worlds drifted apart. Jeremy was offered a lucrative research scholarship at Harvard to further his studies and moved to America. I met my English husband, Robert, in London and we returned together to Australia. I knew I needed to put my explicit sexual past with Jeremy behind me and settle down to start a family and pursue my career academically. Which is exactly what I did.

Although we caught up for the odd dinner here and there, for the next decade or so, we were essentially on opposite sides of the planet. And our lives continued separately ...

I pull my mind back to the here and now and tell myself firmly that camping out in the ladies is just wasting the precious time we will have together — *so get moving!* I take a deep breath to calm my nerves, straighten my shoulders, hold my head high, swing open the door and walk confidently out toward the man who is my best friend and my ex-lover.

As my eyes sweep the lobby bar, my confidence evaporates as quickly as it had been conjured up — he is not here. Disappointment washes over me with such ferocity, I have to lower my hand to the lounge to maintain my standing position. *Typical*, I think to myself; I started the day with butterflies and ridiculous thoughts, like a teenager anticipating seeing their ultimate pop idol for the first time, and ended it talking to myself in the ladies room of a flash hotel.

I do know how hectic Jeremy's life is and that his schedule is ever-changing. Of course it would be highly unlikely for him to catch up with me just because we both happen to be coincidentally in Sydney this weekend. I am disappointed that I have wasted so much nervous energy for nothing, yet a part of me feels pleased that I am still able to feel those sensations when I had thought they were long gone. It serves me right really; I should have stayed and had drinks with Samuel and his colleagues. But I eagerly declined knowing I would be meeting with Jeremy and didn't want to be late.

Jeremy's assistant had said he would be caught up in meetings most of the afternoon. Just as I think to check my phone for messages, a man in uniform with a concierge badge on approaches me.

'Excuse me. Doctor Alexandra Blake?'

'Oh. Yes.'

'A gentleman asked me to pass this message on to you and convey his sincere apologies that he is unable to meet you here.'

My heart sinks as my fears are now confirmed; he can't make it. Disappointment washes over me all over again.

He hands me an envelope. 'Thank you very much, Doctor Blake. If there is anything I can help you with, please don't hesitate to ask.'

I smile as much to myself as to the concierge. Jeremy always insisted on calling me 'Doctor' once I graduated with my PhD, even though he is the true medical doctor and I am the philosophical kind. He knows I'm not good at medical emergencies and have an inherent fear of hospitals, so it was always a joke between us.

I take a seat on the velvet lounge and open the envelope to pull out the typed note inside:

To my dearest friend, Doctor A. Blake,

My sincere apologies for leaving you stranded in the hotel lobby this Friday evening. I had a few unavoidable errands come up at the last minute, which have caused some delays. Everything seems to be in order now and I would very much appreciate you joining me upstairs for a drink. It has been too long!

Please find the security key for the penthouse floor in the envelope.

I eagerly anticipate your arrival.

Love,

J. xo

My stomach flips and turns like a gymnast competing for the Olympic gold medal. Once again I am instantly transformed into a teenage groupie — he is here after all! But what is he doing in the penthouse? The Jeremy I knew always shunned the flashier side of life, preferring to maintain a more austere public persona. Although, if I remember rightly, when surrounded by those who knew him well, he could certainly relax into a mischievous rebel at times, enjoying the finer things life had to offer. Perhaps Samuel's comments weren't misguided when mentioning the bottomless funding of pharmaceutical companies. I can only wonder if the Jeremy of old still exists in the Jeremy of now.

As I gather myself together both mentally and physically, I notice the concierge still hovering in the background — *does he have nothing better to do?* The thought randomly floats through my brain.

'Is everything in order, Doctor Blake, can I help in any way?'

I wonder what expression I have on my face as I turn to look at him. I notice the faintest of smiles at the corner of his mouth, his eyes twinkling. Dumbfounded, I shake my head. 'No, thank you, I'm fine.'

Was I? I am beginning to wonder. He continues to loiter behind me. I change my mind and turn to him.

'Actually, yes. Could you please show me the way to the lift for the penthouse?'

'Of course, Doctor Blake, it would be my pleasure. Right this way and may I take your bags?'

He says it in a way that makes me think he is in on something I don't quite comprehend, and a strange feeling passes through me. Perhaps I'm just not up to speed on the service at five-star hotels these days. Knowing I'm not feeling exactly normal at this point, I push the thought out of my head and conclude that my mind could easily be playing tricks on me.

'Thank you, that would be lovely,' I say politely, and follow him as he leads the way to the lift with my bags in tow.

Seconds later the lift is racing rapidly toward the lofty heights of the penthouse floor. I take a few deep breaths in an attempt to calm my nerves. What a wonderful idea to have a drink while overlooking the city as twilight descends, always a spectacular view with weather like today. I'm not sure if Jeremy is staying in the hotel, but if he has access to the business lounge we may be able to have complimentary nibbles and drinks. Strange how the concept of free drinks still resonates with me, must be left over from uni days … I let out a little chuckle. The concierge must think I'm crazy.

As the doors open, I realise I am genuinely excited about seeing Jeremy; he is an amazing man and a truly great friend. The disappointment of believing he couldn't meet me had hit me harder than I ever imagined possible. Now I feel happy, excited and very much looking forward to a wonderful heartfelt reunion as only best friends can.

I am assaulted by the magnificent views in front me as I step out of the lift and into a carpeted room with floor-to-ceiling windows — I had forgotten how truly captivating Sydney Harbour is from these spectacular heights. I take a moment to absorb the visual feast before my eyes. Sparkling blue water with tiny white flecks. Ferries and yachts curve arching ripples across the silky water, and the buildings imbued with a rosy glow, reflecting the light of the sinking sun. Looking around to orientate myself, it seems strange I can't see any bar on this level.

'This way please, Doctor.' I almost forget the concierge is standing beside me with my bag. I check the security card and notice the symbol on it matches the one the wall. I follow the arrows with my eyes as we walk in silence. Finally I find myself standing tentatively in front of large double doors. Before either of us have a moment to press the buzzer, the door flies open in front of us. And standing before me is Jeremy. More sophisticatedly handsome than I had dared allow myself to remember.

'Hey AB, there you are. Welcome.'

'Hi,' I respond, fairly quietly, almost shyly. 'It's been a while.'

27

'I see Roger found you in the lobby. Thanks for taking care of her for me. I'll take it from here, cheers.' He takes my bag from the concierge and ushers me in, closing the door behind me.

'You're right; it has been too long, way too long in my opinion.' He excitedly wraps his arms around me, almost lifting me off the floor in an all-embracing hug, his eyes twinkling all the while.

'Let me look at you.' He holds me at arm's length and his eyes absorb my face, my hair, my body, my legs, right down to my toes. I had forgotten how penetrating his stare could be and it catches me unawares, leaving me suddenly feeling utterly self-conscious. I quickly look away to avoid seeing any further analysis.

'You look wonderful, Alex, still my young green-eyed Catherine Zeta-Jones,' he says intently, this time embracing me softly, lightly kissing my forehead, as if giving me his stamp of approval.

'And you aren't looking too bad yourself given you're almost forty, Dr Quinn,' I say cheekily, needing to immediately lighten the mood, both because of his possessive words and the intense emotions rushing through my body.

I don't trust myself to fully absorb his appearance but at first glance it doesn't look like much has changed over the years, except a little salt gently peppering his dark hair. Still confident, toned, mischievous ... he does look good. If I'm really honest he looks great, actually; broad, square shoulders, six foot two inches tall, clean shaven. He smells beautiful. It has been many years since I have been this intimate with his spicy, outdoorsy scent but the cloud of arousal it stirs up penetrates deep within my core; his tight round arse looks sensational in his causal trousers. Dear god, I am in sensory overload and I have just arrived ... *Stop it! Look somewhere else*, I scream internally as I command my eyes to slide off his body to the broader environment.

'Wow, this place is amazing. Are you staying here?'

'Yes, indeed I am. I'm here for the week.'

'Well, you have certainly moved up in the world, my friend.' He shrugs his shoulders and grins sheepishly. I love that smile. I love those lips. I love those lips on my breasts. God! *Stop this, now*.

'Come on in. Relax, please make yourself at home.' Jeremy leads me to the lounge room, obviously sensing I'm far from relaxed. Working myself into a right state would be more accurate.

'I thought we were meeting at a penthouse bar for a drink. I wasn't expecting to be in your suite.' I try to keep my voice conversational, tempering my rising level of anxiety.

'Does that cause you any concern?' he asks directly.

'Ah, oh, no.' I stumble the words out. 'No, not at all.' *Should it?* I think to myself.

'Good.'

I hear the pop of a cork, which startles me a little, and Jeremy pours me a glass of champagne. It is perfectly chilled and the bubbles within the crystal glass provide me with a visual representation of how my stomach has been feeling most of the day.

'Cheers, Doctor Blake. I've missed you, my friend, my confidante.'

My heart skips a beat as he utters these words, my mind comprehending the emotional depth attached to them.

'Cheers to you too, Dr Quinn.' We clink our glasses together as our eyes capture one another's gaze for the first time in a very long time.

'How are you, Jeremy? How is your life going? Have you met anyone? Are you enjoying the US? And what about work, you sound so busy with everything ...' God, I can't stop myself blathering! He laughs as he raises his hand to interrupt my inquisition.

'You've never been short of a question, Alexa, have you?' He raises one eyebrow and pauses. 'I suppose some things never change.' His comment is teasing and laced with innuendo.

His look is direct, though somewhat mischievous at the same time. I shuffle uncomfortably at the intensity of his stare and the weight I assume is behind his words. I wish I could read his facial expressions more clearly but as we haven't seen each other for so long, they are unfortunately too masked for me to decipher at this point.

'It's just that there is always so much to catch up on in the time we have. I don't want to miss anything, don't want to waste our conversation,' I reply in my defence.

'We won't, I promise you. Now drink up.'

I notice I still haven't touched my champagne. We both sip a mouthful of the golden bubbles at the same time. It tastes so delicious, initially dry with a sweet aftertaste and I feel the bubbles pop on my tongue. I can't help but take another.

'Now, before I attempt to answer your myriad questions, tell me, what are your plans for this weekend? Who has the pleasure of your company?'

Happy to ease back into conversation, I comfortably rattle off the details of my weekend, particularly as he knows most of the people I am seeing. I tell him about Robert and the kids being away on their great adventure and about my catching up with Samuel at the university, my family and my old school friends. He listens attentively, without interrupting, and I barely notice as he refills my glass. I can't say whether it is nerves or excitement that keeps my chatter going and the champagne flowing.

'Enough about me.' I realise Jeremy hasn't spoken in some time and we have plenty to discuss other than my plans for the weekend. I stop to look at him more carefully and notice his tense expression. 'You're very quiet, Jeremy. Is there something wrong?'

He stands up and walks deliberately toward where I'm seated on the lounge. Silently, he squats on the floor ensuring he is looking directly into my eyes and places his hand on my stockinged knee. A mild electric current travels straight up my leg and I jerk at the sensation. The hint of a smile emerges on his face at my reaction, as if pleased he still has this impact, before it quickly disappears and he regains focus and control of the moment. I immediately blush, blending perfectly with the rose cushion at my back. There is no way he can't notice that I am practically beside myself at his touch. Completely embarrassed, I shift my body weight uneasily on the lounge, while his position is statuesque. My rising anxiety immediately prevents me from uttering a sound.

'Alexandra, I want to ask you something and I'm honestly not sure what you will say or how you'll react.'

It must be serious if he is using my full name.

He pauses, staring unrelentingly into my eyes.

'Which is unusual for me …' he muses.

He fixes both hands firmly on my knees, as if anchoring my feet to the ground lest I should fly away like a helium balloon. 'So, I'll just come straight out with it.'

I don't move an inch.

I do nothing except hold his gaze.

I concentrate on moderating my breathing.

I wait for him to continue.

'I would like you to stay the weekend here with me and cancel your other plans.' He pauses, looking at me from beneath his long, thick eyelashes. My heart literally skips a beat.

Or two. Or maybe three.

As his gaze intensifies, I become lost in his eyes.

Our shared, ancient memories come flooding back into my brain: flashes of university days, ridiculous pranks, lust and love and orgasms and sex, friendship, tears of laughter, tears of pain, experimentation, stolen moments. It was fun, it was edgy, exhilarating and exciting, and there seemed to be no other way with Jeremy.

The look in his eyes conveys all of that and more to me in a few long seconds. I never knew quite what was going to happen next with Jeremy and here I am, all these years later in the same situation. Albeit with very different life circumstances. Our silent dialogue continues dancing between us. Once again daring us to take a risk that would never be taken with anyone else, only each other.

My mind begins to race as fast as my heart. What if I did stay? Would it be the worst thing I could do? People always talk about living life to the fullest, expecting the unexpected … Wouldn't a weekend with Jeremy make me feel more alive than I have in years? Given the effect of his touch on my knee, I can only imagine how I would respond to, well, his touch on other parts of my body …

Finally, my motherly instinct anchors these abstract and fleeting thoughts so commonsense can prevail. My children. My life isn't just about me any more; there are consequences for my actions. The guilt … the betrayal … Robert …. My stomach is in knots. How can I feel such anticipation and remorse simultaneously? It doesn't make sense to me. My clinical mind quickly shifts a gear and makes a mental note to explore the psychology around such intense emotions and the resulting change in my physiology. My immediate situation renders my clinical experience redundant. God, what am I doing, thinking, feeling? Jeremy still has his hands on my knees as his eyes bore into my soul. Moments pass until, as if reading my thoughts, he releases his hold on my eyes and withdraws his touch, rising to step toward the panoramic view.

I immediately inhale as if I have been released from a spell. I must have been holding my breath for quite some time. As he continues to stare out toward the harbour, he says, in a bemused voice: 'Let me guess. You are currently analysing every angle of this situation.' He turns to look into my eyes once again before returning his gaze outward and nods, as if to confirm for himself that he is on the right track before continuing.

'You are weighing up the pros and cons of accepting my offer. One side of you is excited, enticed almost, about the possibilities of the experience, the other is fully grounded in the responsibilities of your existing life, giving rise to endless questions and what-if scenarios and which mean you need more time for consideration and reflection. Truly, Alex, it would take many lifetimes' worth of experience to answer your questions and even then, never reach a satisfactory conclusion. Am I right?' Once again, looking toward me for confirmation.

All I can do is nod my head in agreement. He is reading me like a book. Actually, if I'm truly honest about it, he is reading me better than I can read myself, which disturbs me no end. The accuracy of his words catches me off-guard, his summary both measured and precise. Am I that easy to read or does he really know me that well? I thought he would have forgotten over the years … but if I haven't, how could I naively assume he had? That is a truly scary consideration given my current predicament. He continues with his barrage of my presumed concerns.

'What about your family? Do you really want this? What will it mean if you stay? What would your friends think? How would you justify your decision? Could you live with yourself? And dare I say it, what would happen if you truly let yourself go, even if it were just for one weekend?'

I sit before him, embarrassed at the truth behind his take on my questions, by the depth of his knowledge of my thought processes. But I also know he isn't playing fair now and is deliberately pushing my personal boundaries.

His last question was the summation of many of our conversations throughout our relationship. He knows I put others before myself and always castigated me about it, particularly if I chose paths he could see ending badly for me. He always made me ponder the question of 'what if'? What if, just once, I didn't try to control or orchestrate myself and others, didn't play it safe? What if it was a good thing to not know what was going to happen next or how someone was going to feel about it? Could it still be worth the risk?

My immediate concerns were, unfortunately, way too easy to summarise given the moral dilemma I faced. The real issue for me is, in reality, quite simple — can I say no to Jeremy?

He is playing me well. I know it and he certainly knows it. Even though I try to erase any distinctive emotion, he can read my face intuitively, see through any mask I put on. His understated smirk causes me greater anxiety than the myriad other feelings I am filtering through my head.

My voice arrives quietly but firmly.

'That's really not fair, Jeremy. Do we have to have this conversation right now? Can't we just catch up and see how things go?' My voice trails off at these words. He knows I'm trying to hedge my bets and he can easily see through my attempted poker face, never a good position to be in with him. I unconsciously brace myself for our battle of minds, knowing that *my* brain is in a boxing ring with the right side fighting with the left, both deftly defending their position without understanding they are both on the same team — not helpful.

He walks slowly and deliberately away from the glass panels over to the champagne bucket, carefully picks up the bottle and walks back toward me. He silently notices my hands trembling as he slides his hand down along my fingers and removes the glass I'm holding, refills it and places it carefully on the side table next to the lounge. He kneels in front of me, holding both my hands in his and lets out a sigh. The power and presence emanating from him is in stark contrast to his apparently submissive position on the floor. I can barely breathe the air between us it is so thick with tension. I feel like a deer caught in headlights.

'Now Alex, listen to me, and please listen carefully.' His voice is slow, firm, commanding. 'You and I go a long way back and I want to spend the next forty-eight hours with you. I don't want to have a few drinks and have you disappear into the universe again.

'I know it has been tense between us since you arrived and that's because we're constrained by time. If we know we have two full days together, we will be able to really get to know each other again. Let it be just about us, no one else — just this once. It's important to me, Alex, I wouldn't ask if it wasn't. I don't want to argue with you, I don't want to scare you, I just need to know now that we will have this time together, time we haven't had for many years.'

My ears are ringing in confusion, as is my heart. The electric current running from his hand into mine lands straight between my legs, so much so, that I almost believe he can feel it.

He wraps his fingers around my wrists, his eyes pleading with mine. 'Please. Alex, I'm begging you ... forty-eight hours? Tell me you'll stay.'

My mind has gone AWOL. I can barely breathe, let alone speak. What is he doing to me? I have never heard him sound like this, so needy, so longing. I think to myself that maybe he is in some type of trouble or pain and needs to talk about it. My heart says, *Yes that's it, he is my best friend and he needs me*. Of course, I should have picked up on it before. Why else would he sound so beseeching? He probably doesn't have too many close friends he can talk to like he can with me, particularly given the pressure and responsibility of his job and research commitments. He *obviously* needs to talk otherwise he wouldn't be putting me in this situation. And here I am, contemplating not being there for my friend, my best friend, just when he needs me.

Needless to say, I lose the battle as my voice concurs with my heart's logic. And I hear myself say ever so softly, 'I suppose ... I could ...' I can barely get the words out of my constricted throat as they form an almost inaudible whisper.

But because Jeremy is still so close, he hears them. With eagerness written all over his face he asks, 'Did you say what I think you said?'

Is he really trying to make me say it again? It was hard enough the first time.

'I need to know you're committed. You have no idea how important this is to me.'

I take a deep breath.

'Yes, I will stay for the weekend,' I confirm, a little more clearly.

A smile instantly washes over his face as he releases my wrists, sweeps me off the lounge and embraces me tightly as he spins me around the room. I can't help but laugh as the tension vanishes between us.

'Thank you, Alexandra. You won't regret it, I promise.'

He excitedly reaches for the waiting glasses of champagne. 'Let's toast. To the next forty-eight hours.'

To which I can't help but think, *Oh dear*, but toast him nonetheless and allow the bubbles of the champagne to join their butterfly friends in my stomach.

Before I can come to terms with the reality of my agreement, he says, quick as a flash, 'Right. AB, where's your phone?'

Of course, I will need to let others know of my sudden change of plans, the forthcoming consequences to my family and friends finally dawning on me.

'What am I going to say? What will they think?' I am talking out loud as I fumble around in my congested handbag and locate my phone. Reservations once again creep into my thoughts. Am I doing the right thing? Was it a moment of weakness or desire that made me say yes? Undoubtedly both!

'Jeremy, maybe I shouldn't ... it's not right ...'

'No buts, no regrets, AB!'

Jeremy bounces right next to me on the lounge, as if sensing my apprehension and second thoughts. He snatches the phone out of my hand and strides to the other side of the room. The excitable puppy is turning panther-like with frightening ease and grace.

'Let me take care of that for you,' he says with a huge grin on his face.

He has completely regressed. Where is the distinguished, globally acknowledged and multi-award-winning medical research doctor? I am apparently back at uni with my cocky mate, still teasing and tormenting me.

'Please give it back.'

'Not on your life, sweetheart, you're mine for the weekend. You just said so yourself. Don't worry, I will send through a message on your behalf.'

I have no idea whether he is serious or not.

'I am more than capable of sending a message from my own phone.' I walk over to where he is standing, my hand outstretched, waiting. 'Give it to me, now.' My voice is stern as he ducks and weaves, manoeuvring himself away from me like a complete idiot.

'I need to call home. JEREMY!' I scream at him as he continues his childish movements around the room.

'No, you don't need to call home. You just told me they are in the wilderness, with no phone reception for the next week. There is absolutely no reason you need to call them or worry about it.'

So that explains the intense interest with which he was listening to my plans. I should have known he had an ulterior motive.

'Jeremy, stop mucking around.' Panic starts to permeate my voice as he runs into the bedroom closing the door behind him.

'This is *not* funny. Give me my damn phone, you bastard.' I furiously pound on the door he is obviously leaning against to keep me out.

'Ah, there's the feisty Alex I know. There's the spark I've been hoping for … Now, whom do we need to inform of your intriguing change of plans? Your brother. And Trish, she can then send to the others … oh, and Sally. That should just about do it, shouldn't it?'

'Jeremy, don't you dare!' I am seething.

He comes out from behind the door, ensuring I am well away from him as he reads out the message. Before I can respond, he presses Send.

'You didn't?' I gasp.

'There, you are officially mine for the next forty-eight hours.' He looks like the cat that swallowed the canary.

He then turns off my phone, walks over to the cupboard, opens the door, presses a code to open the safe while blocking my view, places the phone inside and promptly locks the door.

He spins around to see the look of absolute shock on my face.

'What the hell do you think you are doing?' I explode. 'I need to have that phone with me. Anything could happen.'

I feel as if he has temporarily disconnected me from my life. I realise that is exactly what he is hoping to achieve. I find it a very strange, weird sensation, being completely uncontactable.

'Explain to me, AB. Are you saying that the world won't survive with your phone switched off for a couple of days, or you won't?'

The tone of his voice and the look in his eyes clearly tells me that any arguments regarding this matter will be futile.

'Why are you doing this?'

'Simple. I'm being selfish. I know that you are always available to your family and friends and I have no intentions of sharing you with anyone else this weekend. That means no interruptions.'

I stare at him dumbfounded. 'When did you become so bossy and controlling?'

'I had a good teacher at university, and I've been practising for the past few years,' he says, winking at me.

As I move toward the cupboard, his octopus arms grab me around the waist and hoist me into the air before firmly depositing me on the lounge.

'I don't think so.' He is grinning now.

'We are not at uni now, Jeremy. I'm a grown woman, for god's sake!' I sound like a school teacher. He stands over me, eagerly anticipating my next move.

'Fine,' I say, folding my arms across my chest, clearly not happy. 'Well, you put your phone in as well — that's only fair.'

He laughs. 'You always did have to have the last word, Alexandra, didn't you?'

He turns his phone off and with elaborate arm movements, opens the safe, places his phone next to mine and swiftly locks it again.

'Done.'

Part II

'Don't be too timid and squeamish about your actions.
All life is an experiment. The more experiments you
make, the better.'

— Ralph Waldo Emerson

Part II

'It's exciting, isn't it? When was the last time we had an opportunity like this, to catch up, play, explore and talk into the early hours of the morning? It will be great fun. I have it all planned.' His energy on the lounge next to me is almost infectious as I attempt to maintain a nonchalant demeanour with him.

'I'm not sure whether that makes me feel better or worse.' Although my comment is said lightly, there is a heavy truth underlying my words. He notices my fingers trembling again and my glass balancing precariously in my hand. He takes it from me, presumably as a precautionary measure.

'Honestly, Alex, all will be well. I know this is a big decision for you but you know I would never hurt you and that deep down, we have both wanted this to happen for ages. We just haven't had the opportunity. Let's just seize the moment we're in right now, as per Eckhart Tolle.' He pauses as his grin steadily pries his lips open. 'Thanks for the books by the way, there was a lot of truth in them.'

I roll my eyes in utter disbelief but can't prevent the smile curving at the edge of my mouth.

I had sent him *The Power of Now* and *A New Earth* for Christmas a few years back. I remember talking to him on the phone, overflowing with praise for the books and their life-changing messages. Serves me right, I suppose; maybe it is karma coming right back at me, to challenge me. Here I am, thanks to Jeremy, well and truly living in 'the now' for the next forty-eight hours.

'Okay. You win.' I concede. 'Let's have another drink so I can at least take the edge off my decision.'

'Your wish is my command.'

'Hmm, I'm not too sure about that,' I say, accepting yet another refill. The champagne is definitely going down far too easily.

'Come here; let me show you around the rest of the penthouse so you feel more comfortable.' I accept the offer of his hand as he lifts me from the lounge.

The penthouse is certainly impressive. It looks as though it has been recently refurbished in some funky, retro '80s style, nothing like my place but it certainly works in this environment. The master suite is decorated in an ultra urban-modern style and is a masterpiece in its own right. The king-size bed is encased with industrialised steel, the bed head is incredibly masculine, but its intricate detail gives it the sense of delicate feminine undertones — of thickened, metallic lace, almost. I can't say whether I am relieved or disappointed at the existence of a similarly decorated second bedroom. I'll worry about that later. The entire space is larger in size than the average house. After our tour, we finally relax into our friendly banter about old times and share a lot of laughs. This was the catch-up I was hoping for and my mind finally relieves me from worrying about the implications of my decision to stay.

Jeremy tells me about his research and the work he has been doing with certain global movers and shakers, which really inspires him. He says he's had the opportunity to meet some wonderful people although others are just after glory, fame or money, sometimes all three. He looks a little agitated as he considers this.

'But that's the life I have chosen and I won't let anything stand in the way of what I'm trying to achieve. It's just too important.' The determination in his voice is almost frightening. I sense there is more to it but the tension in his face prevents me from exploring further and he quickly reverts the topic back towards me.

He asks me about my work and study and seems exceptionally interested in the topic of the lectures I am giving. I try not to bore him with the details but he seems genuinely fascinated in our perceptions being directly influenced by each of our senses. He even wants to explore further the impact of visual, auditory, olfactory, kinaesthetic and gustatory senses on shaping our perceptions and experiences. He adds considerable medical insight to our discussion, which I value immensely. I had forgotten what a gracious conversationalist he can be, putting people at ease, encouraging them to open up and never making them feel inferior, even though his knowledge is so immense. It is the sort of discussion you can only have with a few people in life, those who know you well enough to question and challenge and who have enough intellectual and emotional maturity to be truly authentic.

With an active listener like Jeremy, coupled with my passion for the subject matter, our dialogue continues for some time. I figure I have had more than my share of air time so I stop to give him a chance to change topics. I notice again the mischievous twinkle in his eyes and his lips trying to hide a smile.

'What is it? I'm sorry, I've been talking way too much. You should have stopped me.'

'Not at all, you know I love to see you like this. Hearing you speak so passionately about your work is just wonderful. Not everyone feels that way, so it's special when it happens.' He smiles a bashful grin at me. 'I just need to come clean about something and I haven't yet.'

'Oh, what's that?'

'I was actually there today.'

'Where?' I ask, not fully understanding.

'At your lecture, this afternoon.'

I stare at him, eyes and mouth wide open.

'You were there, today, at my lecture?' I am completely astonished.

'Yes, yes and yes. I know I should have told you earlier, but I just wanted to see you in your world.' He turns to me gently. 'You were fabulous, Alexandra, you really engaged the audience and stimulated such thoughtful discussion. Both the students and faculty were mesmerised by you and your work. As was I.' His voice oozes sexiness.

This time I am truly speechless. The great Jeremy Quinn attended my lecture. Unbelievable! I subconsciously pick up my glass and take a gulp that finishes the rest of my drink. Jeremy tilts his glass toward mine, gesturing a silent cheers and does exactly the same. I suddenly feel the full impact of the champagne in my head, which is quite pleasant actually, and more immediately, my bladder — not so pleasant. I excuse myself and go into the bathroom. After relieving myself rather urgently, I notice the bathroom is bigger than my bedroom at home, with grey, white and blue marble in an attractive pattern. It is stocked with all the luxuries you would expect from the penthouse suite of a five-star hotel — mini bottles of body lotion, shampoo, conditioner, shower gel, as well as soap, grooming kits and shower caps in little pastel boxes that look so gorgeous it would be a shame to open them. I look longingly at the sparkling-clean oval bath when I hear Jeremy tap on the door suggesting that he run a bath for me.

'Have you become a clairvoyant as well in our time apart? Is there anything else I should know?'

He laughs. 'I know you've had a big day and if I remember correctly, one of your favourite pastimes is having a bath. Also, I have a vested interest in making you feel as relaxed as possible, so I'd be more than happy to run one for you. Just like old times.' Strange that his words sound so familiar given so much time has passed since this last occurred.

'That sounds delightful. Are you sure? I'm more than happy to do it.'

'Alex, please just do me a favour and go with the flow this weekend.' He enters the bathroom.

'I don't want any resistance and I plan on maximising every hour I have with you. Now, it will be my pleasure to run you a bath, so why don't you go and get your things together and settle in.'

Once again, I look at him, completely astounded. Am I dreaming? Is this really happening? I walk out and head toward the exceptionally large walk-in robe where my wheelie bag has been placed. I hear his voice over the running bath water as I take a moment to absorb the sheer opulence of the master suite.

'Please unpack your belongings. I need to know you're not going to run out on me this weekend.'

As I start doing exactly as he requests, I wonder whether he was always this directive. I suppose he was. Not in a bad way, just in a way that makes it awkward to go against. Surprisingly obedient, I unpack my clothes, shoes, take out my toiletries bag, and leave my work papers in my briefcase.

I'm about to walk out of the room when I notice the phone on the bedside table. Given the noise of the bath running, I quickly go over to the phone and pick up the receiver. It won't hurt to leave a quick message for Robert and the kids, just in case they haven't quite lost reception.

A female voice answers. 'Good evening, Dr Quinn. How may I help you?'

'Oh!' I say into the phone, taken aback by the voice at the end of the line.

I didn't expect an operator and I'm obviously not Dr Quinn. At that precise moment Jeremy comes up behind me, wraps one arm around my waist and removes the receiver from my hand.

'Sorry to disturb you, we don't need any assistance at the moment and please don't connect any calls from the penthouse suite unless I speak to you personally.'

I hear the lady say, 'Yes, of course, Dr Quinn. Enjoy your evening.'

'Thank you. I intend to.' He gently replaces the phone.

I feel like an errant child who has been caught in the closet by a grown up eating someone else's candy and immediately turn a deep shade of red. I have never been able to hide my embarrassment or shame from anyone, let alone Jeremy. I can't believe I'm feeling so culpable about trying to make a phone call. I don't utter a word.

He wraps both arms around my waist so I am entrapped in his strong arms, snuggles his face into the side of my neck and inhales deeply before saying in a low, quiet voice, 'Try anything like that again and that cute arse of yours will be the same colour your face is right now.'

My heartbeats faster at his words and the blood pumps through my body, and to my surprise and horror, even my nipples can't ignore the intent of his words through my blouse. How does he do this to me? He lightly kisses my neck and then leads me silently out of the bedroom.

As we walk back into the lounge area, I notice he has music softly playing in the background and there is a plate of voluptuous dark chocolate-coated strawberries on the round table. I decide it is probably wise not to acknowledge his previous comment.

'May I?' Indicating the strawberries.

'Of course,' he nods, 'they are there to be eaten.' How does he make his words sound so enticing?

'They look delicious.' I realise I have only had champagne since lunchtime. They taste as scrumptious as they look and the thick dark chocolate coating is delectable. I close my eyes, enjoying the sensation. Jeremy places a serviette to the corner of my lip, gently dabbing some strawberry juice that had obviously escaped. This simple movement feels so seductive that my legs quiver as my own juices begin to form between my thighs, even though I vehemently deny their existence in my mind. He smiles deliciously at me while offering the plate as if he is fully aware of the intentions of my body.

It is as if I have morphed on to the big screen and I'm playing the lead role in a sophisticated Hollywood romance. I let out a nervous giggle at the unlikelihood of the whole situation. It's not as if this sort of thing happens every day when you are doing the washing up, the laundry and picking up the kids from school. He looks at me quizzically as if unable to decipher my thoughts.

'Don't worry, just reflecting on life for a moment.'

I'm relieved he hasn't mentioned the phone call as I don't want to spoil the mood.

'Well, unless you would like more strawberries right now, your bath awaits.' As he opens the door, the scene surrounding me is becoming more Hollywood by the second. Is this my once-in-a-lifetime version of *Pretty Woman*? Would it be fair to stop now because of the nagging guilt I feel continuously tugging at the bottom of my heart? I literally have to pinch myself as I walk into the bathroom.

'Wow, this looks truly ... is completely ... perfect ... amazing.' I am so taken aback by the romance of the vision before my eyes, I can barely articulate the words.

'Stunning Jeremy, absolutely stunning.' I glance around the bathroom, which has been transformed into a fairyland by sparkling tea lights. The smell is intoxicating but not overwhelming, with scents of lavender and jasmine, perhaps a hint of freesia — all my favourites. How could he remember such intimate details about me after so long? I feel delightfully light-headed with the whole experience he is creating for me.

'Enjoy, it has been a big day for you. Now it is your time to relax.'

He gently raises my hands to his lips, places a light kiss on each and removes himself from the bathroom. Leaving me to stare in wonder at my surroundings. I carefully undress, slipping off my high heels, stockings, and skirt, finally unbuttoning my shirt. I slowly unclip my bra, remove it from my breasts and allow my underwear to fall to the floor. I don't want to disturb the scene with any rushed movements. I can't wait to soak my body in that gorgeous, steaming, aromatic bath. As I lower my body into it, my tension automatically starts to ease. There is nothing I love more than a bath at the end of a big day, and this day has certainly been full of unexpected surprises. As I melt further into the deep milky water, I notice it isn't just my body that is tired, but I have been in an emotional whirlwind most of the day as well. I am very grateful to have some time alone to just relax and attempt to quieten my mind. I release a long sigh. As my body stretches out in the depths of the bath, tranquillity surrounds me. Exactly what I need, I close my eyes and let all thoughts dissipate from my mind … Pure bliss …

I'm not sure whether I drift off to sleep but I barely notice a soft ripple in the water, which is not enough to disturb my relaxing sensation and I keep my eyes closed until I feel a hand raise my foot from the bottom of the bath to commence a slow and steady massage. I open my eyes and I am stunned by the sheer audacity of the vision in front of me.

'How did you? When did you?' I stammer.

'Shhh, just relax. You look so peaceful. I don't want to disturb you, I want to add to the experience, not detract from it,' Jeremy says gently, quietly.

'But, but, you're actually *in* the bath!' I am astonished.

Or am I? Is it such a shock that Jeremy would smoothly glide into a bath with me? Many years ago it was a very common occurrence and would not have been a shock at all. And if I am truly honest with myself, what was I expecting this weekend to bring? The memories floating around in my head are very different from the reality I am now experiencing. The present has far greater repercussions than the past we once shared. I am completely confused.

My surprise eases into a dreamlike haze with the aroma infiltrating my nostrils and brain, mystical steam entwining our bodies. Jeremy's foot massages were to die for and their intensity hasn't diminished over the years. Indeed, quite the opposite. His magic fingers work deeper into the soles of my feet at the other end of the bath. I relax my head back on the inbuilt cushion and let out a long sigh, succumbing to the experience. Who was I kidding?

'That's right, sweetheart, just let go ... Stop fighting so hard. I will take care of everything.'

Although Jeremy is a massive physical presence, there is still plenty of room in the bath for both of us. It could perhaps fit three or four people, but I don't want to think about that. As my other foot completely dissolves as well, releasing all pressure points under his meticulous touch, I barely notice that I am sliding effortlessly toward him. I am cradled between his legs in this exotic bath where the water between us is now a perfect temperature for two.

I'm in a complete state of lethargy given the heady combination of champagne, the heat of the bath, the candles, the aroma, now the foot massage. I can barely raise my voice in protest, let alone a limb.

Jeremy gently washes the length of my arms with a small velvet cloth, then my chest, slowly and carefully. I notice we are breathing in unison, and the water leisurely rises and falls as we inhale and exhale together. That is, until his hand begins to caress my breast. I tense as his fingers lightly flutter over my nipples, teasing them to attention. They instantly oblige. Once he achieves this desired result, he continues to massage my breasts in the fullness of his hands. My breath becomes short and my pulse quickens. I can no longer deny the impact his touch has on my body. I hear a sigh being released before I recognise it as mine; it is a strange sensation, as it seems to escape from my body without notice or warning. Was I already this out of control?

'That's better,' I hear him say. 'Not so scary after all, is it?'

'Is this how you want to make me feel?' I reply breathlessly, as his hands continue on their quest.

'How *are* you feeling?'

If I had been in a more stable mental state, I should have known that question was coming. I knew he would expect an answer.

I think about it and answer him honestly. 'On edge, intense, relaxed, incoherent, pleasured ... all of these words come to mind ... and my body seems to be relieving my mind of its duties.'

'Hmm, yes, that is almost exactly how I want you to feel. Do you like it, this feeling?'

'I think so, but I may have to get back to you on that one.'

His lips caress the nape of my neck as his fingers weave and explore further down my body, past my belly and linger between my thighs. The dull ache between my legs is now swelling with the anticipation of more.

The room becomes hazy as I melt into his touch, his body still firm, smooth with a comforting sprinkling of hair. My body responds fervently to every caress. Just as he is about to arrive at the desired destination, his fingers pause, linger.

'Doctor Blake, can I ask you something? I'd really appreciate your professional opinion.'

'Sure,' I try to say as calmly as my shortened breath allows. I can't quite believe he has chosen this precise moment to have a 'professional' conversation. My heart pounds in unison with the throbbing ache between my legs.

'Great, thanks.' He sounds pleased with himself.

'You see, I have a beautiful woman staying with me for the next forty-eight hours.'

I moan in disbelief as he continues. 'We are staying in the penthouse suite of the best hotel in Sydney. She's as sexy as hell and I don't want to waste a moment of the time we have together.'

'I'm sure you wouldn't waste a second, Jeremy! What's the problem specifically?' I roll my eyes as I try to make my voice sound as even as possible, which is essentially impossible given his carefully orchestrated strokes. I try to respond as if I'm going along with his game, but hope he will also move the conversation along a little faster.

'Well, you see, she finds it difficult to switch off. I don't think she will fully immerse herself in the experience I want to give her this weekend. A once-in-a-lifetime experience, mind you.'

I try to manoeuvre to put some space between us so I can see his face. However, he has me in a position where I am firmly anchored between his legs. One of his arms is around my chest and the other underneath my arse, between my legs, all the while his fingers, playing, teasing, caressing … God, I had forgotten just how good he is at this. He tightens his grip when he senses my attempt.

'She says she will,' he continues rhythmically, 'but you see, I know her well. I know that what I am proposing goes against her nature, potentially even her values, and that's why it is so difficult for her to let go, even though I know she deeply wants to experience what I can offer her.'

As he continues his controlled, even monologue, his finger work intensifies below.

The strength of his grip remains unrelenting.

His smell, his touch, his words, I'm delirious.

I must be dreaming; this can't be happening in real life, can it?

'And then I attend a lecture this afternoon given by some professional psychologist, Doctor something or other, in the hope that she would give me some ideas, you know, to help solve my problem. By the way, you should meet her, I think you'd like her,' he adds offhandedly.

Oh, he is enjoying this! I am in no position other than to play along.

'And did she?' I almost squeak out as I groan inwardly, unsure of whether the sound derives from frustration or pleasure. Either way, I am utterly lost in his hands, his words.

'Yes, in fact she did, so I'm going to follow her advice.'

Additional fingers join down below and now the other hand is pinching and pulling at my nipples as if commanding my body to attention rather than my mind. His touch intensifies as my nipples and loins throb in unison. The motion of his movement makes me weightless against him in the bath. As the water is cooling, I am heating up like a steaming kettle hanging over an open fire.

'So, I have decided I should remove one of her senses this weekend. The doctor's empirical research assures me that this would achieve two things. Firstly, significantly heighten all her other senses, which can only be a good thing given what I'm talking about, don't you think?'

He pauses.

I can't respond. I am unable to focus on his words any longer.

'And secondly, that her experience would therefore exponentially increase beyond all preconceived boundaries and perceptions. I couldn't believe it, all my problems had been solved by this incredibly insightful woman.'

I gulp, gasp, perhaps even choke, at his words. He tweaks and teases my nipples as if testing their elasticity, causing my back to arch in synchrony.

He continues, almost lost in his own words. 'I have considered the five senses and finally decided on the one that was the basis of her research, which will definitely have the greatest impact.' With his other hand, he probes the inner depths of my vaginal passage, gently and carefully massaging, purposefully avoiding the area in greatest need of his touch. Precision fingers.

I am way beyond a deer caught in headlights; I am now loaded and strapped to the roof of the car. Damn him for doing this to me. Damn my body for responding! My breathing becomes uncontrollable, while I am held captive by the intoxicating spell of his knowledge and experience.

'You see, she is a highly visual person and I honestly believe if she lost this sense ...'

I can't hear his words any more. My breath is shallow and swift as I desperately attempt to secure more oxygen into my lungs, into my brain. His fingers come to a standstill.

I am going to hyperventilate.

'God, Alex, you have become even more acutely attuned to physical touch, if that's even possible. Sensations are rippling through your body. It is really distracting me from my conclusion.'

I am distracting him? Insane!

The pause is long enough for me to breathe again. Not long enough to prevent his words, nor his intentions.

'Therefore, all she needs to promise is two things. To relinquish her vision for the weekend and not ask any questions for the next forty-eight hours. A weekend that will exceed all expectations; break through her preconceived boundaries. A truly sensational experience that I have no doubt she will love ... so obvious in hindsight, I'm disappointed I didn't think of it myself ...'

His voice wanders off and his breath is hot in my ear as his tongue tickles and his teeth nibble my lobe. His fingers are relentless in their mission, penetrating, but falling short of securing the relief I urgently desire. My body prepares to explode. Then his voice registers in my ear with profound clarity.

'Alexandra, promise me this, right now.' His words are strong, deliberate. My body is quivering in anticipation. 'It's simple. No sight. No questions. Forty-eight hours.'

I have too many feelings and emotions to fully comprehend my circumstances. My brain, my body, my heart are all focused on one thing and one thing only — release! I'm not sure whether I love or hate that he can do this to me, has always been able to do this as no one else has. I always feel so helpless, so dependent on his next move. It's as if my body renders my mind irrelevant.

'Promise me.' The deep low voice penetrates my haze, my stupor.

Oh god, my throbbing lust becomes agonising as the room starts spinning. It is too hot for me to handle, heat erupting from within, steam billowing around me. I try to thrust my hips forward to create friction where I so urgently need it to relieve the intensity he has so cleverly masterminded. I am physically prevented from doing so. My jolting movement hardens his resolve, his body strengthening its grip around mine.

'Promise me, right now.' The strong voice sends its final command.

'Whatever. I, I, prom—' I can't manage to complete the words as they stutter out in a tangle. 'Ohhh god,' I sigh. He is relentless!

'LOUDER.' His voice booms into my ear like a tribal drum quickening its pounding beat ...

'I promise,' I pant. 'I promise.' I sigh. 'I'll do whatever you want … this weekend. Whatever, just …'

At these words, his fingers plunge deeply into my vagina sending me into the orgasm my body so frantically, so desperately, so completely desires. A primal scream escapes me …

'Thank you, sweetheart, problem solved.' I hear a seductive, distant whisper in my ear.

He finds the sweet spot of my clitoris, which sets alight a new series of convulsions that milk my juices for all they are worth, while pinioning me through relentless spasms of mindless release. Without considering for a second the implications or consequences of the words that have just escaped me, I greedily allow myself to pass through the gates of pleasure he has so carefully constructed, then guarded, then ultimately controlled.

* * *

I'm not sure how long I have been in my own faraway world when I drift back to reality. I notice my skin is starting to wrinkle prune-like, so some time must have passed. I slowly float back to consciousness.

'Are you okay? You were amazing.' I hear the wonder in his voice. Ah, yes, in Jeremy's arms, in the bath. That's where I am, becoming fully aware. I am soft and full and voluptuous, still floating in a decadent haze of delirium.

'Mmm … I'm wonderful, how are you?'

'Let's get you out of the bath before you catch a chill.' He steadily lifts me up and out of the bath and wraps a towel around my shoulders. It is thick and soft and I embrace its warmth.

As he stands behind me with his arms wrapped around me, we face each other in the reflection in the mirror. Seeing him like this, our height difference appears exacerbated and for some reason, I wish I were wearing high heels to compensate for the disparity between us. I am acutely aware of his nakedness behind me, which makes me literally weak at the knees.

He slowly unravels the towel as our eyes maintain contact in the mirror and lets it drop leisurely but deliberately to the floor. I am left staring at our naked forms in the mirror. His eyes are rapturous. We say not a word but regard one another with a deep sense of lust and history that has become more astonishing and complex over the years than we ever could have imagined.

'You are even more breathtaking than I remember.' Jeremy finally breaks the silence.

'You have always been and continue to be too beautiful, Jeremy,' I say, not wanting to acknowledge his comment.

'Alexa, open your eyes, and really look at yourself.' He notices I am trying to look anywhere but at my own reflection. He steps us closer toward the full-length mirror so I have no option but to be face-to-face with myself. Sometimes it is a wonderful thing that others see differently to what we see of ourselves. Interestingly, I find myself looking for any obvious signs of childbirth. It's strange that I have never had that thought before this moment. Thankfully, the light is good to me. As these thoughts flitter through my mind, Jeremy clasps my hands together and lifts them from my side to high above my head, lifting me slightly off my heels. Bending my arms backwards so my elbows are the highest point in the mirror, there is nothing obstructing my face as my body rests against his. Jeremy is utterly irresistible in this erect, virile form. The sight of both of us standing naked before the mirror, embraced by candlelight, becomes more sensually heightened and more emotional than I could have ever imagined.

The electricity between us is palpable. It fascinates me, this closeness, this intimacy and I allow myself to linger at the image before my eyes. What a remarkable exercise, staring at each other like this, I think, taking a professional perspective. Instead of it being something to avoid at all costs, the intensely erotic nature of our steaming bodies in the mirror emanates sexual energy, even more so as I am still reeling from a delectable orgasm.

'I want you to capture this moment in your memory. Take a moment to understand and absorb how much beauty is within you. Your flushed cheeks. Your buoyant, full breasts. Your glistening thighs. Your eyes, wild with lust and desire. Remember this is who you are, an infinitely sexual and sensual creature. I have never desired anyone as much as I have you.'

I can feel the intensity of the truth in his words as much as I feel his manhood swelling thickly behind me.

I barely recognise my reflection in the mirror.

Who am I?

Time stands still.

The moment is utterly intoxicating, breathtaking.

I can't say how much time has elapsed between these moments and when he eventually releases me to wrap the towel around my shoulders.

'I need to organise a few things and it is probably best if you have some space. Take your time; you'll notice the cupboards are well stocked. I have a surprise waiting for you out here, when you are ready.' Jeremy kisses the inside of my wrist and closes the bathroom door behind him. My stomach once again makes its presence felt in my body, as does the heat between my legs and my swollen breasts. How does he do this to me?

I steady myself, placing both hands on the cold marble of the basin bench. I stare at the mirror, looking directly at my face, into my eyes. My body feels energetic, euphoric. I can't remember a time I felt this physical and alive. My mind is desperately trying to maintain balance and perspective. What am I doing? Unfortunately, my body appears to be the weightier component as I let out a surrendering sigh and embrace the fullness of the moment.

Jeremy was right about the bathroom being well stocked; once again his memory for detail is astounding. Little handwritten notes scattered here and there, Jo Malone perfume — one beautifully designed large bottle of my favourite fragrance blend, with enough room to add any finishing touches from the collection of smaller bottles. Body lotion that my skin devours so quickly, I indulgently allow myself a second helping. Yves Saint Laurent make-up bag with foundations, concealer, eyeliner, lipsticks, lip liners, mascaras, all in hues complementary to my skin tone — everything I could need for the weekend and more. Wow. I decide to let myself go a little crazy and enjoy all of them, thinking how much fun it is, like being in cosmetic boutique heaven and helping myself to anything from the skin care and cosmetic range. I let out enthusiastic little yelps as I open boxes, experiment and test an array of gorgeous products featured regularly in high end glossy magazines but never before seen on my bathroom shelf.

I must have been lost in my own cosmetic wonderland for quite some time when I hear a light knock on the door.

'Alex, you are still alive in there, aren't you?' Jeremy's voice softly permeates my hedonistic atmosphere.

'Oh, yes, ah, sorry, I can't believe all of this. When did you have time? How did you know? I mean, well, it has been so long … This is absolutely amazing, I feel like a child opening all of my favourite presents …' My words tumble over the top of each other.

'Questions, questions,' he says with a chuckle, although I detect an undertone of threat in his voice, which stops me dead.

My thoughts immediately drift back to his words in the bath, the promise I made in a moment of weak, lustful desire. The hair on my skin automatically stands on end; my posture straightens like a cat tensing to sense imminent danger. What was it he was talking about in the bath? He wasn't really serious, was he? Wanting me to be blind for the weekend and something about questions? Surely we're too old for such silly games. Aren't we? My intuition doesn't help my apprehension as my mind instantly conjures up the memory of the first and only time I tried to get out of a promise with Jeremy back in our university days. Strangely, in hindsight, I am vague on the details of the promise itself; however, the consequences were embarrassingly clear.

'So, you are absolutely positive you are going to renege on our agreement?' Jeremy asks incredulously as he towers above me. We are in the quad at uni, just outside the Great Hall. I nod. The next second, he hauls me over his shoulders, grabs my ankles and slides me down his back. I am left dangling upside down, looking out toward everyone behind me.

'Put me down, you embarrassing bastard!' I scream, flapping around, trying to haul myself up. 'You can't do this, it's pure brutality. Put me down!' I scream louder.

'I can and I will, until you follow through on your promise.'

*People are looking at me, laughing. Everyone knows
we are best friends and are just mucking around. My
T-shirt is down around my shoulders thanks to gravity
and I quickly hold it up so I'm not giving everyone a
free bra show. I try to bash him with one hand and hold
my T-shirt with the other. Thank god I have jeans on.
Jeremy starts walking off.*

'What are you doing? This is insane!'

*It is difficult to project my voice as loudly as I'd hoped
given I am bouncing along behind his legs, upside down.
I am completely incensed. He casually chats to others
as we proceed along the corridor as if there is nothing
unusual about me being slung over his body. His friends
have a little chuckle as he informs them he is just giving
me a lift to my next lecture. If I could, I would really
hurt him very badly right now. Blood is rushing to my
head by the second, making me look like a ripe tomato.*

*We arrive at the lecture hall and he carefully lowers
me down on to a seat in the front row. He acknowledges
the Professor behind his lectern, as if everything is in
perfect order. He bends down to where he has placed me,
holding my hands together and says with a smile, 'I'll
pick you up after the lecture.'*

'You can't be serious.' I almost spit the words at him.

'Oh, indeed I am, Miss Alexandra.'

*I give him my best death stare as I hear the Professor
say, 'Right, well, let's get started, we have a lot to cover
today.'*

*With that Jeremy plants a kiss on my cheek,
releases my hands and waves goodbye. I am so deeply
embarrassed that I sink as low as I can into the seat, not*

willing to make eye contact with anyone. As I move my feet, I notice my bag resting underneath the same seat I had been delivered to. Nothing like advance planning.

I can't concentrate one bit on the lecture. Instead I am fully preoccupied, focusing on firstly, avoiding Jeremy and secondly, revenge. How dare he do that to me? I scribble a note to a friend asking if I could have her notes for the rest of the lecture. I decide making an early escape would be the safest option, just in case he was serious about 'picking me up' afterwards. Fifteen minutes before the end, I slide out of my seat as discreetly as possible. I move silently toward the back door, which I think is my safest option. As I walk out and glance around the empty hallway, I secretly congratulate myself for out-manoeuvring Jeremy. I start walking determinedly down the corridor, furious with him, absolutely steaming. As I gather speed and lengthen my stride, my legs suddenly fall from underneath me so fast it temporarily winds me.

'What the—' I exclaim.

'Hey, gorgeous, you didn't really think I'd fall for that, did you?'

Jeremy scoops me up into exactly the same position as before. Where the hell did he come from? He carries me by the ankles, over his shoulders all the way to the cafeteria. Blokes are clapping and cheering all the way, congratulating him for being a real man. I am seething, to say the least. He deposits me on a chair and holds me with a firm grip around my shoulders and wrists. He knows too well I will run the second he lets go of me. I stare scathingly at his mates positioned around the table, all with smirks on their faces though their eyes pretend to look elsewhere around the room. Patrick and Neil arrive and place a tray in front of me — presumably my lunch has been pre-ordered so Jeremy has no reason to take his hands off me. Their giggles leave me with no doubt they think this situation is highly amusing. He senses me waiting for any opportunity.

'Don't try it, AB, it will only get worse for you very quickly.'

'And exactly how long do you think you can keep this up, Jeremy?' My voice is icy.

'Exactly the same amount of time it takes for you to keep your word, my friend,' he states. And damn it, he is true to his word.

This 'carry on' continues for the rest of the day. Eventually the thought of being hauled like a sack of potatoes and deposited into my last tutorial for the day and favourite subject, 'The psychology of sensation and perception', is too much for me, given it is a small class of twelve.

'Okay, enough, Jeremy. No more. I have learnt my lesson. You win.' He places me gently on the ground, the right way up.

'I'm so pleased you have come to your senses, AB. I'm sure you didn't want to experience what I had planned for you tonight.'

'God, you are a relentless force!'

'Not to be reckoned with I agree, although I'd rather define it as "persistent when required".'

'Whatever, I just need to get to class.' I try to fob him off.

'You're sure you don't need a lift? My legs move faster than yours.' The smile on his face is so cheeky I can't help but laugh at his cuteness even though I'm trying hard to appear disgruntled.

'Very funny indeed. Goodbye!'

The memory is so clear, so strong, it's as if it had only happened yesterday. Where did that come from? I haven't thought about anything like that in years, decades even. I shake my head in an attempt to dislodge the past from my thoughts and remove any potential significance it may hold.

* * *

'Do you think you might be ready any time soon?'

'Yes, absolutely.' Relief rushes over me. He didn't mention anything about my promise, thank goodness. I quickly scoop all the packaging together into one of the bags and carefully place the lids back on the jars. I'm particularly careful with the perfume as the scent is truly gorgeous and I'd love to take it home with me.

'I'll just dry my hair and be out in a minute.' I locate the hair dryer, flip my hair over my head and quickly blow-dry the damper parts underneath. It is wavier than usual, but I decide to leave it out anyway, hanging just below my shoulder blades. My face and body are glowing and I can't help but smile back at the person grinning at me in the mirror. Nothing like a five-star hotel, French champagne, an orgasm sent from heaven in a luxurious bath and every beauty product under the sun to make a woman feel utterly pampered, at least for a while. I grab a giant, thick bathrobe (they never seem to be made for the average size woman), wrap it all around me and then some, before stepping out from my confined euphoria of the bathroom into the cool elegance of the hotel suite, and Jeremy's arms.

'You look excited,' he says as he squeezes me tight.

'I feel as guilty as sin in a wonderfully decadent way.' I return his embrace and the passion in his eyes leaves me momentarily breathless.

'Come here, you, time to feel a little more decadent. I want to show you something.'

His arm drapes over my shoulders and he steers me quickly through the master suite and into the walk-in robe. We are like young puppies finding a basket of new toys to play with. I gasp when we come to a sudden stop. A grin explodes on his face.

'I have always wanted to do this, Alex, but wasn't brave enough at uni. Would you wear this dress for me tonight?'

I walk over to an exquisite dress, simple, elegant, sophisticated and the most beautiful colour — deep red, blue-red. It is cut on the diagonal and across the shoulder, leaving one shoulder bare.

'Jeremy, it is simply gorgeous, I'm … I'm speechless. Why are you doing all of this? I feel like I'm missing something. I don't understand.'

'There's no need to understand. I want to do this, I've wanted to for a long time and now I can. Everything you need should be there to get dressed. I can't wait to see you in it and I'm so pleased you like it. Try not to take as long as you did in the bathroom, or I'll have to help you speed up the process,' he says with a grin. I stand motionless, staring at him, then the dress. He slaps me lightly on my bottom to reinforce his words.

'Okay, okay,' I reply as I move into action.

I walk over to the dress and run my fingers along the satin; it feels silky smooth and soft. I quickly remove my robe and slip the dress over my head. It slides easily over my body and I'm grateful to find it has a built-in bra that just happens to fit my bustline beautifully. It slithers along my waist with the left side of the dress cascading exquisitely down my legs before coming to a stop; just long enough to tickle my ankle. I find an accompanying box of stunning stiletto-heel shoes that I'm almost not game to try on. I haven't worn shoes like this since my twenties and I silently wonder whether I will be able to maintain a stylish sense of balance in them.

I have never worn such a bold colour and I stare at myself in shock. The creation is tantalising. The person in the mirror is sexy, confident, alluring. I notice an intricate, antique-style clasp on the bench so I pull my hair up into a loose chignon on the same side as my bare shoulder and clip it into place. Now the reflection in the mirror has an added dimension of unanticipated sophistication. No question about it now, I am well and truly living my version of *Pretty Woman*, and so far, for me at least, it is better than the original.

I can't remember the last time I was this dressed up — I could be walking the red carpet at the Oscars perhaps, with a little more make-up, possibly, and a professionally-coiffed hairstyle. After allowing myself one last look at my reflection, so glamorous I hardly recognise myself, I steady myself to walk out into the lounge room.

Jeremy stops and turns toward me. His mouth opens as I enter the lounge room. I desperately try to be the sophisticated, confident woman in the mirror, rather than the causal, clumsy uni student he had once known, as his eyes rake in my appearance. His sharp intake of breath and the open admiration in his eyes tell me that he likes what he sees.

'Oh my … oh,' he says slowly. 'Oh, Alexandra, now I'm speechless, you look … absolutely breathtaking.'

'The dress is beautiful, Jeremy. I don't know what to say either.'

'No, sweetheart, you are beautiful. The dress merely complements your best assets.' I laugh a little apprehensively at his words as his eyes linger appreciatively on my breasts.

'It does a little more than that, Jeremy, it hides all the worst … Oh, by the way, there was only one thing you forgot.'

'Really?' he asks, sounding surprised. 'And what was that?'

'Knickers.'

He remains expressionless.

'Undies?' I continue.

No response.

'Panties, if that is what you prefer to call them?'

I had looked everywhere for them in the walk-in robe but they had all mysteriously vanished.

'Oh, right.' He finally seems to comprehend. 'No, I didn't forget them, you are wearing everything you need.'

He turns his head, his stare penetrating my eyes.

'You know I appreciate access, Alexa, at all times. Just the thought of it makes me hot.'

He winks at me and I blush again so hard that the dress and I become indistinguishable.

At that moment I notice several dozen roses in a vase on the table. I have never seen so many together. They are unopened and deep, blood red, exactly the same colour as the dress I am wearing. They are magnificent, each and every one of them perfect. I walk over to study them in detail and inhale their heady scent. I sense Jeremy move as he positions behind me, his breath light against my neck. I am a little taller in high heels so he conveniently doesn't have to bend so low.

'Each one of these roses represents the experiences I want to give you this weekend. Imagine what they will look like when they have all fully blossomed, every layer opened up. They are beautiful now, just as you are, Alexandra, but just imagine what they will be, as one by one they explode into their full potential.'

His lips lightly caress the exposed nape of my neck as he speaks. Oh my goodness, his lips and his words ensure my knees almost buckle beneath me.

My voice is slow, breathless. 'You are certainly well on your way … I can honestly say I have never experienced anything like this before, Jeremy, ever.'

'You ain't seen nothin' yet, babe.' He instantly lightens the mood with his newly acquired, light American twang.

'We need another cheers,' he states ceremoniously and turns his back to me as he starts to concoct something set up on the buffet with some elaborate glasses and lots of ice.

'Oh no, not vodka shots?'

'Not quite, but good memory though. Something different this time, you'll see.'

The tone of Jeremy's voice and the look in his eyes takes me directly back to one of the most playful, surprising and tantalising sexual encounters I have ever participated in and probably ever will in my lifetime …

Jeremy and I have finally finished our mid-semester exams and we can't wait for a night off; it feels like we have been hitting the books non-stop for the past few months. Just as we are heading out to the pub a few blocks away to meet some friends for a few ales, a cracking electrical storm hits, resulting in a thunderous downpour. Jeremy and I take one look outside before deciding against going out and settle in for a few quiet drinks and a movie at his place instead. It suits us, as we are both pretty knackered from burning the midnight oil. Although relieved that the stress of exams has passed, we haven't built up enough sleep surplus to be in full party mode. As we settle ourselves on the lounge with cider and popcorn, Jeremy's friend and fellow med student, Patrick, bursts through the door, dripping wet.

'Mate, how's the storm out there?' He shouts the words over a crack of thunder that almost shakes the walls. 'Oh, hi, Lexi, didn't see you there. How's things?'

I've always thought Patrick is cute. He has a boyish charm, is just under six foot tall with quite a muscular build from playing rugby on the university team. And he calls me Lexi.

'Hi, Pat. I'm well, thanks.'

'Come in, mate. Looks like you copped it pretty bad out there, you're saturated!'

'Thanks. I was just heading to the pub to meet everyone and got caught in this. Hope you don't mind.'

'Not at all. We just decided to watch a movie, couldn't be arsed going out in this weather so just slothing about instead.'

After we put his stuff in the clothes dryer, he sits on the lounge with us, a white bath towel tied firmly around his hips. His tanned body looks good, tight with muscle from the many sit-ups and chin-ups and whatever else

footballers do for training. Oh yes, you can call me Lexi,
I muse … He opens his beer and we settle in for the
movie.

I sit at one end of the lounge with my legs draped over
Jeremy's lap and Patrick at the other. After our second
round of drinks, Pat rolls up a joint. He goes to light up
outside when Jeremy stops him.

'No worries mate, it's still pouring outside. Have it in
here and we won't have to stop the movie.'

After he has a long drag, he hands it to Jeremy who
also wastes no time in sending the essence of the joint
directly to his lungs. He allows the impact to settle,
takes a smaller drag and offers it to me. When I hesitate,
Jeremy encourages me.

'Go on, you've finished your exams, loosen up; we're
not going anywhere tonight and we have the next week
off.'

All true, so I take the joint from him and concentrate
on doing it properly. It is always so embarrassing if
I stuff it up; it seems everyone is willing to offer their
expertise on the correct methodology for smoking a
spliff. I exhale all air and slowly inhale the smoke deeply
into my lungs, resisting the urge to cough and splutter
it out. The sensation instantly goes to my brain as I
continue to talk myself through the process — hold,
hold, hold and very gently exhale. Jeremy removes the
joint from my fingertips just before it falls, as my body
goes momentarily limp and flops further into the corner
of the lounge, feeling comfortably numb.

I have one more drag and that's enough for me. I'm
content in my own little space for a while and I have no

idea how much more the boys smoke or what they've been doing. My consciousness returns toward the end of the movie to see the boys lost in laughter at something. Not sure what, but it only takes me a minute before I find it hysterical as well. After the movie finishes, some music videos come on and Pat starts dancing around the room in his towel and Jeremy joins in. It is very funny to watch with the strobing lights of the TV and the sound of pelting rain in the background. At least no one would complain about the volume. Jeremy tries to get me off the lounge to dance with them but I have barricaded myself in the cushions instead.

'No, you two look great up there by yourselves, let me enjoy being a voyeur.'

This sends them into an array of ever more complicated dance manoeuvres that look completely ludicrous given the state they are in. They eventually disappear into the kitchen to return with a tray full of vodka shots. I shake my head.

'Oh no, not after a spliff!'

'Definitely after a spliff, Lexi, it's the only way. After all, this is a post-exam downpour party,' Pat declares to his own laughter and Jeremy endorses his sentiments with his own hysteria. They attempt to high five each other, but miss. This really does just keep getting funnier to watch and my stomach hurts from laughing.

'Okay, Alex, down two shots now and we'll let you stay on the lounge behind your barricade,' Jeremy offers.

'Absolutely. You can sit there like the gorgeous princess you are, in your comfy castle,' Patrick adds.

Pure genius — what a perfect solution. All I want at this moment is the soft comfort of the lounge and all the cushions I have collected over the course of the evening.

'One?' I should never have posed it as a question.

'Two. One for Pat and one for me, then you're safe on the lounge, for a while anyway.'

'Done!' I exclaim as if their logic makes perfect sense.

'Cheers.'

'To *new* experiences,' Jeremy adds, as we all connect our glasses making eye contact, as was the custom between us.

One shot, down. Second shot, down.

'Jeez, vodka is strong when you have a double shot like that.'

Patrick hands me some lemonade to help take the burn away. 'Very considerate of you. Thanks, Pat.'

'We're here to serve, m'lady,' he says with a cheeky, mischievous smile as he attempts a courteous bow.

'And that pleases me no end,' I agree with a wink.

I'm thankful they leave me to wallow in my soft, smoky, vodka haze while they continue their dancing and parading around.

When I look around the room again, I notice Jeremy, like Patrick, is only wearing a towel low on his waist.

'Do you think you belong to a male harem? Look at you both. You look hilarious.'

They do look absurd, but as I watch them I find myself noticing more and more how their muscles move and how firm their bodies are. I flush at the thought of having them in my own personal harem.

Then suddenly, they are either side of me on the lounge stealing all of the pillows.

'What are you doing?' I holler at them. 'Give them back, they're mine, you can't, it's not fair.'

They think this is hysterically funny as they strip me of my pillows and I try to retrieve them.

'Come on, AB, you've been there for ages. The pillows can't be more important to you than us, can they? Let them go ...'

And Jeremy then plants a kiss on my lips, his tongue penetrating my mouth.

I am a bit stunned that he would do such a thing in front of Patrick. I look toward Patrick and notice the same lust in his eyes as there is in Jeremy's.

I notice too late that they give each other a quick nod and before I know it, Patrick has my legs and Jeremy my upper body and they carry me towards Jeremy's bed.

'Boys!' I'm laughing and squirming as the heavy rain continues belting down. 'What are you doing?'

'It's only fair that you be in a towel, too. We just want to play a little.' They toss me lightly on the bed. Jeremy unbuttons my jeans and slides down the zip. 'Lift her up a little, Pat.'

He arches my back so Jeremy can slip off my jeans.

'That's it, sit her up.' Jeremy lifts the shirt over my shoulders and arms.

I look straight into his eyes, questioning, unsure of what to do or how I should be feeling. Or exactly what is going on for that matter. He then pauses and asks me quietly 'Do you want us to stop?'

'No.' I slowly shift my head from side to side. I don't want them to stop. Who in their right mind would say no to being pleasured by two buff, virile men on a dark and stormy night? Certainly not me! The heat in my belly immediately spreads to more sensual areas.

He unleashes a massive grin. 'It's okay, GG. I know you want to play as much as we do. We promise to give you our undivided attention. Just relax and enjoy the ride!'

'GG?' This is new.

'Gorgeous Girl, of course!'

Great, my list of nicknames is growing exponentially tonight.

He then turns to Patrick. 'You undo her bra and take her knickers off while I hold her in position.'

I can't quite believe this is happening and am utterly mesmerised by the hot naked maleness surrounding me — completely tantalised by the thought of what might happen next. Is this really happening to me? Apparently so, it seems to be my lucky night! So I let them lay me back on the bed, fully naked, eagerly anticipating their next move, and allow them to play with me, caress my breasts, nibble my earlobes, kiss my stomach, share me, suck me, probe me. I close my eyes, open them, and see Jeremy sucking my nipples. Moaning, I close my eyes again and then open them to see Patrick languidly drawing a line with his tongue along my inner thigh. They explore parts of my body together, then separately and then together again, each finding their own unique ways to take me to uncontainable heights.

For many hours.

And it is spectacular.

My head is resting in Patrick's lap, still wrapped in the towel as they engage in some anatomy-type conversation that I am not even pretending to follow. He is stroking my hair and fanning it out over his crossed legs as Jeremy lies sideways next to us. Patrick lowers a spliff to my lips and I inhale lightly, looking up at him. Quite relaxing as I'm already lying down, and happy to have a break from the intricate attention their hands and mouths have been giving to my body. I'm floating in both body and mind.

Pat feels my forehead. 'Lexi, you're burning up. Are you feeling alright?'

'Yeah, great, I think, although it does feel quite hot and stuffy in here.'

'Not surprising.' *They laugh.*

'Let me get the thermometer,' *offers Jeremy.*

'Not necessary, J,' *I say, laughing with them. Patrick's fingers continue to caress my hair and it feels serene. I take a deep breath and let myself float off into a cloudy haze. I am brought back to stark reality as Jeremy throws my legs over his shoulders, spreads my butt cheeks and inserts the thermometer up my arse, presumably lubricated as it has no problem sliding in. I attempt to hoist myself upwards only to be kept calmly in place on Patrick's lap as he pins my shoulders toward the bed.*

'Jeremy!' *I exclaim.* 'What are you doing?'

'Taking your temperature, AB. We wouldn't want to let anything serious happen to you when we can take necessary precautions. We're both nearly doctors, you know.'

77

'I'm absolutely fine. Get that fucking thing out of my arse.'

'Just hold still another minute or so. It wouldn't be good to have mercury leak into your sweet spot now, would it?'

His words, believable or not, ensure I don't move a muscle until he removes the invading object.

'Oh yes, esteemed colleague, you are correct. Thirty-eight point five. Well diagnosed. Lucky I have just the remedy.'

'I do not have a temperature, Jeremy, you idiot.' I recommence my squirming.

'Please calm the patient, Doctor McCluskey.'

Patrick swiftly clamps my mouth shut with his thick fingers. Jeremy shifts my arms above my shoulders, which Patrick obligingly pins to the bed with his solid football legs. I groan without much success of creating any real noise.

What now? I think. They must be exhausted. I am.

Apparently not.

Jeremy reveals an ice bucket overflowing with ice cubes that he sits up on the bed. He then ever so slowly works the ice over the skin on the inside of my arms, round and round my underarm, across my chest and then repeats the sequence on the other side. My body begins to react to the sensation of the freezing ice sliding and dripping over my overheated body. As he reaches my breast, he circles and circles, needing new ice cubes as they disintegrate into droplets over my burning skin. At the same time as Jeremy is tantalising my nipples, Patrick has ice rolling languidly over my lips, teasing ice into my mouth and playing with my tongue. My arms are numbing under the weight of his legs, becoming useless weapons of protest. I am thirsty for the ice in my mouth so I let him torment me until he relinquishes each cube down my throat. So focused am I on this that I barely notice Jeremy finishing with my nipples and continuing his mission further south, leaving a small bundle of ice jiggling around my belly button. Patrick doesn't allow my nipples to feel neglected for a moment and continues where Jeremy left off. I am literally drowning in sensory stimulation. Jeremy begins thoroughly and completely icing my vulva, sending shivers all over my body, until he eventually slides a cube skilfully into my vagina. My back arches instantaneously at the sensation.

'Please ...' I say breathlessly, to someone, anyone.

Jeremy slides another ice cube deeply into me. The sensation of the frozen cube being pushed into a tunnel so hot sends my body throbbing internally as it tries to reject the frozen, harsh invader biting into my over-sensitised flesh. Before it has the chance, he gently coerces another ice cube along the same path, his eyes completely absorbed with the impact his actions are having on my body.

Just as I can't take any more of the fire and ice competing within my body, Jeremy squeezes my legs together tightly, bound either side by his and devours my mouth in his. As Patrick holds my head in his lap, I can feel his throbbing erection next to my skull. He repositions himself to once again ice my surprisingly sensitive underarms before slipping my arms out from underneath him and pinning each arm to my side,

*thereby trapping the ice in position. Jeremy had ensured
my mouth and southern tunnel were inundated with
ice as his body restricts and limits my movements. I
feel like an inside-out igloo. The sensation of so much
body heat on the outside and being trapped frozen from
within is like nothing I have ever experienced. My entire
being ripples with the sensation of freezing and burning
simultaneously, ripples with uncontrollable tremors as
the heat from my body aggressively devours the ice in my
oral and vaginal cavities. The frozen intruders compete
with the natural habitat they are invading as my brain
becomes numb with the sensory overload my body is
experiencing.*

I can't scream. I don't scream.

The boys don't release me until I achieve meltdown.

*When I do, Jeremy lowers himself to dramatically
exhume the diluted juices he has created, wholly and
completely. Although consumed with frost, I am wet
with lust and desire and erupt volcanically.*

*'See, Alex, I have told you many times only good
things come from a sincere vodka cheers. Quite an
experience, wouldn't you agree?'*

I am too fervently spent to comment.

The strange thing is, I never did find out whether they had
planned it that way, or the whole experience just happened
during the flow of the evening …

I attempt to dislodge the salacious memory from my mind
and focus on exactly what Jeremy is doing.

'That looks very technical. What on earth are you preparing
over there?'

'Not as technical as it looks, but we may as well make it worthwhile. It's not like we're together very often, after all. I hope you don't mind, I've opted for the Hemingway version given it is Friday afternoon. It is a little more involved than the French version and the Bohemian version is sure to set off the fire alarms.'

His explanation doesn't help my confusion.

He ceremoniously scoops up two frosted glasses of opalescent milk and hands one to me.

I lift the glass to my nose to sniff the contents as I raise my eyebrows in suspicion. It smells heavily sweet with an anise or liquorice undertone.

'It is the drink of Vincent van Gogh, Oscar Wilde, Ernest Hemingway.' If this is meant to enlighten me, it fails. Before I have a chance to question him further, he makes a toast. 'To you, Alexandra, to exploring and discovering the enlightened version of yourself. And of course, to the blossoming of your roses,' he adds with a mischievous and knowing wink.

I may be wearing the most beautiful dress I have ever worn, feeling more glamorous than I have ever felt, but all of a sudden, we are back at uni, about to embark on some playful, boundary-breaking adventure together — again. I am as excited and apprehensive as a small child going to their first theme park and I allow myself to be swept away in the alluring, mysterious unknown of this weekend, knowing Jeremy would never do me any real harm.

And I know better, for many reasons, than to decline him at this point.

'Skol.'

'Slainte,' I respond, as per our tradition of saying cheers in the language of one of the countries we have visited together.

I look up directly into his eyes, before allowing the icy-cold liquid to slide smoothly down my throat, its potency striking alarmingly fast, warming my blood without delay.

'That's the spirit, I knew you wouldn't disappoint me. This weekend is meant to be.'

'What on earth was that, Jeremy?'

'Absinthe, sweetheart, the green fairy.'

Jeremy sets his glass down and walks over to me slowly and assuredly. I can't accurately pinpoint the look in his eyes.

'So, Alexandra, are you ready to say goodbye now?' I look at him quizzically.

'We've only just said hello. I thought you wanted a full forty-eight hours.' The rush of the absinthe permeates my brain as I wonder what he means.

'It means it is time to deliver what you promised me.' He takes my hand and strokes ever so gently beneath my palm, his fingers barely touching the skin. I take a deep breath and try to stay as calm and even as possible.

'You mean to stay the weekend? Jeremy, you know I've already promised you that, it's okay. I will still stay.' My words sound weak and wasted in their attempt to sound conversational. Jeremy can feel my pulse start racing at his previous words as his fingers are cleverly positioned on my inner wrist. What was I thinking? Trying to fool a doctor. Trying to fool Jeremy!

'You are toying with me, Alex. You know exactly what you promised.' He continues keeping track of my pulse as I attempt to look elsewhere, anywhere but him.

'Oh, you mean in the bath? Is that what you're talking about?' He shakes his head in condescension, but still has a smile on his face.

82

'Yes, GG, that is exactly what I'm talking about. You didn't think I had forgotten, did you?'

His words are loaded with innuendo from our ancient past whilst melding perfectly into this present moment. I pull away from him, attempting to put some physical and emotional distance between us.

'What was it again? I wasn't fully focused on our discussion at the time. Something about the lecture ... senses, was it?' I say flippantly, trying to lighten the mood, although something inside me wishes I hadn't asked given his furrowed brow, his silence intensifying the moment.

'You weren't serious, Jeremy? You can't have been. I thought you were just teasing, you know, just wanting to heighten the experience ...' He interrupts me.

'I asked you to promise me two things. No vision and no questions.' He pauses for effect. 'For forty-eight hours. Simple really. Nothing a smart, intelligent, woman such as yourself can't understand I'm sure.' My palms moisten at his words. He continues, in a serious, no-nonsense manner.

'Alexandra, you know better than anyone that I don't ever, ever joke or tease about promises.' He looks at me intently but allows me to keep my distance. Oh god, he was serious, he honestly wants to follow through with this. Typical, just when I'm starting to relax and have some fun. Such a Jeremy thing to do, to take the situation to a whole other level that puts me on edge all over again. I know full well that he is right. He takes promises more seriously than anyone else I know. What was I thinking? Making stupid mindless promises, all for the short-term satisfaction of a mind-blowing orgasm. Ah, but what an orgasm ... and I haven't had one for soooo long ... And the promise of more is almost too much to bear. *Focus!* I castigate myself.

'Well, Jeremy,' I say in a serious voice, attempting to harden my resolve and stand my ground. 'You did make me promise under duress and you know as well as I do, that it doesn't count.' I can only hope I am matching his language and energy as a last resort at getting out of this.

'Ah. So you do remember. We have progress. Would you really call that duress, sweetheart? It certainly seemed to me like you were more than enjoying yourself.' His words are as wry as his smile.

'Even so, it doesn't mean that it wasn't duress. You knew I was in a situation of weakness and just played on it.' I'm trying to sound convincing.

'Are you ready?' he says firmly. Obviously the time for discussion is over.

'Really? You want to go through with this stupid promise thing? It's so silly, nonsense really. We don't need our time together to be like this, Jeremy. It would be so much nicer to spend time together without ... well, without ... having this tension between us, without playing games. We've grown up, there is no need for this. It is just childish,' I say, my rising alarm giving way to a little exasperation.

His eyes narrow and zero in on mine as he steps toward me. I automatically take a step back; I can't help myself, as if erring on the side of caution, attempting to avoid the enveloping sense of danger, as enticing as it may be. He continues to close in on me. As I step back again I realise I have reached the edge of the table. What was I meant to do now, run? It seems ridiculous, running away from my best friend, my ex-lover. I don't want to run and therein lies the problem. I have to reason with him.

'Please, Jeremy, please, must you do this?' I say urgently, almost begging for both time and space. He places his arms on either side of my body, wedging me firmly against the table. His body presses against mine, my personal space vanishes and I have nowhere to go other than hold firm or lie backwards on to the table. I feel his eyes penetrate me, seeking my soul with their glare and know I must avoid looking at him at all costs, knowing that if I do, they will bore straight through me and penetrate my inner sanctum. There is no need for him to feel my pulse now; he can sense it all over my body. Like a Formula One racing car driver, my pulse only has one pace — fast.

'Alex.' He is close, firm, dominating. I sense his patience is diminishing rapidly. 'You promised; you know what that means between us. You know we never promise something we can't commit to, to ourselves or to each other. It has been that way since we met. Our word is our bond.'

The intensity of his words and the force of his response momentarily stun me. I hadn't anticipated the heated emotion trapped within them. A deep shiver runs down my spine. Once again my mind replays the promise memory again as if on cue, conjuring up the same images as before. I remember his words had a similar tone and finality.

'You know I am serious, Alexandra, I won't let this go.'

But will you let me go? Do I want to go? These silent questions float through my head.

I know he is not to be messed with whenever he uses my full first name.

The air between us is thick with pent-up energy, emotion, and anticipation. There is so much I want to say, so much that isn't coming out of my mouth. Where are my words? Where is my protest? Where is my escape? Why am I still here, accepting this? There must be something I can do. My mind is blank. Could I want this reality? Do I desire it? Is he tapping into something I've been denying in myself for years?... Oh no, my own mind has just given him the opening he is looking for.

I continue to search his eyes in an attempt to find further explanation as to why this is so important to him? Why so persistent? I know it is in his character; he has always been determined, always the winner, but why now, what is he winning? What could I be losing? I just don't understand. He must have sensed my analytical mind switching into gear because his voice interrupts my thoughts in their tracks.

'Enough! The time is now,' he proclaims in a booming voice. 'Make your decision.'

'Is it really my choice, Jeremy?' My voice shakes with emotion.

'It is always your choice, Alex, never forget that. You didn't have to promise and I am not forcing you to stay. I am simply outlining the conditions if you do.'

Oh, Jeremy, the supreme mastermind.

He takes my hands and gently leads me to the second bedroom suite. I can feel my heartbeating faster by the second. I can't decipher whether it is due to the absinthe, adrenaline or sheer emotion. I try to twist slightly away from his grip, without success. *Oh god,* I think, *what have I gotten myself into?* As my eyes scan the room, I notice an elegant silk blindfold cascading over the edges of a petite, expensive looking box — it is the same colour as my dress and interwoven with delicate black lace. Alongside it is a velvet face cloth, a tiny bottle of ointment and some eye drops laid out on the bedside table. My heart pounds erratically as my feet become firmly planted at the door.

There is a voice in my head screaming *Walk away now, right now! Move your feet and run. You are giving him complete control. It is wrong, you don't want this. You are a mother, a wife. Move, get going. Do not become a part of this.'* Another voice says in three simple words *Bring it on!* I begin to tremble. Jeremy hugs me possessively. Like a big brown bear paradoxically in love with its prey. My arms fall limp by my side.

'Why is this so hard for you, Alex? It is meant to be exciting, intoxicating, not make you shake like a leaf on a tree defending against gale force winds.'

His voice is low, caring, caressing. His words sum up my feelings more eloquently than I can describe them myself.

'Why is it so important that I comply, Jeremy?'

'You made a promise.'

'I feel this is about so much more than that, so tell me, please, just tell me what is going on. Why is this so important to you?'

'Let me have this moment with you, it won't last forever. I will look after you, I promise you that. When have I not?'

I let out yet another great sigh knowing his last statement is true. We have had some wild times together but he has always looked after me. I feel as confused as any human being on earth. Jeremy is telling me I have a choice, but I don't feel like I have one — if I want to stay, that is. Is that a true perception or merely my imagination? I honestly don't know. I am drowning in my thoughts and emotions when I notice a bowl of perfectly formed red apples sitting in the middle of the round table. Strange how I didn't notice them before, their symbolism being so obvious. For a fleeting moment I reflect how Eve must have felt when being tempted by the snake to eat the apple. Perhaps knowing it was the wrong thing to do, but also knowing intuitively that fate was clearing her path forward regardless of her own actions. Was she destined to play her role in the biblical story because the temptation was predetermined, beyond her control? Or was the choice she made solely of her own accord and she wanted to eat the apple to see what would happen? This internal debate is not helping my immediate dilemma.

'I'm not sure what to do, Jeremy, I just don't know.'

Deep down, I know these words are the wrong ones to say to the man standing before me. Nonetheless, his response catches me completely off-guard.

'I know I'm asking a lot, but remember; it was inspired by your lecture this afternoon. At the very least it will be a learning experience for you and I know you have never turned your back on continuing your education. I know how important it is to you. Think about what you ask your clients and students to go through to achieve personal growth. Is this so different? Except that I am asking *you* to go through it, instead of the other way around? I'm giving you the opportunity to understand first-hand the impact of lack of visual stimulation, to explore sensory deprivation for yourself, the very topic of your expertise. It may be the beginning of a whole new thesis for you, important research based around personal experience that you may have otherwise never considered.' He pauses, assessing my response to his line of argument, which is at least thought-provoking. I reluctantly admit to myself that his proposal intrigues me, though I'm just not sure I'm brave enough or have the strength to explore it on such a personal level.

'I don't want you to leave here now. I want to be with you, to touch you, to connect with you. You look divine, and I know you believe it, I see it in your eyes. I want you, Alex, and for the next forty-eight hours I want to send you where you have never let yourself go. I want to remove all your boundaries, I want to tap into the essence of your being, introduce you to yourself again. I know in my heart this is how to achieve it. Please, trust me. Let me take you on this journey of discovery. Give yourself to me.' Jeremy's voice is hypnotic, my brain and heart absorbing his words as if liquid to a sponge. His charisma, his presence, is both seductive and intoxicating.

I am lost in his words now, just as I was in his touch when we were in the bath together. He leads me to the edge of the bed, lowering me to a seated position. Everything becomes trance-like, tranquil. I feel energised, yet calm.

'You know I have always loved you, Alexa, I would never hurt you.' His voice is smooth, caressing my body to relax, for my mind to give in. I nod slightly, as if to say *I know, I understand*, but my words remain within, unspoken.

'You know that from the moment we met, I have never met anyone like you and I know I never will again.' His fingers caress my forehead, his palms settle on my temples.

'Lie still, Gorgeous Girl, let me look after you.' The fear that previously restrained me has mysteriously left my body and has been replaced by a peaceful awareness. My body is in a serene state while my mind is dependent on Jeremy's every word. I'm not sure I could lift myself from the bed even if I tried at this moment.

'Will you let me do this now?'

I feel my head nod slightly.

'You won't fight against me?' My head moves from side to side. His hands press firmly but gently on each of my shoulders as he slowly lowers my back on to the bed.

'Look at me, Alexandra.' I meet his gaze.

'Are you ready to say goodbye to your vision for forty-eight hours?'

'Yes,' I respond softly. As my response enters the air, a tear rolls slowly from my eye onto the bed, perhaps due to the anticipatory emotion contained within the decision I am making. He meaningfully kisses the trace of the tear on my cheek as if acknowledging the power I am granting him over me. His fingers guide my chin upwards, tilting my head back in to the palm of his hand.

'Thank you.' He softly shifts the loose hair that has fallen around my face to the side and masterfully places two drops of the ointment into each of my eyes. As I blink, the room quickly becomes dull and blurry.

'Close your eyes for me.' I take a deep breath as I slowly close them. I feel a light brush ever so gently stroke the ointment on to my eyelids and they become profoundly heavy. It only takes a few moments for the world to completely recede from my vision as darkness surrounds me.

What have I done?

Part III

'Life is a succession of lessons which must be lived
to be understood.'

— Ralph Waldo Emerson

'How are you feeling?'

'A little disoriented.' I sit up on the bed carefully. It definitely feels weird, like I'm in a black dream. I can't open my eyelids; they are dead weights on my face. I keep turning my head, searching for light, but of course, there isn't any.

'Now, was that really so difficult?' Jeremy teases.

'It wasn't easy, I can assure you. And I can't recall you volunteering in my place.'

'This weekend is about you, sweetheart, not me.' I don't want to go there again.

'What was it? That you put on my eyes?'

'Rest assured, nothing that hasn't been approved by the strictest pharmaceutical standards. I wouldn't put you in any danger. I'm a doctor, remember, I take my oath very seriously.'

Great, moral standing and access to any drugs he so desires.

'That's very reassuring, Doctor Quinn, given my current situation.'

He laughs. 'Honestly, are you alright? Can I help you?'

'I'm sure I'll need a lot of help with everything now that you have made me one hundred per cent blind! Are you sure this isn't permanent?'

'The drops last twenty-four hours give or take. I'll redo them tomorrow. Let me know when their impact is fading.'

'No problem. I'll be sure to let you know the second any light comes in.' My voice is laced with sarcasm. I raise my hand wanting to feel my eyes first-hand. They feel so heavy, so bizarre.

'Oh, no you don't.' My hand is guided away. 'No touching whatsoever. That is why you will also be wearing this blindfold, as a reminder to leave your eyes alone.'

'No way! That won't be necessary. I can't see a thing.'

'It is and you will.' He places it over my head. It fits snugly against my eyes and feels silky soft.

'Well, well, another perfect fit. Did you have it made especially?' I say jokingly.

No answer. 'Jeremy?' There is a long pause.

'Yes Alex, as a matter of fact, I did.'

* * *

'Come with me.' Jeremy holds both my hands and assists me carefully up from the bed. I forget I have high heels on and stumble a little before I regain my balance.

'Wow, this is really, really weird.' He places his arm around my waist and leads me out of the second bedroom rather precariously. I feel like an invalid. I am stunned this has happened, that I am now blind and fully dependent on Jeremy for the weekend. It makes me feel nervous and tense, but also excited somehow, not knowing what to expect. My dreamlike state has evaporated so I can only hope I'm not entering into a dark nightmare.

'Here, let's sit on the lounge.' He guides me down into the soft velvet cushions. I feel either side of me for armrests but there aren't any. I wonder how blind people do this every day of their lives? Not knowing how or when things are happening. The positive voice inside me is quietly grateful I had spent some time in the hotel suite earlier. At least I have some familiarity with my surroundings.

A knock on the door startles me.

'Stay here, I'll be right back.' His hands leave mine before I can respond. Jeremy briefly greets whoever is at the door as I sit on the lounge silently like a complete idiot with a blindfold on. I am deeply embarrassed.

I hear noises of plates being efficiently set up and arranged and a bottle crushing into ice, perhaps refreshing the champagne? There is a vague aroma of food in the room. There is no discussion between Jeremy and the 'door people' as they go about their business and they remove themselves as quickly as they arrive. I hear Jeremy thanking them and securely closing the door behind them.

He sits beside me on the lounge and places a glass of champagne in my hand.

'Thank you, Alexa, this means everything to me.'

It is so strange not being able to see that I find myself utterly lost for words, so I don't say anything. I hear our glasses clink together and feel a desperate need to gulp the bubbles down fast. I swallow as much champagne as physically possible, so urgent is the need for me to drink it. I suddenly feel completely out of control, reality hitting me like a brick on the head. I find myself wishing for another shot of absinthe to numb me from it all. What have I done? Anything could happen ... I have literally handed myself to him on a platter. Oh well, what possible difference could another glass of champagne make? At least if I pass out I won't be conscious of how freaked out I am. The rational voice in my head quickly questions the sanity of this particular logic. I keep tipping the glass up but it must already be empty given nothing is coming out.

'Whoa, Alex! You never drink that fast!'

'No. I don't, Jeremy.' I finally find my voice. 'But extreme situations can result in extreme behaviour.' I place my glass out into the space in front of me.

'Would you mind filling up my glass again, please? This champagne is delicious.'

'Are you sure?' he asks tentatively.

'Oh, yes, I am very sure I would love another glass of champagne. I would be very happy to pour it myself if you would be kind enough to direct me to the bottle, although I would hate to spill any on the lush, five-star carpet,' I say pointedly.

'You're mad at me?'

Such an emotional rocket scientist, I think to myself sarcastically; maybe his EQ isn't quite what I thought it was after all. Or maybe it is? I'm not so much mad at him as angry at myself for allowing this ridiculous situation to occur in the first place. The reality of being blind has caught me completely off-guard. It's one thing to be enticed by the concept, the sensuality of the idea, quite another to know I'll be living like this for the next forty-eight hours. My emotions are threatening to overwhelm me as the significance of what I have just done settles in to my bones.

As I can't see him, nor read his emotions, I just keep holding out my empty glass, waiting for him to provide the refill, needing the alcohol to fill the void.

'Alexandra, are you really angry with me? Honestly?'

Another Alexandra moment. I wait with my glass extended toward his voice. He takes it, refills it and places it back in my hand. Thank goodness. I'm relieved as I raise the bubbly liquid to my lips. I decide to ignore his question, believing it at least gives me some control.

'Lovely champagne, Jeremy. What is it? I'm not sure I've had it before.'

I sense he is bemused at my avoiding his question. Unfortunately, he knows me well enough to recognise the more polite I am being, the greater the emotion I am hiding. Basically, he knows me almost as well as I know myself, if not better. Which is no doubt why I am sitting here in a ball gown, with a blindfold on, in the penthouse suite, trapped for the weekend. It is just all the more frustrating.

'It's Krug. We had it when I graduated. You loved it then as well, said it put you in a really great mood and —'

'Oh, yes, I remember.' I cut him off, not wanting his version of a trip down memory lane right now. My emotions are in overdrive, all the hypnotic calmness having taken its leave.

'Well, all the more reason for drinking it now.' I say as I take another sip. At least I am not gulping it now. I hear him sigh.

'Will you at least have some *hors d'oeuvres* to go with your champagne?'

I have to agree some food wouldn't go astray. Even though my mind is spinning and my emotions are all over the place, I'm sure my rational brain wouldn't be encouraging me to drink any more alcohol without food.

'That would be lovely, thank you,' I say very politely, formally. I can just imagine him rolling his eyes at my behaviour.

'Open your mouth, please.' He is close to me.

'In my hand will be fine, thank you.' It feels good to assert myself.

'Alex, this is ridiculous.' I take another sip of champagne in defiance. Maybe being blind doesn't result in complete dependency after all. I can't help but allow a small smirk to ripple across my face. He quickly snatches the glass out of my hand.

My smirk vanishes immediately.

'Open your mouth and I will give you your glass back.'

I am just about to answer back when something small and delicious lands on my tongue. Taken aback, and with a mouthful of food tickling my tastebuds, I decide to close my mouth and eat it. After all, it would be a shame to waste such tantalising cuisine. Another one arrives not long after. Blini — absolutely delicious. I can taste the strong flavour of smoked trout against the light buckwheat pancake and feel the salmon roe slide around my mouth. The slightest hint of fennel confirms they are just like the ones we had in Russia all those years ago, amazing! Though I'm pleased we are drinking champagne rather than vodka as we were back then. My stomach is very grateful for the food.

'More?' I hear him ask. I nod and turn toward him, not really wanting to give him the satisfaction of my words. Something warm and soft arrives this time with an aroma of garlic and herbs.

'Mmm.' This time I can't help but let out a groan in delicious delight. 'Gorgeous. Scallop?'

'Indeed it is.' He dabs the corner of my mouth with a linen serviette. 'Another?'

'Yes, please,' I hear myself answer. After I swallow it he hands me back my glass of Krug. I sense he is happy that my frustration is dissipating alongside the food and champagne. Something about good food and wine that lifts the spirit, I think to myself.

'Care to share your thoughts?'

I eventually come to the conclusion that my anger is a result of my anxiety about losing control, particularly as I am so used to being in control of everything. I allow the emotion to leave me, as it is serving no purpose. Given my current predicament it would make the next forty-eight hours downright miserable for both of us, so I relent and share my thoughts with him. Although I am still on edge with my blindness and the dependency that surrounds me, it feels better being at ease with Jeremy and allowing the conversation to flow between us.

After a few minutes of banter, Jeremy sidles up against me.

'So tell me, honestly, how do you feel? Are you having fun?' He lifts me slowly off the lounge to my feet.

'Oh. Let me get this straight. You are allowed to ask as many questions as you want but I can't ask any, is that the way it works?' He caresses my neck and collarbone with his lips, oh so slowly, his breath like a feather against my skin.

'Yes, that's the way it works, for this weekend, anyway. There will be plenty of time for your questions later. So tell me, does this excite you?' he asks again as his lips locate the top of my breast and I feel a little light-headed as my breath becomes radically uneven for the umpteenth time this evening. His touch engages the rest of my body and my vulva swells and moistens in anticipation. I can't withhold a slightly muted sigh at the sensation.

'Oh, so the answer is yes,' he whispers into my ear as his teeth nibble my lobe.

'Yes,' I say breathlessly, 'it excites me a little.' Not wanting him to take away my words as he has my sight. His kisses feather and tease my lips.

'It does me too, very much,' he says as he lowers my hand to feel the bulge fighting against his trousers. It takes all of my concentration to prevent me from falling to my knees and devouring him then and there. The power of this raw, sexual emotion almost cripples me. I wonder if I know myself at all ...

The phone rings at that exact moment which startles me from my fantasy back to reality. He continues to hold my hand so I blindly follow him as he answers it, taking exaggerated, careful steps to balance on my heels.

'Wonderful, thank you. We are on our way.' He hangs up. 'Alex, you look panic-stricken, what's wrong?'

'Oh, nothing, nothing at all, why do you ask?' I say nervously, wringing my hands together. Can it be that even with a blindfold covering my eyes, he can still read that much expression on my face?

'Good, are you ready to accompany me to dinner?' With these words, the panic infiltrates my bones. He can't be serious, can he?

'We aren't really going out to dinner, Jeremy ... I can't possibly go out like this. Please, please tell me you're joking.'

'Of course we are. Why on earth would I waste you looking so exquisite and keep you confined to a hotel room? That would be absurd.'

I feel my breath shortening again. *Keep calm, breathe*, I say to myself, but I hear my words tumble out regardless.

'How many times are you going to send me into overdrive tonight, Jeremy? I can't take it, it's too much. I try to get my mind around one thing you are asking of me, leading me into, and wham, then comes the rush of another and another.'

I draw breath momentarily before continuing on my verbal rampage. 'I don't know what I'm thinking or feeling or even what I should say to you. This situation is too strange for me, unreal, surreal.'

I hear myself talking erratically, quickly, searching for words to account for the emotion that is threatening to totally overwhelm me.

'I have no filters, Jeremy. You've taken them away, or maybe I've allowed them to be taken. I don't know. Either way, it can't be good. I've trained myself for too many years to give considered, thoughtful responses and now listen to me. I don't know what I'm thinking or feeling or doing. Why are you putting me through this?'

Jeremy doesn't answer, but I sense his closeness and know intuitively that he is staring at me intently. I take a moment to catch my breath and attempt to regain some form of composure. I feel like a child lost in the wilderness, not knowing who to trust or where to turn.

He places his arm around the small of my back, while holding my wrist and firmly steers me toward what I assume is the door of the penthouse. I hear the door open.

'Oh no, please, Jeremy, let's stay here. What's the time, anyway? Isn't it too late for dinner? I'm not really hungry, we've had *hors d'oeuvres*. Really, it would be such a waste ...'

I ramble on, wedging my heels deep into the carpet, as I attempt to throw excuses in his unrelenting path.

'We can't possibly be seen in public, don't you understand?' I'm scrambling for words as he edges me closer to the door.

'How could you even think about taking me out like this? I'm blindfolded for goodness' sake and I have no knickers on!'

My heels wave the white flag as they surrender their grip on the floor and I catapult into his arms, and presumably out the door. I try to steady myself as best I can and he holds me firmly in his arms.

'Where are we going anyway?' I ask him, desperate for some form of verbal response. His silence is exasperating. He suddenly pushes me firmly against the wall, his face close to mine, his body pressing powerfully against the silkiness of my dress.

'I know you have questions, Alexa, you always do. As I have told you, this weekend is not about your questions. I have been counting how many you have asked so far and I strongly advise that you stop, as there will be consequences for each one. Now behave yourself!' he adds sternly. 'I am taking you to dinner; you look beautiful and you have nothing to be embarrassed about. Now, one more thing … as we are on my time this weekend, I never want you to ask the time again. Do you understand me?' He is so close I am dizzy with his questions and demands. I am dumbfounded at the sharpness of his words as his heady presence and aroma invade every facet of my space.

'Have-I-made-myself-clear?' He emphasises each word purposefully. I am at a loss as to this change of mood, the darkened edge to his voice, so much so that I am astonishingly not willing to risk an offhand or flippant comment in response. It is too strange, the tension palpable. So I defiantly remain silent, considering this to be the safest strategy, even though his erection continues to swell intensely against my belly. He grabs my shoulders and spins me around, pushing my breasts deliberately against the wall and swiftly slaps my arse so hard I am left with a stinging sensation that I cannot remotely fathom. This is the last thing I expect from him. I'm horrified. He just spanked me! Blindfolded, in the corridor of a hotel. He spins me back around just as rapidly, seemingly to inspect the look of utter shock on my face as a result of his handiwork.

'I asked you a question, Alexandra. Are we clear?' he says in his stern, metallic voice. All I can utter is 'Perfectly!' my knickerless arse sizzling against the wall. This is something new; he has done a lot of things to me over the years but never anything like that.

'Good. Let's go.' He takes hold of my elbow and steers me firmly down the corridor, my heels clattering against the hardened floor to keep pace with him. The sensation of being spanked is not something I am familiar with. I can't remember the last time it was done to me, even in childhood. Robert had certainly never done anything like that. He was always serious in the bedroom — perfunctory, never playful. I realise then and there that Jeremy is the opposite of Robert — playful, unexpected and oh, how I've missed this unpredictability in my life. Even now, humiliated in a hotel corridor, though I feel out of control, at the same time adrenalin is pumping through me in a way I haven't felt in years. I am truly alive.

I hear a 'ding' sound and the lift doors open as he guides me in. I take a deep breath and pray. Please don't let us bump into anyone I know. Please, please, please! The doors close and Jeremy doesn't skip a beat before his hands are stroking my thighs, coercing the softness between my legs to moisten further and become even more accommodating, which started the second his swift hand slapped my butt. An unexpected insight ... how can I be in shock yet so highly aroused and horny at the same time? Jeremy knows each and every one of my sensitive spots as well as any doctor knows the anatomy of the human body, and he isn't missing a single opportunity to use my body as his personal radar, testing and paying attention to the response, to great advantage.

It is such a weird sensation not being able to anticipate arousal; obviously visual stimulation plays a major role in this. Stranger still is having no true sense of what is coming next. Being so frustrated you could scream, then wham, one light, smooth stroke and your body roars into gear proactively endorsing the sting and the caress and leaving you begging for more. How does that work? The problem is, I'm not sure whether my body is betraying me deliberately or whether it knows my mind far more effectively than I could possibly imagine.

'Please stop it, Jeremy. It is hard enough to focus on what's going on, let alone having your hands distracting me at every opportunity.'

'The whole idea of this weekend is that you don't focus on anything, Alex.'

'Well, it is just not possible,' I say, exasperated.

The lift door opens and we step out as a rush of air blows my hair back. Jeremy is greeted. I feel the blood rushing to my face and am sure it is flushed.

'Dr J, how wonderful you could join us this evening, it's been too long.'

My legs quiver beneath me as Jeremy holds me securely upright.

'Lovely to see you again, Leo.'

'Let me show you to your table.' I am chaperoned to a lounge seat where Jeremy settles me into position. I quickly cross my legs, given my lack of underwear and inwardly curse Jeremy for making me feel as uncomfortable as I ever have in my entire life.

Who is Leo anyway and why can I hear the faint hum of voices around me? I can feel my forehead developing minute droplets of perspiration as my anxiety rises at the unknown yet again. Why am I so on edge anyway? *Relax, enjoy*, I tell myself. *Impossible*, comes the response.

'What will sir be drinking tonight?'

'We will have two martinis, extra dry, stirred not shaken, with a twist.'

Jeremy's response instantly surprises me. He has just ordered my perfect martini, even though I haven't touched a martini in the past ten years. Unbelievable.

I try to keep myself calm enough to at least decipher my surroundings and congratulate myself on maintaining a few moments of self-control. I notice the carpet is thick and lush and the voices are very low; some nondescript music is meandering around the room. As the fact that we are not alone comes to mind once again, my apprehension gains momentum until Jeremy's voice interrupts its predetermined destination.

'I'm assuming you are happy to have a martini? That is the way you always liked them in Europe.'

'A martini is the least of my problems.' I try to calm my voice as much as possible. 'How could you have brought me here with other people around? What if someone recognises us? I can't believe you are compromising me like this. You are putting both of us at enormous personal and professional risk. How could you? It is totally unacceptable.' My tension builds like a tsunami through my bloodstream. My heart pumps faster than it can reasonably handle, perspiration not cooling my body temperature as effectively as it should be. He has gone too far, this is not right. My hands are twisting and palms sliding with sweat on my lap. My breath short and shallow, I easily diagnose my state as an imminent anxiety attack. Jeremy cups my hands together.

'Calm down, everything is fine. You are overreacting.'

Overreacting? My internal voice is incredulous. 'Nothing is fine!' I exclaim, control almost lost. I rein it in as best I can as I have no idea who is in the room, who these people are. Does it matter? *Yes, it does, damn it.* I answer myself. And no doubt Jeremy knows this, knows I will attempt to contain my emotions in public.

'How could you put me in this situation, Jeremy? How dare you? Who are these people?'

I feel vulnerable, alone and completely out of control. My body trembles as it experiences the invading cocktail of emotions. This is not nearly as easy as I thought it would be, and I'm a little disappointed in myself for not handling it more professionally. But what is professional about being at dinner with a frigging blindfold on? Goodness knows what they are thinking, seeing a blindfolded woman arguing with one of the country's, make that the world's most renowned medical researchers. Or maybe this just happens to be 'Blindfold Friday' at the InterContinential — as if!

Suddenly, a moment of complete clarity and confidence sweeps through me. I realise I am in control. I still have legs that can walk, hands that can at least remove the suffocating blindfold that may enable some form of blurred, dark vision, and a voice to say 'No!' — the one thing I have never, ever been able to say to Jeremy. If luck is on my side, I may even be able to engage some innocent bystander to help me escape from this outrageous situation. As I let these thoughts rapidly flow through my body, I suddenly feel empowered to act.

'I can't do this, Jeremy. I know you were hoping that I could, and I have tried, but I can't. I'm sorry I promised you, but it was a stupid mistake. This situation is proving impossible for me to manage.' At these words, I stand up and raise my hands to remove my blindfold and be free of the embarrassment and submission it causes me. Just as my fingertips touch the silky layer, Jeremy launches himself over my body sending me flying back into the lounge seat. He grabs my hands and roughly pins them behind my back. With his legs now straddling mine, I am anchored to the seat and breathless at the suddenness of his plunge. The emotion between us is sizzling hot. He secures his grip around my wrists and ensures I literally can't move from under his physical presence.

'You will do this, you promised me, you consented and you haven't even given yourself time to adapt. You don't need to manage or control anything. That's your problem and until you stop trying you will be feeling like you do now. Let me be very clear — I will go to any extreme to ensure you keep your promise. I want you like this, Alex, and I won't let anything stand in my way, including your insecurities.' His voice is low, demanding, unrelenting. I can feel his muscles surrounding my legs, my thighs; I can feel his excitement swelling above me. My god! Now I can feel my own in response. How does he do this? He wants me, and how long has it been since I've heard that? Since forever, it seems. And I want him, but like this? And what *about* my insecurities?

Dumbfounded, I squirm ineffectively beneath him.

'You will have your chance to remove the blindfold when we have been together forty-eight hours. You are not touching it, nor are you going anywhere.' There is an irrevocable determination in his voice that is unyielding and compellingly X-rated. God, what happened to the empowerment I felt only moments ago? No eyes to see, no legs to walk, no hands to move. He really is taking every bit of control away from me and his physical response clearly tells me he loves it. And apparently so do I.

'Well, you are certainly using over-the-top measures to ensure that I don't.' I acknowledge for his benefit that I can barely move. Even as I question why I am secretly thrilled that he is going to such extremes, my arousal skyrockets with each passing second.

'Trust me, Alex, the fun is yet to begin and I know you will love it if you just give yourself the opportunity to embrace it.'

Is he my therapist now? I decide that struggling is futile, as it just seems to strengthen his resolve further both figuratively and physically; he tightens his hold on both my wrists and thighs. My brainstorming mind clicks into gear weighing up potential options. As if sensing my thoughts he states calmly, 'Don't fight me on this, AB, you will lose.'

Just as I'm about to speak Jeremy's mouth comes hard against mine with his tongue forcing its way through my lips, probing my tongue, invading my throat, harder and faster as I am pinned beneath him. He smothers my face, leaving me literally gasping for air. His power is a carnal force that my body has no urge to reject.

'You are mine for the weekend. Stop fighting so hard, you are wasting precious energy that could be put to much more effective use.' His voice is laden with suggestive undertones. 'God, you look absolutely irresistible. Shame we have company or I swear I would take you right here, making the most of the access under your dress.'

I am left melting beneath him; the hot, pulsing ache in my groin ensuring I am breathless and wanton.

'So beautiful, but she does struggle so …' he reflects, and for a long moment his palms cup my chin and cheeks as he straddles my body. I feel his erection harden against my thigh. He releases a long sigh as I anxiously await his next move.

'You leave me no choice. Leo, please cuff her.'

'Certainly, sir, right away.'

Jeremy pulls my shoulders toward his body and slides his hands down my arms to my elbows ensuring they don't bend as they are anchored behind me. Leo, whoever he is, quickly straps something that feels like padded handcuffs around my wrists and clasps them together in record time.

I am left gasping, speechless, bound and blind as Jeremy secures the blindfold back into position. What on earth is going on here? This isn't just some university prank that we can laugh about together. Jeremy said he would go to virtually any length to make this happen. Why? My thoughts are pulsating in my brain in tandem with my heart, trying to decipher what has just happened to me. I can feel the intensity of the energy in the room as if it is pumping through the air. What is driving him to be so dominating? What exactly am I missing?

'I'd forgotten just how very stubborn you are. It's quite astonishing.' The old Jeremy is back, having a normal conversation with me. Unbelievable.

'Stubborn,' I shriek, emotion still overwhelming my muscles, my voice. 'How can you …'

'Please, keep your voice down. I won't be able to feed you with a gag in your mouth,' he states calmly.

'You wouldn't dare —'

He cuts me off immediately. 'I've come this far, my love. You know I would. The sooner you surrender yourself to me, the more freedom you will experience,' he whispers as if we are co-conspirators. What does he mean by that?

I shuffle around on the seat while trying to fully absorb the reality of my wrists being bound behind me. Although we have had an exploratory sexual past, Jeremy has never taken things this far before. There has never been this urgency, this underlying non-negotiable tone. I recognise now that perhaps I am in well and truly over my head. I just don't understand what is driving this situation, and why ...

One minute I feel so close to him, in every way. The next minute I have to wonder if I know him at all. I am a mother for god's sake; how the hell did I let myself get into this situation? What if I really can't get out of it, now that I'm here? Is he joking, playing? Is he testing me? Pushing me to the limit? If so, it is working. I am confused and panicked, and contradictorily and frustratingly, extremely bloody aroused.

* * *

'Now, let's not waste these martinis.'

Jeremy holds my chin upwards and carefully slides the cold liquid into my mouth. I don't speak to him; I honestly don't know what to say. I can barely move. I am petrified of going against his wishes after what has just happened, which is no doubt exactly what he intended, so I sit in silence, like a mannequin. It's as if every cell in my body is electrified, awaiting his next move, on high alert. It's strangely invigorating. I can feel his stare attempting to penetrate my thoughts. I try to calm my breath, my emotions, my thoughts ... I fail. More silky liquid finds my tongue and slides down my throat. I don't encourage it. I don't prevent it. I'm frozen with some sort of fear of the unknown that I can't define; it's exciting and tantalising even though I feel utterly vulnerable with only Jeremy to rely on. What choice do I have, but to temporarily accept this bizarre sequence of events without protest or complaint? However, in accepting this fate I am also forced to concede that I have never felt more special or cherished by anyone in my life.

Presumably we have finished our martinis because I am guided to a standing position. Jeremy slips his arm around my waist through my bound arms. We walk away without words. Suddenly, my feet are swept out from beneath me and Jeremy carries me easily up some stairs. It makes me feel very small, even more fragile and dependent, when he can scoop my body up so effortlessly. I have no physical defence against him and my emotional ones are being systematically infiltrated. I have never relied on someone so completely. I am usually so self-sufficient and this gesture of complete possession makes me quite literally go weak at the knees.

I hear a door open and feel a flood of fresh air surround me. He lowers me directly into a chair. I can hear the noise of the city below and feel the warm humid air on my skin. I imagine the evening is as beautiful as the day was earlier. It feels good to be out of the tense energy of that room. My entire body shudders with relief at this new environment and sense of space around me.

'Are you cold?' He is obviously watching me as intently as I had supposed he was. Before I can stop myself, I shake my head, acknowledging his question. So much for ignoring him. I continue to sit as still and straight as possible. I sense that he continues his attempt to decipher my every mood and reaction.

'Would you like some music, or would you prefer to sit in silence?' He always had a knack for procuring an answer other than yes or no. I sigh inwardly but don't answer him. This is his game, his rules, so I assume he will decide.

'Music it is, then.'

Some light, mellow jazz music instantly commences at the end of his words. I am surprised — the music sounds live and I tilt my head in the direction of the sound. The music is smooth and melodic, vaguely familiar although I can't quite place it at this stage. A light aroma teases my olfactory sense and I pause to consider its identity. I can detect wonderfully fresh coriander, chilli, some ginger, perhaps sesame oil. I realise Jeremy is allowing me to smell and absorb one of my favourite Thai dishes. He raises it carefully to my lips, teasing me a little. I let him play his silly games.

'God, you look so gorgeous sitting here, so beautiful, so vulnerable, so stubborn. The night is spectacular, let me describe it for you. There is a full moon rising from the east, looking magnificent, not a cloud in the sky. The city lights are shining neon everywhere around us. We're on the rooftop of the hotel, and we are the only guests here, so you don't need to worry about anyone recognising us. The table has been set simply but is sophisticated, like you. I have ordered your favourite foods, your favourite wine, your favourite music. We are finally able to share these things in style with no expense spared. Alexa, I have longed for this moment with you and it is even more perfect in reality. I have you all to myself. You sitting there so still, bound and blind, being so brave, it is just melting my heart. I would release your wrists, but the vision of you sitting before me like this is giving me such a surprising hard on, I am selfishly savouring the moment a little longer.'

His words leave me speechless, my body responding as it would to his touch. I hear music floating around my ears.

'May I have this dance?' It appears to be a rhetorical question as I am escorted to my feet. He releases my wrists from behind my back only to refasten them together around his neck. It seems as if I'll be dancing regardless. Does he honestly think I'm going to run away from a high-rise rooftop when I'm blind? The thought flitters flippantly through my mind … My brain finally recognises the riff that has been playing since our arrival. His hips start to move, I clumsily move with him, I don't have much choice. He holds me close to him until we gain some form of synchronicity. He places my head on his shoulder and I can feel the smooth fibres of his shirt and, behind that, the heat from his chest. I'm intrigued by the specific choice of the song. I don't resist the rhythm of his body. I inhale. I exhale. Words float into the music that he knows I love.

The saxophone, guitar, drums and percussion caress away the anxiety I experienced before, and I effortlessly glide in his arms as he leads me confidently around the dance floor. Jeremy carefully and skilfully dissolves my tension until I am literally melting into his arms. His touch is exquisite, not too much, not too little. The sexual chemistry cascading over our bodies is once again impossible to ignore.

We dance, we eat, we drink, we talk, we kiss, we laugh.

I am blind but no longer bound.

I allow myself to compartmentalise any fear I felt downstairs into a distant, shrunken corner of my mind. Maybe tonight is as much for him as it is for me, maybe it is about us, I don't know. Finally the scales tip and I can say I am here now more by choice, rather than force. After feeding me dessert, an extravaganza of taste sensations: smooth, silky chocolate ganache, with a hint of something — orange perhaps or some other citrus — in crisp, buttery pastry, accompanied by a sticky dessert wine that leaves my tongue thick in my mouth. I am floating on air.

'Alex, would you sing for me, while we have the band still with us?'

I smile at his question. 'It's been years since I have sung anything.'

'Please, it is only us. Any song you choose. There is a guitar here for you.'

Jeremy used to love listening to my girlfriend Amy and I jam together on rainy Sunday afternoons. I was embarrassed at first but we became used to his presence on these occasions. Even though I have consumed a considerable amount of alcohol since my arrival, I'm surprised that I feel only a little tipsy, not drunk. Perhaps more hours have passed than I realise, or the degree of sheer emotion and nervous energy scorching through my body has burned off the alcohol. The idea of doing something I haven't done for years suddenly appeals to me.

'Why not? Just one song.'

He sounds surprised and excited that I agree so readily. I want to keep the mood this way rather than revert back to my previous antagonism. I think of the words of the songs we have just been dancing to and wonder what our relationship is really about, what it means to him? I remember a song we sang and which he used to love to accompany us with improvised percussion on saucepan lids. It was about best friends and was always special between us. Jeremy assists me with the guitar and I ask him to leave me with the band.

'I'll wait by the table. Enjoy!' he encourages, as he kisses me on the cheek. It takes me a little while to get comfortable with the guitar and establish the right key. My fingertips have softened over the years from lack of playing; the strings feel raw and hard against them as I adjust to the sensation and slide my hand along the neck of the guitar. I have to go on feel rather than sight but thankfully I know the words and chords by heart. I begin …

A tear trickles out of my left eye as I finish the song to resounding applause from the band. It felt incredible, to sing again, to play, to do something I thought I'd forgotten. I loved it! I'm euphoric as I blindly thank the band for the opportunity and they help me to put the guitar down. I can't help but consider I would never have done this if I could see … As I stand up Jeremy swoops in to give me an all-encompassing hug.

'That was fantastic. You were amazing!' He pauses. 'Is that emotion I detect on your cheek, Dr Blake?'

'I think I found my voice again.' I wonder why I use these words.

Another drop of emotion finds its way from my eye to my cheek. I can't understand why I am feeling this way but singing and playing somehow strikes a chord in me, one that hasn't been accessed for many years. I remember reading once that it was important to understand where your tears come from as they have a direct connection to your heart.

What is he doing to me? Another layer removed.

Jeremy lowers his lips to mine and before I can say anything, he kisses me so exquisitely and delicately, the effect so heavenly, that the feeling and memory will be etched in my psyche forever.

* * *

Our night on the rooftop comes to a close as I hear the members of the band pack up and say their goodbyes. I feel like I have been on a roller-coaster from the second I arrived in the hotel foyer. I have never experienced such intense emotions in such a whirlwind period of time. I wallow in the sensation of the warm, gentle breeze and relax in Jeremy's arms. To be honest, I feel exhausted fighting him and exhilarated being so close to him. Maybe I should just let go, like he wants me to. What would be the worst that could happen? He'd never put our professional reputations at risk, it means too much to him. And apart from that, I want to be with Jeremy. Mother, woman, wife, academic, all parts of me want Jeremy, have always wanted him if I'm completely honest with myself, and my body certainly requires no rationalisation. I desperately want to prolong the perfection of the moment we are sharing.

I am considerably calmer now. The ambience of the music, the singing, dancing, dining, kissing, and maybe even the darkness — though I'd never dare admit it — is simply intoxicating, like floating on air. I feel a warm, light energy within me, a sparkling essence that I don't believe I have experienced before. It is an unnatural sensation for me, though I happily absorb its presence.

'What are you thinking right now?' Jeremy asks as he plays with my hands and lightly places his thumb over my bottom lip. I can tell he is in a playful mood.

I answer him directly. 'I'm thinking I want you, right now.'

'Oh, really?' He laughs. 'And do you think you can have me?'

'Mmm, yes, actually I do, now that I have my hands back.'

I find his belt and unbuckle it, quickly undoing his fly and sliding his trousers down over his firm, round butt cheeks.

'Do you need any assistance?'

'I may not be able to see, Jeremy, but I know what I'm looking for.'

I sense his smile as I feel the considerable bulge rising from inside his underpants. I play a little before removing the obstacle they present. My palms longingly stroke the flesh of his cock, my fingers desperate to knead his balls. He groans in unison with my touch.

'You still like it like this, after all these years?' I inquire.

'Some things never change.'

I lower myself to my knees, continue fondling his balls while firming my grip on the base of his penis and ever so gently dart my tongue back and forth on his tip, eliciting a slick of salty juice that casually cascades over his rim, and pause. His hands have caressed my hair until this point; now he firmly holds my head — for balance? From need? I steady myself with my palms gripping his firm, muscled buttocks and I continue to tease, taking a little more of him in my mouth, stroke by stroke. My tongue loses its focus and becomes hungry for him. My mouth is all-encompassing, his length teases the back of my throat and I readily welcome him in, his smooth, hard cock filling my mouth as I take him deeper and deeper.

I love doing this to him and I can't deny the burning flame it ignites between my thighs as I continue to suck, now long, deep and strong. Jeremy groans loudly and I know he is close, nearly there. I ease off a little, playing, revelling in his need for me, before thrusting him wholly into the back of my throat and wrapping my lips around his base. I feel the throbbing before the explosion that almost comes into my mouth. At the last second, I pull my mouth away, still maintaining my grip on his balls. He convulses at his climax, while his liquid must be landing somewhere over my shoulder. I remain kneeling until he recovers and returns to reality and lightly kiss his tip before standing, licking the remaining residue. His breathing is heavy, uneven.

'Why do you always pull out at the last minute? I would love you to swallow.'

'You know I don't like it.'

'Have you ever tried?'

'Not exactly, and I'm not planning to.'

'So it's not just me.'

'No, not just you, Jeremy. It's just not something I do.'

'But it feels so unbelievable when you do everything else. It would be heaven if you swallowed.' Ah, here is an opportunity; I wonder whether he is willing to negotiate.

'Would you give me my vision back, if I said I'd swallow?' I tease.

'Ah, as tempting as that would be … well, let's just say I'm loving you blind.'

'Well, here we have an impasse,' I conclude.

He kisses my mouth, long and deep as his hand creeps underneath my dress, finding and fondling my inner lips. His fingers begin to explore, to probe. I sigh, ensuring my hands are entwined around his neck, trying to resist the temptation to join him.

His fingers continue their magic and my legs loosen their grip and stability on the rooftop. 'You will take me wholly and completely that way one day,' he states with confidence.

'We'll have to see about that,' I retort while sighing, attempting to stay upright.

'Indeed we will.' He laughs, as he eases his fingers from their mission and once again scoops me off my feet and carries me back to the room.

My dress is discarded before I register its removal and his fingers resume their conquest with greater intensity than where they left off on the rooftop. Jeremy's skill and precision is even more highly tuned than I recollect. Every shred of concentration leaves my mind and my moans echo within the silence of the room. As my brain has exhausted itself in its attempts to grasp the reality of the past few hours, my body greedily embraces the physical experience on offer. Eventually, I fall asleep, warmly snuggling into Jeremy's embrace. A deep, calm, strangely gratifying sleep.

* * *

There is a strange sensation on my feet. I try to push it away, dream it away, but it is like an itch I can't get rid of. What is it? Someone? Something? I roll over trying to ignore whatever it is but this persistent tinkering with my feet is relentless.

Damn it, it's still there … a finger?

No, too hard.

A brush? No.

A feather perhaps? Possibly.

These silly thoughts are making me lose my slumber. It is still dark so no need to wake up yet. I try kicking it away this time, ah yes, that works. I settle back into the gorgeous softness of the bed, crisp sheets and feathery pillow. Although, very different from my own. The thought makes my mind consider where I am. No, I think, as weird memories flood my mind, it must have been a really, really bizarre dream … My hand reaches out, wondering whether I will confirm a presence on the bed next to me. Nothing. No one. I have no idea how long I have been sleeping when suddenly it hits me. Where I am and who I'm with.

Reality strikes. I try to prise open my eyes, momentarily forgetting my current situation and hesitate before touching the blindfold, the memory of the same action from last night and the repercussions that followed preventing me from doing so. This was no dream and from what I understand, for me at least, it will be dark both night and day.

The persistent aggravation at my feet recommences, meandering its way past my ankles, along my lower leg, and toward my knee. A very ticklish spot for me, it has always been intolerable to be tickled there. I sit up, fully alert.

'Hello there.' Jeremy's voice. Definitely not a dream.

I laugh nervously. 'Hello there. How long have I been asleep?'

'You ask a question in the first seconds of waking up. Be a good girl for me, Alex. No questions. Please just lie back down and keep quiet.'

I obey. I don't want to argue. I feel the sheet being whisked off the bed, as I lie there, exposed, naked. The feathers continue their journey, making me squirm as they tease their way past my bellybutton to my nipples. I don't need to see them to know how instantly they respond to this ticklish touch.

'My body betrays me so easily,' I whisper almost to myself.

'It always has; when will you start listening to it?'

I ponder the question.

'Please raise your arms above your head and keep them there.' I do what I am told, his direct instructions for some reason becoming easier to follow as my mind flitters off on other tangents. The feathers play with my arms, my face, my neck. Being blindfolded, naked, and having feathers gently and carefully caressing my body without any idea as to where they could land is like nothing I have ever experienced. Their lightness is like butterflies fluttering in a gentle breeze, barely touching my skin, and the ever-so-mild sensation they deliver on contact sends shivers and goosebumps all over my body.

'Please part your legs,' Jeremy orders politely. Whether it is years of defensive or protective sexual behaviour I'm not sure, but these words immediately cause my legs to press firmly together and my hands lower themselves from above my head to cover my pubis.

'Interesting ...' Jeremy murmurs. The feathers stop their crusade and nothing else is said. I can feel him waiting for my next reaction. My arms slowly return to their original position above my head.

Continued silence. My vulva pulses with so much anticipation I am scared to part my legs in case the throbbing looks as obvious to him as it feels to me. As if it wouldn't be, I reprimand myself.

'I'll ask one more time, please open your legs.'

I sigh, embarrassed but enormously aroused. I slowly inch my thighs apart.

'Further, please.' His voice is adamant. God, he really has to make a point of things. I bend my knees as I open wider for him, the throbbing within me deepening with anticipation. I try not to move as the tickling recommences, but it is exceptionally difficult. I begin to wriggle and squirm, attempting to anticipate his next focus point on my body. An impossible task, but I manage to maintain my overall position as best I can. The tickling is insistent, teasing, yet so light, almost caressing, but not quite. My body yearns for more, longing for Jeremy's touch. In all this time his skin never touches my body, not once. I am literally craving him. My breath grows shallow. How much longer can he keep this going? I can't stand it. I need more pressure, more something, anything. I can't help but lower my hands to my breasts as my back arches with the continuing sensation. I am hungry for him to be inside me, desperate for his physical touch. His patience is beyond what my body can bear and he knows it. He always loved testing my limits, pushing my boundaries further than I ever thought possible.

'Jeremy.' I call his name as I reach out for him.

'Patience, sweetheart, patience. Until you lie completely still and do exactly as I ask, this will continue and relief will elude you. The more disciplined you are, the greater the reward.'

'Oh, god,' I groan, knowing all too well he is completely serious. His ability to tease, tickle and torment every inch of my body has been tried and tested on many occasions throughout our history. I sigh in utter frustration. I am too far gone to say no and he knows only too well I am craving release. I summon all my 'inner zen' to lie still, in the position *he* wants me in and accept the relentless torment without further protest or complaint. I try to count backwards from 100 and lose count as I arrive rapidly at eighty-nine, unable to focus my mind.

I squirm.

He stops.

I lie still.

He recommences feather warfare. I am frantic for his touch while attempting to maintain this position for him.

He is relentless, disciplined and patient.

I am not.

When I'm saturated with frustration and desire, his body suddenly slams on top of me, spearing his throbbing penis into my vagina so completely I cannot withhold the scream that escapes my lungs. My legs are spread far and wide as he penetrates deeper layers, sparing no force as he pins my arms above my head. He thrusts and thrusts, it is hard and it is fast and it is exactly what I need. My back arches at the force of him, flinging back my head. I feel winded without the dreadful pain. My lubricated vagina hungrily absorbs his entry as he explodes inside me.

Apparently his patience had finally reached its limit. Thank heavens!

He collapses on top of me, his weight smothering me into the mattress. We are speechless as we both pant for more oxygen. My tingles below return, deep longing in the base of my belly. This sensation began in the bath and will no doubt stay with me for some time. He snuggles into my neck.

'That was unbelievable. I've never woken up like that in my life.'

'Likewise,' he agrees, kissing, almost eating, my neck.

'Please don't make me wait that long again. You almost sent me over the edge.'

He continues devouring my neck hungrily with his lips and tongue before admitting a dire truth. 'I'm certainly never going to promise you that, sweetheart.'

I groan. Again.

'You must be starving. Let's eat!'

I can honestly say my body has never felt more alive. I have not been this sexed up since my early twenties but this is so much more than it ever was then. How we still have it in us, I don't know. My lips above want to smile. My lips below are buzzing with greed and anticipation. I can feel sexual energy pulsing through my veins, in my blood. It is the weirdest sensation, sated yet hungry for more. What is happening to me? Can it really be the lack of visual stimulation enabling me to feel so much more than usual, or is it the result of the emotional roller-coaster Jeremy has carefully crafted since my arrival? It's as if he is awakening sexual cravings that have been lying dormant within me for years, just waiting to be ignited. I can only conclude it must be the combination of all the above as my ability to conduct further analysis at this stage is without a doubt, defunct. I can't help but ruminate on the irony that my attempts to connect with my analytical mind for research purposes are being constantly annihilated by wave after wave of Jeremy-created sensation.

Jeremy orders almost everything he can think of from the room service menu. We chat and we laugh and we caress and it doesn't seem so weird that I'm wearing a blindfold. His voice is so reassuring and familiar that I almost feel totally at ease. The food arrives and we finally eat. I am ravenous.

'Are you still hungry?' he inquires as he places another strawberry in my mouth.

'I honestly can't get enough of these, they're addictive. There is something about fresh strawberries and five-star hotels. It's like they are designer made, perfect …'

'Well there is only one left. Here, you have it.' He places it in my mouth and then suddenly withdraws it.

'On second thoughts, you have probably had your share. I might keep this one for myself.' He loosens my robe and I feel the strawberry circle my nipples. It travels past my bellybutton before teasing my opening. I feel the juicy fruit enticing my vulva.

'I think this one would like to play hide and seek.'

I whimper as his tongue commences seeking.

Part IV

'Life is not measured by the number of breaths we take,
but by the moments that take our breath away.'

— **Anonymous**

'**N**ow, let's get you dressed. We have a big day ahead of us.'

'A big day? Aren't we just going to hang around here all day and play?' I don't envisage getting out of my bathrobe for quite a few hours so I don't take him the least bit seriously.

'Another question,' he responds flatly.

Not the question thing again, I think to myself. His tone makes me apprehensive. I don't understand what it is about. What is he expecting? A mute? Of course I have questions, what woman on the face of the earth wouldn't, even under normal circumstances, let alone in this situation? I wish he could just relax and chill a little more about the whole question thing.

Rather than saying any of these thoughts out loud however, inwardly congratulating myself from the lesson of last night, or whenever it was, I attempt a different tack.

'So, what will I be wearing then?' I ask chirpily, stupidly.

'You really can't stop yourself, can you?'

'What?'

'Asking questions!' He sounds completely exasperated.

'I didn't!' I say indignantly. 'Oh, I did,' as I remember my last words. 'Slow learner, I guess?' I try to make light of my error. I reach out to find him for a quick all-is-forgiven hug, but the space around me is decidedly empty.

'You will learn, Alex,' I hear from somewhere else in the room. 'I'm just not sure that you will appreciate the lesson.'

'What does that —?' I hear the words leave my mouth before I can prevent them and immediately stop myself short. I don't understand his cryptic comment but I am surely not going to be led into yet another question, just in case.

'Alright then, let's get dressed,' I say as lightly and easily as possible.

'Much better,' he replies smoothly and kisses me on the lips. Happy again. All good.

Although … I can't help but think that I'm being trained for something, like a good puppy.

'The girls should be here any moment to help get you dressed.'

Even after these unexpected words, a knock on the door startles me more.

'Girls. What girls?' I say in a freakishly high voice. 'Sorry, sorry,' I say automatically before he does the 'another question' routine. I'm on edge all over again.

'Just relax, I'll get it.' I'm really left with no choice. I hear female voices introduce themselves at the door to Jeremy, something like Cindy … Candy … He can't be serious.

'Hi, pleased you could make it. Come on in, she's in here.' My mind starts to spin as I urgently feel for the edge of the bed and accidentally roll off the corner, leaving me splattered on the floor. Jeremy comes rushing over asking if I'm okay. I feel like a complete idiot. I'm so embarrassed, I want to curl up in a small ball and disappear through the floor. How could he? My heart is beating so fast, I don't know what to think, do or say. He always had this fantasy about two girls … He wouldn't, he couldn't! He helps me to my feet.

'Are you sure you're alright? You look pale.' I feel green, so I can only imagine how 'pale' I look. Words elude me.

'The girls are here to help you dress for our big adventure,' he exclaims, true blue excitement in his voice.

'I don't want or need any more adventures, Jeremy. I have now had enough for a lifetime,' I say in a harsh whisper, as I don't know how near or far 'the girls' are from where I am. He raises me to my feet and leads me to the bathroom. Oh god, is he insane?

'Don't worry, it's not what you think. They are here to help, I promise.' He extracts his arms from my grip and hands me over to them. I start to tremble. One of my hands is placed in each of theirs. I try to keep hold of him but his touch is withdrawn.

'No, please don't leave me. I don't need their help. I'll be fine on my own. Jeremy?' I hear the door close and I am left alone in a panicked state with two female strangers and their call girl names, who are faceless to me, though I am not to them. I feel long fingernails on the hands gently removing my robe. I instinctively hold onto it, tightening its grip around my waist. The fingernails try again as other hands undo the waist tie simultaneously. I attempt to distract the touching fingernails by talking to them.

'I'm honestly fine, I can handle this. It's okay, really.' They continue on their quest. I am surprised when they remove my blindfold. I am now fully naked. I am placed on the toilet. I cover myself with my arms. The shower is turned on and I am led into it. The water sizzles against my goosebumped skin. My hair is washed, conditioned and massaged so delicately and carefully that I find myself relaxing into it more than I imagined possible. The fingernails become allies as they smoothly lather me up beneath their expert touch. When four hands are skilfully conducting their business over your body, do you prevent them or willingly allow them to complete their mission? I accede to the latter.

The products they are using smell divine and feel rich and luxurious against my skin, leaving me feeling velvety soft as I'm thoughtfully rinsed clean with the steaming water cascading down from above. No words are spoken as I am exited from the shower and thick plush towels dry every inch of my body. Smooth, silky, moisturised hands glide along my legs, arms and torso. They lift one foot at a time and massage between each and every toe sending reverberations to other less obvious parts of my body. Wow, I had no idea toes could have that effect. When their task is complete I am carefully re-robed and I breathe a sigh of relief that they went no further. I feel so soft, so ripe, so replenished and I smell like I've been ensconced in an exotic genie-bottle of Coco Mademoiselle. I would hug myself, if I were alone. My hair is blow dried, then tightly bound into a low French braid. I attempt to open my eyes but my lids are still so heavy it hurts to try, so my grey darkness continues, with or without a blindfold, into the next unknown.

I hear a rustling sound as I am ushered out of the bathroom, into the walk-in robe. I am then zipped and buckled into a leather all-in-one suit with thick knee-high boots, and gloves that just so happen to fit perfectly. Surprise, surprise! Every part of my body is clad in the aroma and feel of leather. Large sunglasses complete the look as I lose all sense of light when they are wrapped around my eyes. Good old Jeremy hasn't left anything to chance.

In some respects, I am thankful I can't see how ridiculous I look. I have no idea what I'm dressed for, except that Jeremy must have some full-on leather fantasy that I was completely unaware of. I jingle as I move because of the number of zips and studs strapping the outfit securely to the contours of my body. I envisage I look quite punk-like, imagining the leather is black but I have no idea. I would roast him if it were any other colour, come to think of it; imagine if it were some hideous hot pink! Although I feel hefty and resilient from the neck down, I am completely vulnerable from the chin up. I have no idea what I am doing in this heavyweight outfit and certainly hadn't considered the prospect of leaving the hotel. But I guess, since I've been having such an extended run of incorrect assumptions, I should have expected as much.

'Wow, you look fierce, Alexa, like a tough biker chick. If I didn't know you I'd be scared shitless.'

'And if I didn't know you, Jeremy, I wouldn't be dressed like this in the first place,' I say, with my hands firmly planted on my hips.

'Fair call,' he says with a laugh. 'Fair call.'

Inwardly, I love the idea of looking 'fierce' and am happy to play the role, even if I am as blind as a bat.

'Let's go, biker babe! There's not a moment to waste.' He grabs a handful of my smooth, leather-clad butt and leads me out the door to the lift. Is this all just a funny charade? Either way, I can't help but find it amusing, so I grab his butt in return and feel that he is in the same material as me.

'Well, well … we must look quite a sight.'

'Indeed we do,' he agrees as the lift descends.

* * *

We arrive and I sense, given the length of the time we are in the lift, that we must be at the lobby or parking area of the hotel. I nudge closer to him, knowing we are entering the 'real world', and my insecurities instantly come back to haunt me. He places me next to a wall.

'Don't move an inch, sweetheart. Just stay where you are and I'll bring her around.'

'Her?' Insecurity rises to fear within the space of a millisecond. I clamber against the wall as he leaves me stranded. The roar of an engine coming to life makes me leap with fright as petrol fumes invade my nostrils. The sound and smell are close enough to touch as Jeremy grabs my hand and pulls me toward the monstrous noise.

'Have you ever been on a bike before?' he yells as he drags my hesitant leg over the throbbing beast.

'Only a trail bike on a farm when I was growing up,' I reply nervously.

'Well, hold on tight, babe, 'cause you're in for one hell of a ride.' He sounds like a teenage kid who is driving his own car for the first time.

'But I can't see!' I scream as he squeezes a helmet over my head and ensures my glasses are correctly positioned.

'You don't need to see, I do,' he shouts back at me over the noise.

The engine growls to life underneath me. He laces my fingers together around his waist.

'You just need to hold on!'

'Do you have a licence to ride this thing?' I yell in his direction.

'You don't need to shout. I can hear you now you have your helmet on.' I hear his voice penetrating the inside of my helmet, straight into my ear. He ignores my question. *Uh oh*, I realise I have just asked another, and hope he hasn't noticed.

'Hold on, sweetheart, and try to calm your breathing just a little.' He could obviously hear my anxiety through the helmet's microphone.

'Easier said than done!' As the beast lurches forward, I'm almost left behind. I have no option but to hold on to him as tightly as possible as we swerve around a sharp corner. The wild ride of this weekend is clearly still in full octane swing.

We stop and start quite a bit for a while and it takes my balance a while to adjust to the unanticipated manoeuvres. Jeremy isn't talking so I presume he is concentrating on city traffic, which is at least a little comforting. Now that I am on a motorbike, I don't feel quite so conspicuous in my outfit. And at least I'm not wearing a blindfold. We pick up speed and the ride eventually becomes smooth, making it considerably more comfortable than the jerkiness of before, where I was continually bracing myself for the next move.

'Are you alright back there?'

As I feel Jeremy readjust his position on the seat, I realise I am squeezing him so tight, he must be having difficulty breathing.

'AB?'

My grip is so strong; I'm not game to loosen it in case I fall off. My legs anchor me to the bike while my arms brace his waist. My upper body is slamming against his back so there is not a millimetre of space between us. Just as I tell myself to loosen my grip and tell Jeremy I'm fine, the bike swerves to the right and back to the left rapidly. Great, now he is overtaking someone.

'Alexa, can you hear me?' His voice pounds into my helmet again.

'Yes, yes, I can. I'm okay. Just concentrating on, well, on holding on, really.' I stammer out the words as we gather more speed. 'Staying alive' would have been more appropriate, I muse.

'Are you scared?' His questions continue to filter through to my headspace.

'What do you think? I never knew you could ride.'

'I've been riding for years. It's great to be finally taking you out for a spin.'

'Well, I'd rather be experiencing the ride with vision.' I can't help but point this out. 'Please be careful, Jeremy. I really need to come out of this alive. I'm in your hands.'

'Indeed you are, Alexa. Finally you are beginning to understand. Settle back and relax into the ride; we are on the open road now.'

'And I don't suppose you will enlighten me as to which open road that might be?'

'You know that would spoil the fun.'

At that, he goes full throttle and lets 'her' embrace the road at high speed, which does take my breath away.

Who would have thought I'd be riding on a boisterous beast such as this, in pitch black conditions? Not me in a million years. Once I let myself relax a little, not too much though, I have to admit it is a great feeling. Thankfully Jeremy's position in front ensures my insulation from the harshness of the wind, which allows me to appreciate the exhilaration and openness of the bike. Imagine if the kids could see me now! They wouldn't recognise me. Jordan would hardly believe it, but would think I was the coolest mum ever. He'd want to take a photo to prove it to his friends and teacher in Show and Tell, although he'd be more impressed if I was riding on my own. Elizabeth would probably be more concerned for my safety and would ask me if I was scared. I can't help reflecting on whether male and female gender roles and values are that predictable from birth when assessing risk. I've never been able to resolve the whole nature versus nurture debate though it always makes for interesting discussion. I wonder how they are going out there in the wilderness and I hope they are having fun.

I don't know where we are going, or whether the ride is itself the destination. No doubt Jeremy has it all sorted out in his plans for our forty-eight hours of togetherness. He is certainly being true to his word when he said he wouldn't waste a minute of it. So I calm myself down, snuggle into his back and rest my head against his shoulders. The engine's rhythm between my legs provides a consistent, pleasant, low-level vibration. My other senses are completely soaking up and absorbing the whole experience. It feels fantastic and I am really, honestly enjoying the ride. I hug him a little from my position behind him.

'Jeremy, this is really amazing. I would never have dreamt of doing this and I'm loving it.' His hand gently pats mine as if to acknowledge my words. I immediately freeze.

'Please, please, please keep both hands on the handlebars. I don't need to be freaked out more than I already am.'

He laughs as he returns his hand safely to the handlebar. 'Okay, fair enough.'

'Thank you.' I can't stop myself smiling, just as I can't deny enjoying the ride. The wind, the speed, the engine, the closeness is awesome ... even the blackness is exciting, in a strange, surreal way. I allow myself to submerge in the exhilaration of the journey, not knowing where it will lead me.

We eventually slow down after quite some time, maybe an hour or so, maybe more. I'm not sure and I'm not going to ask. Jeremy assists me off the bike, my legs slightly numb from the ride, and removes the now-constricting helmet from my head. It's good to stretch my legs, as they are a little shaky from being in the same position for so long. I'm more than a little self-conscious and adjust my sunglasses nervously.

'Don't worry, nobody is looking at us.' He is able to read my discomfort.

'Are you sure?' The words leave my lips before any filtering can occur.

'Yes, I'm sure. Because I can see and you can't.'

'Right, point made.' My nose greedily sucks up the air around us when the fumes subside. There is a real freshness to it. The smell of it, combined with the gentle breeze and birdsong, reminds me of fond childhood memories with my cousins during school holidays.

I remain standing in place until he reaches out and holds my hand in his and we start walking.

'I can't believe you never told me you got your bike licence.' I try to sound indignant.

'There are many things you don't know about me, Alex. Hopefully that will change over the coming years.' Years? I think to myself that even when I try to be light and conversational, he manages to insert a hefty undertone and it keeps taking me by surprise. We pause as I hear him ask for two skim flat whites, no sugar, and could we have takeaway cups, please. Once again, the lack of consultation is a little astounding. *Let it go …* I relax my mind.

'Coffee, how perfect,' I say, thinking it gives me a hint that it must be between 10 or 11, Saturday morning. Or perhaps

Jeremy has orchestrated the coffees to make me believe it is morning tea-ish. *Stop thinking about time*, I lecture myself. *You have no control over it so forget it.*

'I thought this might be easier for you than a cup and saucer. Be careful though, it's hot.' He sounds like me instructing my kids to be careful when I take something out of the microwave for them. He places the container in my hands and leads me to an outdoor table and helps me to sit.

I raise the cup slowly to my mouth, happily anticipating the aroma and taste, although I certainly don't need the caffeine to wake up as my nerves are more than fully engaged. Keeping the adrenaline pumping through my veins doesn't require any additional assistance.

'Great coffee,' I comment, after taking a long, cautious sip. I am beginning to realise how much of human conversation is dependent on questions or visual indicators. My lack of both makes my small talk sound shallow and superficial. It's almost as if we are on a first date that isn't going very well. My conversational flow is dismal and I don't know whether Jeremy is experimenting with this, or leaving me in limbo deliberately. Maybe my whole conversational style is question-based these days and, given my background, I suppose that would make sense. Perhaps I find it difficult to develop other short-term strategies when placed in an unanticipated circumstance? How strange that I have never noticed this about myself until this moment, when I'm sitting next to Jeremy, with my coffee, in leather, unable to see.

'Penny for your thoughts?' Jeremy finally breaks the silence between us and grounds me back to the present.

'Funny you should ask. I was actually just pondering the idea of how much of human conversation is based on questions, either direct or indirect. And whether I actively engage in real conversations in any other way than asking questions. And as I say the words out loud, the concept horrifies me if it is true. It's only an underlying thought at this stage, but the more I consider it in theory, the greater relevance it appears to have for me.'

After my speculating comes to an end, there is an excruciatingly long silence.

'Jeremy?' Has he left me? Gone to the toilet?

'Are you still there?' I ask. Shit, I am prattling on to myself like a lunatic and he isn't even here. I curse my blindness yet again.

'Yes, I am still here,' he says quietly, taking hold of my hand across the table. 'I'm really pleased you're beginning to understand this about yourself. Do you think it is fair that you ask the questions and we don't ever get to hear about you? Your thoughts? Your feelings? You are so caught up in your professional self it has overflowed into your personal relationships. You are so busy trying to work out everyone else, I sometimes think you forget about yourself. Who you are. What you stand for.'

I am a little taken aback. Well, that's an understatement. I am a lot taken aback. 'You really think I'm like that?'

'Yes, I do. You always had that tendency and it has become more acute with your profession. That is why you are finding it so incredibly difficult to refrain from asking questions this weekend, and letting go, as I knew you would.' I suddenly feel much younger than Jeremy, psychologically small somehow. Stuck somewhere between the parent/child and doctor/patient relationship. This paradigm is exceptionally uncomfortable for me. I can't say with any authority how it is for him, although I could calculate a guess.

'How are you feeling, by the way, about not being visually stimulated?' His curiosity has a slightly analytical tone to it.

'It's not as if I haven't been stimulated in other ways ...' I say, trying to lighten the mood.

'No, seriously Alex, tell me.'

Given he has just provided me with feedback on not being open I decide to answer honestly. 'It is really, really difficult, as I'm sure you would assume, Doctor Quinn. Harder in some ways than I ever imagined ... There're times when I just feel like screaming at the complete and total frustration of it and there are other times, when I am totally caught off-guard and it's, well ... it is ...' I can feel my cheeks warming.

'Go on.' He strokes my cheek, gently encouraging more words to flow.

'It's just so strange being unable to anticipate, well, anything really. No actions, no words, I just don't know where the twists and turns are coming from or whether we are coming to a complete stop. Conversations can feel a bit like the bike ride for me, figuratively speaking.'

'And the other times?' I notice I'm fidgeting and almost squirming in my seat. I'm used to being the one asking the questions, not answering them.

'Other times I find myself nervously excited at the thought of not knowing what's coming next, like when I might be touched or caressed, or even spanked!' I blush, remembering the exceptionally swift slap on the arse that took me by complete surprise before dinner. 'I don't know where all this is leading and I'm really tempted to, well, you know, surrender control ... but it is just so hard.'

'I was hoping you would react this way and you've gone way beyond my expectations. If you would just trust me a little more, let me in. I do want you to surrender yourself to me this weekend, more than ever before. I want to reveal the true Alexa, the woman who has been hiding behind a controlled façade for way too long. We know the ins and outs of each other better than anyone else on the planet. We have nothing to lose and everything to gain. And frankly, along with discovering a cure for depression, which by the way I hope to achieve in the next year or two, you are my life's mission.'

How and when did I become his life's mission? His words scare the living daylights out of me, as I know what sort of man he is and he doesn't say such things lightly — ever. Even though his comments are uncomfortable to hear out loud, somehow I sense the truth in them, whether I like it or not. Jeremy has always been able to see straight through me, sense what I'm feeling or wanting before I could put it into words, enabling him to be a step ahead of my thought processes. It seems that this weekend was playing out in the same way. We have never been able to fully let each other go.

'If that is what you believe, then why do I always feel slightly on edge with you, Jeremy? I always have and I can't believe it's still happening after all these years.' A little frustration enters my tone as I continue. 'Look at me now, completely dependent on you. You know how much I value my independence, how hard I have worked for it, and that is exactly what you have taken away from me. You ask me to let you in, but how much further can I go? How much more do you want? Is this really about me, Jeremy, or is it honestly more about you?'

'Interesting insights, Doctor Blake, to which I will give you one, honest response. You know when you are with me to always expect the unexpected. That is what I give you, that which cannot be controlled. Fear, excitement, anticipation, pleasure, the unknown, trust, surrender, all bundled up together. Somewhere in your psyche that combination proves an intoxicating mix. Why do I do it? Because I know, deep down, you love it, and ultimately it will free you from the constraints and boundaries you have set yourself. Think about it, Alex. If I were not in your life, the very thing that would be missing from it is freedom. Even if you get angry or frustrated with me, it is only ever short-lived, so I am willing to take the risk for the phenomenal rewards.' He pauses momentarily as his words hit me like a brick. 'There exists between us the ultimate sexual tension, and honestly, as much as we have tried to ignore it over the years, it will simply not be extinguished.'

'Wow, that is a lot for a blind woman to absorb.' The power of his words creates insightful paths that branch through my mind and pound in my head as I try to assimilate too many thoughts and emotions at once.

Could it be true? Do I love it? The unknown? The unexpected?

What does he mean by freedom? He keeps using this word …

Does he honestly believe we are destined to be this way?

I feel like he is reading me like a book this weekend, coherently, thoughtfully, cleverly and at whatever speed he chooses.

'And rest assured, my dearest Alexa, the promise still stands from last night, and I am still counting.'

'Sorry?' I say, distracted by the sudden change in topic, still lost in the previous conversation. He repeats his statement.

'I'm sure you remember only too well that I'm an excellent statistician!' His tone is fully loaded with innuendo.

'Yes, of course, Jeremy, how could I ever forget!' My response equally loaded. I *do* remember only too well. The memory makes me squirm in my seat — initially uncomfortable, but amazing recollections.

'What a classic night. One of my sweetest victories and ultimately one of our greatest discoveries about your incredible body ...' Jeremy's voice trails off as we reminisce and I return to that time in our lives.

There has always been rivalry between us at uni as to who is best at what subjects and we often place bets with each other. Jeremy and I are both taking an elective Quantitative Methods course and had made a bet —whoever topped the class could choose one thing that the other had to go along with for the night, without complaint. I agreeably shook hands and had thoughts of Jeremy cleaning my apartment naked, preparing dinner, giving me a massage and generally being at my beck and call. Yes, I thought, this is an excellent idea for a bet, even more so because I had topped the class in all of our assignments. It never really occurred to me that I wouldn't win; after all, it wasn't his area of expertise.

The marks are finally announced: Jeremy scored half a mark more than me because he provided a more complete explanation for the final question. I head straight to Professor Jarlsberg's office to go through the exam paper with him question by question. Annoyingly, although understandably, Jeremy accompanies me, unable and unwilling to hide the grin that looked far too big and wide for his face. No amount of argument or protest will convince the Professor to either increase my paper half a mark, or reduce Jeremy's, though heaven knows I try. Jeremy's smirk seems to double in size, if that were possible.

'Not a word,' I said harshly, waving my finger at him before storming off. Jeremy didn't say a word, but his face spoke volumes.

I deliberately avoid him for the rest of the day, or else he wisely leaves me alone. We cross paths later that evening at our friend's birthday drinks at a swanky gay bar just off Oxford Street in the city. I have calmed down and am not as devastated by my loss. An hour or so later, when we are all in a group talking, he whispers in my ear.

'I think I'll take my winnings now.'

'Pardon, what did you say?'

He repeats his words.

'Right here, now?' I question.

I am a little embarrassed about my earlier behaviour as I'm not usually such a bad loser, but then again, I don't usually lose that often.

'Sure, what can I do for you? Buy you a drink?' I start off toward the bar. He quickly hooks his arm around my waist and whisks me around in the other direction.

'This way. Follow me.' I pause, a little confused as to where we are going. It would be rude to leave without saying goodbye and besides, I haven't been there long and was having fun with my friends. He senses my hesitation.

'Now!' His grip tightens as he steers me firmly toward the stairs.

'What are you —?'

He raises his fingers to my lips, silencing me as we continue downwards. I never even knew this area existed

*in this bar. He opens one of the extra-large doors to the
Unisex toilets, guiding me in before him, closing the door
behind us and ensuring it is securely locked. It's as if we
are in a vault. On one wall there is a framed ceiling to
floor mirror, otherwise the whole area is carpeted, floors,
walls and ceiling. It looks and feels rather luxurious,
particularly when you consider its rudimentary purpose.*

*'Helps buffer the noise,' he says by way of explanation
as my eyes gaze around the room.*

'From outside or from within?'

*He raises one eyebrow and gives me a quirky smile.
'Hmmm ... good question.' Oh dear, what does he have
in mind?*

*'Do you need to go?' His question surprises me as he
indicates the toilet.*

*'Oh ... No! And certainly not with you in here.' I
sound indignant.*

*He washes his hands with warm water and carefully
dries them.*

'For goodness' sake, Jeremy, what is all this about?'

*'Me winning, you los—' He stops himself short. 'You,
let's say, not winning.'*

*I give him an exasperated sigh and roll my eyes. His
eyes darken as he steps toward me.*

'Tell me what the condition of our bet was, Alexa.'

Oh, here we go ... '"Without complaint", Jeremy.'

*'Good, I'm pleased you remember. Turn around and
place both your hands on the mirror and above your head.'*

*'What?' He turns me around, so I'm facing myself in
the mirror, with him standing directly behind me. Even
with my killer heels on he is taller than me.*

'Now!' He impatiently grabs my hands.

'Alright, alright.' I sense that this is going to be a very long night.

I do as he asks and wiggle my butt back to where he is standing to lighten his mood. I can feel his erection swelling behind me. Ah, Jeremy, you are very turned on by this! We both let out a small, amused laugh as we catch our reflection in each other's eyes. His eyes are burning with excitement and arousal.

He hitches up my skirt around my waist and pulls my knickers down to my ankles, waiting for me to step out of them. I give him a resigned sigh and lift my left foot. He ensures my legs are spaced wide apart.

'Thank you,' he says politely, as if offering me a chair to sit down.

What is he up to?

He kisses my neck and snakes his arm around my waist not wasting a moment before heading south and cupping my sex.

'This is going to be fun. Don't take your palms off the mirror, Alex. I mean it.'

He takes something out of his pocket and places it on the small shelf close to him, out of my line of sight.

Then he starts to play. One hand on the small of my back, underneath my bunched up skirt — although it is pretty short anyway — the other around my front where his magic fingers begin their tantalising quest. The juices within me enable a smooth gliding path for his ease of access. My eyes start to glaze over as the touch of his internal massage gathers impact and precision. He is watching me intently. I start to moan as the tension of

145

the day takes its leave, only to be replaced by another form of rising sexual tension. My palm slips from its position, leaving a moist handprint in its wake.

'Do not move your hands.' I attempt to splay my fingers more firmly in place, in the hope of securing greater grip. Oh god ... He continues his assault and I know I am close now, hungry for the release only a moment away. How does this happen so quickly with him? His fingers and thumb work in perfect unison and I am on the cusp ... the very cusp ... enter the vastness ... the stillness ... losing all sense of awareness ... and explode into the beauty and wonder of what he can do to my body. My head leans against the mirror with my hands and elbows as my body convulses to the rhythm he has created when I suddenly feel an unexpected intruder — a shocking, warm, full, sliding intruder, in my arsehole. My sphincter automatically tightens around it.

'What the fuck is that?' I pant out the words as I recover my equilibrium, well sort of recover ...

'A butt plug. A couple of mates have just designed it. They want to use their degrees in business and science to develop a business in sex toys, so I offered to test this design for them.'

How can he possibly do the most outrageous things to me then flow immediately on to normal conversation? About sex toys? It even manages to distract me momentarily from my current situation.

'What is it doing up my arse, Jeremy?'

'You have a beautiful arse, Alex. I want to explore it more and since I won our bet, tonight I can. And the *best thing is, I know I won't have a single complaint from you.' As his face explodes into a mischievous grin, I realise I haven't dared to move an inch since he inserted the invader. The more tense I become, the more I feel it and try to squeeze it out but it just won't budge. I'm not even game to put my hand anywhere near it. I am aghast, standing staring at him in the reflection.*

'The theme of our evening is Marco Polo,' he states proudly as I maintain my mannequin position. He cannot be serious.

'Just as he discovered undiscovered territories of the world, so am I going to explore and discover the undiscovered territories of your body.'

Oh god, he is serious and looking quite chuffed with himself.

'Breathe, Alex, and you can move by the way. You will be okay, it will just feel a little strange until your body adjusts to the sensations it creates.'

'Since when did you become such an expert on these things, Jeremy?' I splutter the words at him.

'Let's just say I'm well researched.'

He bends down to pick up my foot. My body jerks in response to the forced movement as he deftly places my knickers back in position. His fingers gently feel the plug, giving it a little push and pull, which makes me gasp out loud before he adjusts my skirt back into a respectable position.

'Perfect. Thanks for wearing a short skirt tonight, very convenient. Are you ready to join the others? We've been in here a while now.'

I stare at him in horror. It hadn't yet dawned on me that I'd be expected to socialise. His eyes twinkle at the look on my face.

'Or would you prefer to go panty-less?'

'God no!' I freeze in fear at the thought. His lips twitch at the corners.

'You can be such an arsehole, Jeremy.'

'Oh, sweetheart, believe me I know, no pun intended I'm sure. And to think, the night has only just begun.'

I look at myself in the mirror and am surprised to see flushed cheeks and a post-orgasm glow on my face instead of the ashen pale face I was expecting due to the invasive plug.

'I can assure you, you look more fantastic now than when we came in here and I have no doubt will continue to improve as we progress into the night.' I look at him with an eyebrow raised, seeking further explanation.

'I fully intend to remove the butt plug the same way it was inserted, but your orgasms will be far more dramatic outside the confines of a unisex toilet, I can promise you.'

His words send my cheeks into an even deeper blush and my vulva into warm spasms that ricochet against the butt plug. As I take a careful step toward the door, I notice the invader's bite has been subdued and is now replaced by a strange tantalising, sexual pull. It surprises me.

'Every time you feel it within you, think of me touching you and what is to come. In the meantime, let's have a few drinks to loosen you up so you don't look like you've got something stuck up your arse!'

He gives me a light slap on my backside and I tense causing the invader to assert its position inside me and then my nipples instantly harden at the sensation. Damn! Jeremy notices immediately.

'God, I love your body, AB. It's as if it talks directly to me.'

I congratulate myself for having eased back into conversation with my lab partners, Josh and Sally, reasonably successfully for the past half an hour, trying to ignore Jeremy's winks and grins from the group beside us. I am resigned to the fact that the invader will be there until Jeremy removes it, mostly because I don't want to touch it. And it doesn't feel too bad, actually, not too bad at all, but I'll never admit that to him. We are in the midst of a very animated discussion when suddenly the fucking plug starts to vibrate deep within me, causing me to jerk and throw my drink in the air. It lands all over poor Josh. The feeling is absolutely like nothing I have felt before and is intense. I try to apologise to Josh, but all I can do is hold on to the bar table, resting my head in my hands as I break into a sweat and start panting. Fucking Jeremy better turn this fucking vibrating monster off! The sensation is so strong I can't even lift my head to throw him a death stare.

'Alex ... Jeez ... what's wrong? Are you alright? Here, come and sit down ...'

Sit down? God no. But how can I explain that to your nearest and dearest friends?

Thankfully, he stops it.

'Really ... I'm okay ... I'll be fine,' I pant out intermittently.

Jeremy strides coolly over to my side, putting on a great show of looking concerned for my welfare.

'Alex, you don't look well. Perhaps I should take you home?'

'Yes, perhaps that is a good idea.' I glare at him furiously for what he just did to me, but for once, I completely agree with him. Another stint like that in public would completely send me over the edge and I'm horrified to find myself in desperate need of his promised orgasm. 'Let's go. Now!' He senses the urgency in my voice and efficiently gathers our belongings. We quickly say our goodbyes and promptly depart.

At home, he carefully, considerately, tenderly and lovingly deflowers my arsehole. It doesn't hurt as much as I thought it would. In fact, the more I relax, the more open I am, and that gives Jeremy room to move within me. It feels tighter, strangely more intimate than vaginal sex, as though he is claiming me, owning me completely. The sensations are totally different, more focused on my lower back and my thighs, while my clit and front passage are being teased and caressed to throbbing intensity by Jeremy's expert fingers. What more can I say? Except that something I feared so much needn't have caused me any anxiety whatsoever. Jeremy assures me such success can be attributed to the appropriate preparation and planning. As we lie naked in bed together, we are in awe of our bodies and the experience we have just shared together. Absolutely mind blowing. Maybe I shouldn't have fought him for so long on this issue ... Oh well, either way, it was worth the wait.

'Guess what? I have decided what I'm doing my honours thesis on,' I state proudly as we caress each other with languid strokes.

'Finally! Do share.'

'I'm basing it on the writings of Sabina Spielrein, specifically examining the connection between masochism and the ego in relation to the female form.'

'Wow, AB. Pretty heavy topics. Has it been approved?'

'Yes, just this morning. I'm really excited.'

'Any reason you decided on that in particular?'

Jeremy looks directly into my eyes, eagerly anticipating my answer.

Suddenly embarrassed by the look in his eyes and the tone of his question, I attempt to dismiss him by rolling on to my stomach and burying my head in the pillow.

'Alexa? You're not trying to hide from me, are you?' He gently tries to pry me back over. 'Oh Alex, there is absolutely no way I am going to let you get away with this.'

Shit, what have I started here? Why on earth didn't I just answer him academically like I did with Professor Webster this morning?

He finally flips my body so I'm face up. He straddles my belly and starts to tickle me mercilessly and I, of course, shriek in response. 'No, stop, please, I hate it,' I gasp out between attacks.

'No way, not until you promise to share.' I'm trapped beneath him as his tortuous fingers continue their assault.

'Okay, okay, I can't stand it, please stop.'

He waits patiently for me to compose my breathing, anchoring my hands either side of my head so he has full view of my face. I decide to make it as fast and brief as possible.

'I've always had this fantasy of being completely restrained and blind and flogged and pleasured and I want to understand the root cause because I'm deeply embarrassed by it. There, end of discussion.'

He looks quizzically at me, a smirk on his face but his eyes wide. I silently beg him to leave it be.

'Interesting.' He stares at me thoughtfully, the silence expanding between us.

'Did you enjoy tonight, Alex?'

'Yes.'

'A lot?'

'Very much.'

'Did you expect to?'

'No, not really.'

'I am more than happy to be directly involved in researching any part of your thesis.'

'Thank you. I'll bear that in mind.'

'Thank you for sharing.'

And I can't believe I'm off the hook.

'Anyway, I'm thrilled that you are finally on your path of self-discovery. It means my plan is working exactly as I anticipated.'

'Oh dear, there is nothing more ominous than you with a plan, Jeremy.'

'Don't sound so cynical, sweetheart. Look how far you have come already and we still have so far to go.' He is just teasing me, I'm sure, although his reply is a little too enthusiastic to instil a large degree of confidence in my assumption. 'Just out of interest, did you ever end up exploring the psychology of your hypotheses first-hand, like we discussed?'

'No, Jeremy, I didn't and besides, you would have known about it if I had.'

'Oh, why is that?'

'Do you really need to ask me that? As if I would do anything like that with anyone other than you.'

'I can't tell you how much that pleases me, Alexa, in so many ways.' I'm not one hundred per cent sure what his comment implies but I am one hundred per cent sure I want to move away from this conversation, quickly.

'Okay, far be it from me to put a dampener on this journey you have so carefully planned for me.' I finish my coffee and place the empty container on the table.

* * *

I really need to use the bathroom after my coffee. This is going to be awkward. I can't believe I have to ask him; it is so embarrassing. It is at these times that being dependent is just plain awful. But what choice do I have?

'No problem, just in here.' He guides me through a door. His hand threads through my legs and pulls a zipper down around my bottom, between my legs and up toward my belly. I can't honestly believe he has just done that.

'The toilet is right behind you. Oh, and don't worry about your knickers. They're French, for easy access.' I can hear the smile in his voice.

'I'll leave you to it and wait outside.'

Is there one minutia of detail he hasn't considered this weekend? Anything left unaccounted for? Probably not, he has always been a meticulous planner and obviously those skills have only been more finely tuned over the years. Zips and French knickers. Good grief! I wonder whether they are for convenience such as this, or did he have something else in mind? The thought shudders through me as I make myself focus on the task at hand.

'Right, all set?' he asks.

I nod.

'Great, come with me. Let's get you harnessed up.'

Oh crap, is all I can think.

My feet remain anchored to the ground as my stomach embarks on another roller-coaster ride of anticipation, fear, calm, fear, calm, fear, fear …

'Harness …' I ask hesitantly. 'And that's a statement, not a question,' I add quickly for clarification.

He leads me silently and blindly forward. 'Don't worry, you'll love it.'

'Love it? Love what?' My voice turns suspicious, as I cast around for something that I love that involves a harness. I draw a blank.

Straps are placed over my shoulders as I hear 'click, click'. I feel rough hands around my legs doing the same thing; around my waist, 'click, click'. It's all I can hear as my anxiety rises.

'Jeremy?' They don't feel like his hands. I can smell stale cigarettes.

'How does that feel, love?' A strange man's voice. I realise he is talking to me as one strap is pulled tighter and readjusted. I am tugged and pulled, clipped and then a final snap.

'That's better,' the voice says. 'Looks like you're both set. Don't worry, love, you'll be right once you get into the swing of it. It's only the first part that's shit scary.' He laughs and pats my shoulder as if to reassure me. My voice leaves my throat and is unable to protest that I can't see through these sunglasses, just as my legs begin to liquefy. Swing of it? Shit scary for the first part? Although my mouth is attempting to shape the words, there is no sound forthcoming. I desperately try to make sense of what is happening minus the visual stimulation. I have clothes on; that has to be good, doesn't it? But the zips, the access between my legs, the straps, the clips, they are all very, very worrying. My mind is filled with images of wild sex games and orgies. How could he? Why would he? This is going too far. I can't do this, I will never do this … It is not who I am. My breath is shallow and my mind freezes as panic sets in.

I hear someone's voice.

'Alex?' It is in the distance somewhere. My knees buckle as my head spins and I struggle for air. I crumple toward my feet and am caught before I hit the ground.

'God, AB, are you alright?'

'No, I am not alright at all.' I'm not sure whether my mind or voice speaks the words.

'Just take your time, breathe.' Strong arms around me keep me walking somewhere as my legs wobble beneath me. 'It's okay, I've got you, that's it, one step at a time.'

Yes, one step at a time, that's right, stop the feeling, stop the spinning. Good advice, my mind confirms, as we continue up some steps and along a little further.

'Here, sit down, would you like some water?' I'm lowered onto a hard, cushioned seat.

Yes, water, good idea.

'Alexa, water?'

I have already said yes, then I realise it's my mind talking so maybe he hasn't heard me. I nod my head. I feel water at my lips and take a sip, then some more. I need to prolong this to gain control over my head and stomach, and tell Jeremy we need to stop what we are doing.

Take a deep breath … My stomach is still churning but the dizziness is leaving me, thanks to the oxygen.

'Keep breathing. Good, that's better,' a voice says, although I'm unsure whether it is the man's or Jeremy's. *Breathe in, breathe out, air in, air out*, I say to myself in concentrated effort.

'Alex, please answer me, are you okay? Can you hear me? I'm not sure what happened to you.'

'I, I'm, I'm a little …' I hear a door close nearby. Sound becomes muffled.

'It's alright, I'm here, right beside you, sweetheart. Honestly, I won't leave you.' Something in his tone is mildly reassuring.

'I can't, I …' Words still find it very difficult to follow the path from my brain to my lips. I take another sip of water. I hear another click around my waist and it sends me off. 'I'm not going to be harnessed up in the air in some kinky sex machine, Jeremy.'

My voice is hoarse, frantic. 'This needs to stop. How could you? With some man smelling of tobacco. I can't believe you would ever put me in this situation. You can't, I won't.'

I feel tears welling up inside me and I swallow hard in an attempt to keep them there.

'It's too much, you have pushed me too far.'

'Alex.' Jeremy places his arm around my shoulders. 'Is that what you're thinking? What you thought I wanted you to do?'

Tears erupt and my shoulders shake. 'I can't, Jeremy, I won't. I'm just not like that.' I sob out the words.

156

'Sweetheart, I'm not asking you to. This is meant to be fun for you, not something that makes you upset.'

'How can it not, Jeremy? Look at me, I'm a mess.'

I hear engines roar into life, a propeller, movement.

'What? We're on a plane?' I ask incredulously as the slow turning stops and we accelerate suddenly forwards. The force pushes my body back into the seat until suddenly we are swept off the ground and the atmosphere cradles the plane as it climbs higher and higher. My tears stop in their tracks. I throw Jeremy's arm off my shoulder and swing my fist into where I assume his chest would be as hard as I possibly can.

'You bastard,' I screech. He catches my wrist just before full impact. 'You absolute bastard!' Holding my fist in his hand, he replaces his arm around my shoulder once again, anchoring me into the seat, knowing I am desperate to lash out toward him again. I can feel his body convulsing with silent laughter. I could explode as I struggle against him. His arms assert their strength and restrain me further.

'Come on, AB, I can't help it if you have a dirty mind. I thought we were just taking a plane ride and here you are, thinking about a kinky sex machine? You'll have to share with me exactly what you had in mind ...'

'Oh, shut up, Jeremy, just shut up.' He is in absolute hysterics, laughing uncontrollably. I snatch my arms away from him and fold them together defensively.

I don't answer him. I am furious, deceived, embarrassed.

I can't answer him, as I am honestly not sure of the answer myself. Where had the thought come from in the first place, why had my mind automatically leapt to that conclusion above all others? That has to be of concern.

As Jeremy is lost in wild hysterics, I take the opportunity to elbow him sharply in the ribs, causing him to choke on his laughter. This makes me feel a little better as I am seething from the inside out. I decide enough is enough with the glasses, the barriers covering my eyes, and desperately hope the potency of the drops has worn off. I quickly move my hand to peel the glasses off my face when just as quickly my hands are, yet again, snatched away from me. Is he ever not watching me?

'Don't you dare, Alex. We went through this last night and you know exactly what will happen.' He pins both my wrists together in his one hand as if he is perfectly content to sit the rest of the journey this way. No remorse. No apology. I seethe in silence for what seems like ages.

His tone lightens again as he snuggles his face into my neck, the humour returning to his voice.

'You must admit though, it is pretty funny.'

I can't believe him.

'There is absolutely nothing funny about it,' I respond defiantly.

'But did you honestly think ... honestly believe ...' He begins to laugh again. The look on my face must be enough to make him stop short and compose himself. 'Obviously you thought it was something really bad. I've never seen you react that way ... you were trembling.' He pauses, softens his tone. 'It's really important to understand how and why you are going through these emotions. It's all part of the process. You'll learn so much about yourself,' Jeremy says more seriously.

Condescending prick is the only thought that enters my mind at his words, regardless of any potential truth in them.

'Was it really that scary for you? Was the fear too much?'

'I don't want to do this any more, Jeremy. Please don't make me. I can't take it any more, I'll have a heart attack.'

'Then it is lucky for you I'm a doctor and I'll save you. Besides, you are in perfect health.'

'Perfect health means nothing under these conditions, and besides that, how on earth would you know?'

At this point, I feel a sudden gush of wind and am deafened by a forceful roar.

What now? I am being tugged and pulled again, clipped and checked.

'You haven't guessed yet?' Jeremy is screaming into my ear above the blast of wind and engine noise. 'We're skydiving, just like we did on your twenty-fifth birthday! Remember, you tried to renege on that, too, but you loved it once you did it.' Given the noise of the engines and the rush of air surrounding me, I know he isn't joking. Relief, fear and excitement flow rapidly through my veins. I shake my head in disbelief.

'I need to make sure you have enough adrenaline pumping through your system so you have energy for later!' he shouts. There is both cheekiness and sincerity in his words.

'Well, this ought to well and truly achieve that,' I say nervously. 'But blind ...?'

'All part of the process.'

I desperately grip hold of Jeremy, standing attached to me and try to brace myself within the plane as I scream toward his voice. 'Just because I've skydived before,' *and loved it*, I admit privately, 'doesn't mean I want to do it again, right now. Not like this!'

The pressure of his body intensifies, pushing me forward, and I know the moment to jump is near.

'Okay Alexa. Three, two, one ...'

I am flung into the air. We are tumbling, tumbling, tumbling as air penetrates every orifice of my face, snatching my breath from my lungs and causing my stomach to somersault. Suddenly, my arms and legs are forced by pressure to their extremities, coerced outwards. The noise of the wind quickly overtakes the continuing distancing of engines. All sounds of man-made engineering rapidly vanish as we fly free.

There is nothing quite like the experience of plunging out of a plane, full of hope and completely attached to the person pulling the strings. The force of oxygen pounding into my head overwhelms my entire body. My stomach immediately shifts to my throat as I plummet downwards, and I lose all sense of stability. Instead of lasting a second or two it keeps going and going as I eagerly anticipate the catch of an opening canopy, but it doesn't and I continue to free fall. The descent takes forever as my stomach continues to flip and turn while my body spears through the nothingness of the atmosphere. How can it be nothing when it is forcing every muscle, every bit of skin, every cell back up against itself? Yet I continue to fall. The noise is huge and my ears could explode. For the first time, I'm thankful my eyes are sealed and covered as the pressure is so intense. I suddenly feel dampness surround me and shiver as I presume we fly through a cloud. We are still falling, falling. Finally my stomach adjusts and I allow myself to relax into the rush, the velocity, wholly and completely. It's even better than the first time. It is overpowering, all-consuming, an in–the-moment adrenaline rush. My form of ecstasy, heroin, speed, whatever … As I think this a memory floods my brain. I distinctly remember a client telling me that they tried heroin once and would never, ever touch it again. I asked if it was that bad and they said, 'Just the opposite, it was way too good —

so unbelievably awesome that if you went back a second time, you'd never stop.' Only Jeremy could know that my anger and fury would dissipate rapidly with the intoxicating rush of sheer adrenaline. The thought flashes through my brain that I could easily become addicted to Jeremy.

At this, I want the falling to stop. I suddenly don't want to allow myself to love the feeling any more. Shouldn't our fall be halted by the release of the parachute by now? Now I'm not at all happy with my lack of sight. I need to see how far from the ground we are. We have been falling so long my lungs are almost unable to accommodate the oxygen being forced into them. My heartbeats faster at my thoughts, my fear accelerates. If it is adrenaline Jeremy wants for me then he has certainly achieved it. I'm pumping, pumping, pumping, harder and faster. I feel like everything about me is in free fall during these seconds of my life, everything at risk, everything has the potential to be destroyed. And I am in no position to prevent it, to stop it, to control it. I have had many dreams like this before, of falling, falling, desperately waiting for the fall to end, to wake up, to be saved, whatever it takes to not hit the ground. In the dreams I always wonder how I happen to arrive in this position, what causes the free fall in the first place.

Have my conscious and unconscious mind finally collided? And is this the consequence, the conclusion? Were the dreams prophetic, or have I missed some warning? Where is Carl Jung when I need him!

Please, I pray, to myself, to anyone, *please let nothing go wrong, please let me live to see my children again, please, please, please get me through this in one piece*. I don't want to die; I'm not ready to die … How can we still be falling? How high were we? 10,000 feet? 15,000 feet? Did we fly that high, higher maybe? I realise now I was too stressed and distracted to take any notice of anything else at the time, including the discovery of being on a plane in the first place. Surely we should …

We stop, abruptly.

Silence.

The harness pulls tight between my legs and it feels like we have come to a complete standstill. My ears are deafened by the silence after the pounding vibrations only seconds ago. We begin to float … softly, quietly. *Thank you*, I say silently, *thank you*. Overwhelming relief permeates my being.

I am very aware of my heart pumping blood through my veins, but the noise has calmed, the pressure has eased and my limbs are not being forced outwards. They fall limp as the tension fades. We are floating calmly, beautifully, wonderfully and freely in the world. It is so peaceful. My stomach resettles itself somewhere near my bellybutton, although I can't confirm it returns to its original position. Close enough, though. I am smiling now, relieved and thrilled with the experience. I'm happy, free, exhilarated, overwhelmed to be alive. Warm tears flood my eyes as emotion releases from within.

Thump, thump, my knees buckle underneath me as the ground pushes up into my body with a jolt and then … nothingness.

Unsure of my consciousness, I find myself wrapped in a hug with my feet barely touching the ground. Arms securely around me. A hug. A real hug. I feel him unclipping me and turning me to face him. I bury my head deeply into the chest I know to be Jeremy's and allow the intoxication of adrenaline and relief to wash over me. I shake. I bury my head harder. Arms tighten around me. I sob. And sob. I can't stop. I'm overflowing. Trembling. Shaking. Long, hard, full body sobs. For a long moment in time.

There are no words shared.

The arms don't let go, still holding on tight.

They don't let go. There is no need to speak. These arms won't leave me.

Breathing eventually returns to normal via deep sighs.

After a long time, a finger lifts my chin, lips lightly brush my lips and linger for a moment. The arm securely wraps around my body and leads me away, half walking, half carrying.

No words are necessary as our bodies move in unison. Then quiet preparation going on around me as I am lowered onto a blanket. The sun is warm, the breeze gentle. I am still blind. I know that I will be until the forty-eight hours are over. I'm at ease with it now. I no longer have the will or desire to fight it. I accept it. I am calm.

The preparation noise has stopped. I remain still.

No noise. No words. Just the wind, the birds, the smell of salt in the air, ocean waves gently moving back and forth to their own universal rhythm. My shoulders are lowered to the ground. A light touch on my cheek. I feel a body closing in on mine. I try to find a face. I do. I pull it close to mine and inhale its scent. I pull it to my lips, to my tongue. I need this face. I need to kiss it deeply, to penetrate its mouth. I need to convey the depth of the emotion I feel. To transfer the longing, the urging, the deep force within the core of my being which has lain dormant for so many years, so this face has some understanding of what it has done to me in the past, what it is doing to me in the present, of what I am going through.

My body is writhing and throbbing under his body. There are too many barriers between us, physical ones. I'm not close enough. It's intense and it's frustrating. I struggle to find ways in, to find some way to remove the barriers. I need closeness. I crave it. I can't. I'm foiled. My hands don't make it, they are lost, prevented, kissed. The throbbing continues deep within me. My hands are held tight, trapped under the weight of his body. Like the sobbing earlier, the throbbing also eases with time. My breath returns, my heartbeat slows, eventually. As does his.

'You are overwhelming, all-encompassing, all-consuming.' He slowly breathes into my ear. His words heighten the intensity between my legs as I again wait for the ache to subside. He could always trigger this pre-orgasmic feeling over the years with a look, a touch, a comment. But rather than being diluted over the years, it has now reached a concentration I never imagined possible.

'Do you feel the same way?'

I nod, too overcome to speak, not daring to acknowledge the underlying truth in his words. 'What have you done to me?' is all I can manage to barely whisper.

'You do know I love you, Alexa.' His tone is serious, his voice overflowing with emotion.

'Yes, I do. You know I love you, too.'

'It's strange, isn't it, having a love like ours that isn't based on traditional love per se.'

'It always has been … strange between us … intense … playful … intoxicating …'

'Our unexplained, unreconciled love …'

'At least we understood that at a very young age.' Or did we? I wonder silently.

Jeremy's mood seems to have shifted. I'm used to him switching from playfulness to challenging, from forcefulness to reflection, but this is slightly different. He seems to be talking to me on one level and lost in his own thoughts at the same time. The dark undercurrent still lingers beneath his words. I don't know if I'm unwilling or unable to explore further. Not being allowed to ask questions doesn't help especially as I keep getting in trouble when I do. And now he says he loves me. My roller-coaster of blackness is becoming as much emotional as it is physical.

I feel exhausted, numb.

Alive.

Calm.

Intense.

Light.

Energised.

Overwhelmed.

Frightened.

Lustful.

Special.

* * *

I lie down on my back with my elbows propping me up. Jeremy offers me some water. Basic needs become an urgent priority as I realise just how thirsty I am. I splash it down my throat and gulp and gulp and gulp.

'Thank you.'

'Are you hungry?'

'I'm not sure.' He hands me a sandwich and I take a bite. 'Hmm, maybe I am.'

We eat and chat and chat. And chat and eat and drink as the wall I have carefully constructed to protect me from my feelings for him over the past decade crumbles more completely.

'Can I ask you something?' the voice beside me says.

A flash of anxiety passes through me for a millisecond and I send it away.

'Sure. What would you like to ask me?'

'Do you ever do it back there, any more?' I must have looked as confused as I felt because his hand slips under my crotch and gives a little push toward my butt. 'You know, back there.'

'Of all the things to ask! No, I don't. Not since you anyway,' I explain, not in the least expecting this change in topic.

My arsehole must remember the feelings of the first time as it starts to react to our discussion.

'Why not?'

'Why should I?'

'Alex,' he says flatly.

'This question thing is ridiculous!'

He returns to the subject he wants to discuss. 'But you loved it.'

'*You* loved it and that's why you did it. You were obsessed with it, ever since the butt plug night and still are by the sounds of it,' I add.

'But your body loved it.'

'I'm not so sure ...'

'Oh, but yes it did. Your body loved it a lot.'

He rolls me over on to my stomach and simply cups his hand over my leathered behind. Tingles immediately zap through my body as if to prove the point.

'Well, it may have, eventually, but *I* didn't,' I say quickly, attempting to close the topic. Why is he talking about this?

'Isn't it one and the same?'

'Obviously not,' I reply.

'Really? So you are actually admitting that your mind and

body might be thinking and feeling different things?' Oh, here we go, our age-old discussion …

'Why are you trying to trap me with your words, Jeremy? Honestly, you are making me doubt every assumption I've ever made in my life this weekend. It is really disturbing me.'

'Ah, this just keeps getting more perfect by the hour,' he says, laughing with confidence.

'I don't find it even vaguely amusing, actually.' I say nothing more in the hope that he will move on to another topic of conversation.

'I'm only asking because I'm involved in some research that deals with exactly this issue.'

'What, arseholes? And back door entry?' Now it is my turn to chuckle as I consider exactly what this sort of research might have involved back at uni. No doubt Jeremy would have eagerly volunteered.

'No, not arseholes, Alex,' he says more seriously, then jokes, 'Well, not yet anyway, but I am happy to experiment with yours whenever you're ready.' He strategically strokes my leathered behind. 'More about that later. Right now, we need to get going.'

'Oh, do we have to? The sun feels so good it would be lovely just to stay here a little longer and have a siesta, don't you think?' I settle into a sideways sleeping position.

'It would be, but it is not going to happen. I'm not wasting my hours with you sleeping when we are on a time limit. I am making the most of every minute.'

'How much more can we fit in, Jeremy? Drinks, baths, dinner, dancing, singing, sex, orgasms, breakfast, bike riding, coffee, *skydiving*' — I say with great emphasis — 'and now a picnic. Isn't that enough for a week, let alone one day? We've already done everything. Let's rest a little, just half an hour or so. There's still plenty of time.' I say the words although I've no idea how much time is left or where we are. I place my hand out to try to find him and pull him toward me but he has moved.

'You haven't changed, have you? There's so much more to experience, to awaken within you and so little time.'

'Isn't skydiving the ultimate experience? I promise you, Jeremy, I feel well and truly awakened, probably more so than I have for many decades.' My mind wanders back to this morning and the pulsing sensation reignites in my groin from the memories.

'I can assure you, sweetheart, I have barely begun.' He strokes my cheeks and lightly kisses my lips. Shit! Barely begun? What more is there? My heart starts racing — again.

'There is an amazing innocence about you, Alexa, even after all these years.'

I'm not sure whether to be offended or not.

'We need to get moving now so we can rectify your innocence. There is no time to be lost.'

'No. I'm not moving. What innocence? What are you talking about?' I would never use that word to describe myself. I stay stubbornly seated.

He completely ignores me. 'If you're not going to move, I'll just have to do it for you. A man's work is never done these days.' He sweeps me up from the blanket, his hand firmly grabbing my arse in the process as if to reinforce our conversation. After taking a few steps, he places me on a warm seat, fastens a seat belt around me and readjusts the sunglasses to ensure they are in the correct position, once again ensuring I am utterly in the dark.

'We're in a car?' The engine roars to life, as does the rhythmic, tribal trance music coming from the speakers and off we go. We must be in a convertible given the wind once again whips around my ears as we hit the open road. At least this will be a little more comfortable for the journey back to the hotel. Although on second thoughts, after a long bike ride, a plane trip, the parachute jump and now being in a car, I have absolutely no idea where we are or where we could be heading. We could have crossed state lines for all I know. My curiosity regarding our whereabouts is peaking, as I'm sure is Jeremy's intention. Even so, I dare not entertain asking the question. So I sit silently, enjoying the psychological space the music freely offers my mind.

Part V

The eye — it cannot choose but see
We cannot bid the ear be still
Our bodies feel; where'er they be
Against, or with our will

— W. Wordsworth 1847

Our journey continues and I am surprised at how energised I feel given my presumed emotional exhaustion. It is as if Jeremy has discovered and unleashed a fertile oasis within my body, which I'd previously regarded as a barren desert. The pores in my skin feel like they are oozing pheromones. I have never felt this intensely alive, so sensual, so sexual, so female. I consider my marriage to Robert as a contrast and my feelings are numb, almost non-existent. But how could they ever compare to the magnitude on the Richter scale that Jeremy creates — could anyone else create such emotional seismic shifts for me? My thoughts are interrupted by Jeremy's voice as he places his hand on my knee.

'Do you mind if we talk about some aspects of my research now, while we are driving?'

'No, not at all.'

'Just wanted to check, as you looked deep in thought.' I shake my head to dislodge my feelings.

'Please, I'd love to hear about it.'

'Okay, great. As I mentioned earlier, there is a group of doctors and professors from around the globe collaborating to research the connections between physiology and cognitive neuropsychology in regards to sexual activity. I am now heavily involved as a result of my research into the explicit links between sex-related issues and depression. To cut a long story short, I had the good fortune of meeting up with Samuel a few months ago in Hong Kong when both our flights were cancelled due to volcanic ash, so we had the rare opportunity to discuss our work in detail.'

'Ah, so that explains why he was so up to speed with your work.'

'No doubt when you met for lunch Sam informed you of their research into the female orgasm and the scientific discrepancies and medical controversy regarding ejaculation.'

I nod in confirmation, fully absorbed in his words. I love it when he is in professional mode and his work fascinates me. I can hear the passion in his voice.

'We ended up brainstorming the possibility of developing a formula produced from natural serotonin that would not adversely affect the chemical balance of the human brain in the medium to long-term. After much testing and analysis in our labs, we discovered there are potential links between our areas of research, given certain scenarios, that significantly reduce the likelihood of depression — particularly involving the concept of "adult play". This indirectly led us to analysing the secretion of fluids from female orgasm for each blood type.'

'Wow, that sounds amazing.' This is Jeremy at his best, why he is recognised globally for his research. I can't help but be in awe of his capabilities and the way in which his tangential mind operates to find solutions others completely miss. He is always open to exploring the unlikely.

'We believe there is another potential link, one that we haven't explored in detail as yet, which relates to our discussion earlier.'

He pauses and I sense a slight hesitation in his voice.

'It involves sensory connectivity, the neural pathways that may exist between the body and brain in relation to sexual activity, and the corresponding hormones secreted and released. We need to secure a Research Psychologist before we can progress with our plans for experimentation. Your specific expertise is highly sought after, particularly on a project of this nature and our review board specifically asked me to discuss it with you and assess your interest in the role.'

Jeremy knows full well that professional flattery will get him everywhere and this subject is close to my heart. He is playing his cards well and his timing, as usual, is perfect, especially given the state I'm currently in — that he, in fact, is responsible for.

'You really are a clever man, Jeremy.'

'Thank you, as you are a clever woman,' he says with a smile in his voice. 'I can provide you with more information, if you're willing to consider it. It would mean you'd be working closely with myself, Samuel, and Ed — Professor Applegate in the US, that is — and Dr Lauren Bertrand in France, she's a prominent chemist, along with Professor Schindler, a German neuroscientist, and one or two others from the UK we are in the process of confirming. It would involve a bit of travel, you know, from time to time ...' His voice trails off, as he knows this has been an issue for me in the past. 'We'd all immensely value your involvement, Dr Blake. You come highly recommended regardless of your connection to me and you are the team's first choice in filling the role. Your lecture on Friday sealed the deal from our perspective,' he adds seriously.

'Gosh, I'm not sure what to say … It sounds incredible, Jeremy.' I am secretly thrilled they are even considering me and so pleased we can still have a professional conversation after everything we have been through for the last however many hours. What an opportunity, to work with such distinguished minds in their chosen fields. It sounds like a professional dream come true. I consider Elizabeth and Jordan. They are both older now, at school full-time and have their own friends and activities. I think of the endless pick-ups and drop-offs — soccer practice, piano lessons, dancing, gymnastics. Kids have busy lives themselves, these days. They are more able to cope with me being away now, I reason, and a little time away here and there would be exciting, good for me to be living my own life. Robert's job has the flexibility to work around school hours more easily than my career. I have put so many other opportunities on the back burner for my family, maybe now is the time to finally say yes. How would I feel if I let a chance like this slip by?

'Actually, I'd love to be involved. Count me in,' I say decisively.

'Honestly? Hey, that's great! We've no doubt having someone like you on the team will make all the difference to the practical applications of our analysis.'

He really is in flattery mode, I think to myself.

'Thanks, Jeremy, I really appreciate it.' It's like receiving accolades for years of hard work — I'm completely chuffed.

'And just so you are perfectly clear, I'm expecting you to be personally involved in both the conceptual development of our theories *and* their application. So, no more sitting on the sidelines, Alexa. Do you understand what I am saying?'

My stomach does a full somersault as I realise the meaning of his words.

'Really?' Do I still want this?

'We don't break new ground and make life-changing discoveries without challenging convention, and that has to begin with ourselves. Your willingness to engage in and experience both sides of the experimentation process will be paramount to our success. We are depending on it, so it is non-negotiable for us.'

My lover has instantaneously transformed into my new boss. Incomprehensibly, my groin warms in anticipation of what could be ahead of me. Oh, jeez, Louise! Both sides of the experiment?

Our journey suddenly comes to an abrupt end, as does our discussion. I'd anticipated a much longer ride back to the hotel. Jeremy is at the door in seconds and carefully guides me out of the car.

'Well, here we are. How are you feeling?'

'Slightly shocked by your last comments, still blind, of course, but perfectly well otherwise.' He chuckles as I stretch.

'Can I take care of the car for you, sir?' The voice startles me. I haven't heard another voice for quite some time.

'Of course, thanks.' I hear the tinkle of keys whizz past.

He takes my hand and leads me up some steps. I feel him reading my face and he no doubt wonders when I'll ask something about where we are, but I keep deliberately quiet. I hear a door open.

'Greetings, sir, welcome.' A chirpy male voice greets us from nearby.

I'm disappointed there isn't a good morning, afternoon or evening to give me a sense of time. Is everyone conspiring to keep me in the dark? Where could we possibly be now? It's all sounding very formal. I feel conspicuous about being blind in yet another new environment and tentatively raise a hand to my eyes.

'Stop fiddling, Alex, you look fine. Nobody will notice anything.'

'Easy for you to say.' I hold on to his hand a little more firmly.

'Please make your way to reception, sir. Your luggage has been taken care of.'

'Luggage?' I whisper toward him, as we move on. 'We don't have any.'

Our footsteps echo around the expanse of the room. The rubber soles of our boots are squeaking against a hard marble floor.

'Welcome, Dr Quinn, we have been awaiting your arrival. We are so pleased you have made it on time. Everything is arranged, so please follow me. If we can be of service in any way, don't hesitate to ask.'

'That's very kind of you. Thank you.'

We take a few steps as someone presses the button for the lift.

'Have you had a good day thus far?'

'We have had a great day, thank you, and very much looking forward to settling in here.'

'Excellent, sir. We certainly hope you enjoy the experience we have to offer.'

I feel like I'm somewhere between being the invisible woman and the giant pimple on a face that everyone can see but is carefully choosing to ignore. Butterflies commence their flight once again in my stomach ... you would think I'd be accustomed to their presence by now. The lift doors open, and for some reason I have the sense that we are travelling down, not up. I'm steered out of the lift.

'As discussed, this entire floor is yours and there will be no disturbances unless otherwise arranged. We hope you have a very enjoyable stay.'

'Thank you very much. We certainly intend to.'

I hear the lift disappear into the distance. I realise I'm on shaky ground again, being in a new place. I had memorised most of the layout of the penthouse suite which had at least provided me with some reassurance of my surroundings.

Jeremy takes my hands and leads me to a lounge. 'Here, have a seat, try to relax. Would you like a drink?'

'Yes, that'd be great, thanks,' I say, relieved.

He hands me a chilled glass filled with a mix of berry flavours. I can taste the likes of cranberries, raspberries and blueberries blended in creamy yogurt. Not at all what I was expecting.

'Certainly a potent mix of antioxidants in this.'

'You are no use to me sick, Alexa. I need to keep your immune system humming.'

What a strange thing to say.

'Do you mind if I take a quick shower after this drink? I'd love to get out of these clothes.'

'Yes to the former, and I'll help you with the latter.' He sounds a little distracted, although I have no idea why. He puts my drink down and unzips and unbuckles here, there and everywhere. It is such a relief to have these heavy clothes removed, I feel at least five kilos lighter.

He assists me in putting on a T-shirt and gym pants and I'm grateful not to be left solely in the French knickers. I stretch my feet and allow my toes to sink into the luxurious thickness of the carpet. It feels good to be free of the boots.

He hands my drink back after guiding me back to the lounge.

'Shower?'

'I said yes, I do mind if you take a shower. It's not time to wash yet.' I'm a little stunned by his controlling response.

'Well, you certainly are on a strict schedule, Jeremy, aren't you? I didn't realise we were being timed to the minute!'

'There are many things you haven't realised yet, sweetheart,' he whispers close to my ear, his voice sounding shadowed, dark. A shiver races right down my spine to my tailbone.

'Do you feel more comfortable now?' His voice is back to normal.

'Oh, ah, yes, much better, although I'd still love a shower.' I find his thigh and caress it with my hand. 'Are you sure I can't persuade you to take a shower with me?' I start edging my way off the seat.

'No. Now sit.' This time I am aghast at his order. His hands push me firmly back into the lounge. My mouth is open in shock. 'Please, sit down. We need to conclude our discussion, come to some agreement.' His tone is only slightly more gentle.

Oh, great, I need a shower and he needs to talk.

'Fine. I'll smell and you talk,' I say as defiantly as I can. 'Then I'll shower.' Making sure it is a statement rather than a question.

He places my drink back in my hands and shifts closer to me on the lounge.

'You know I respect you?'

'Most of the time, I suppose.'

'Alex!' He can sound so commanding with one word. If only I had that skill. Obviously this is to be a serious conversation.

'Yes, okay, I know.'

'I want to play with you, create some edginess. I want to take you to a place you have *never* dared to go, give you an opportunity to embrace your sexuality like you truly never believed possible.'

Seriously in overdrive, yet again! His voice is engaging and tantalising, teasing my sex and my mind simultaneously. How does he do this to me? Just using words, for god's sake. I temper my breathing as I take a moment to absorb his statement.

'We have been playing with each other since we first met, Jeremy, and this weekend has been a never-ending physical, mental and emotional roller-coaster of "play", to use your word. Where else could you possibly take me?'

'But you've enjoyed it so far, haven't you? You've said so yourself.'

I sigh before answering.

'As much as I hate admitting it to you out loud, yes, I've loved it. It scares me, though, at the same time.' I pause as I reflect back on our conversation in the car and how it links to theories of play. 'You know some psychologists believe that play is perhaps the most powerful source of joy humans can experience — as it encompasses both fun and fear. Some believe it can even protect against depression —'

I stop myself as the word leaves my lips and it finally dawns on me. I've been so comprehensively distracted by him that I have been embarrassingly slow on the uptake. 'This is what you want to explore further. This is what you have been doing, ensuring I'm kept on a roller-coaster ride of fun and fear!'

'Exactly, Alexa, hopefully now you understand. The concept being that "real" play is essentially a simulated anxiety attack.'

'Well, you've given me plenty of those since Friday. So, if that is what you have been hoping for, you have well and truly succeeded.'

I can't help but wonder if I'm still missing something ... is there more to this? I feel like he has been deliberately keeping me in the dark, literally and figuratively since we met. Now he is doing the slow reveal on the real purpose of the weekend. Is he creating experiences enabling me to learn more about how I handle stress, or 'play' as he calls it, or am I merely a pawn in some greater game?

'I have been involved in the studies analysing the amygdala, the cell clusters in the brain specialising in fear, and how they relay messages to the frontal lobes of the brain.'

Of course he has.

'And I'm particularly interested in investigating dopamine reward circuits and the release of chemicals such as opiods. Our initial data analysis shows an unexpected correlation to Sam's work from a pleasure perspective. This is why we need to study it more thoroughly.' His comments put me on a new learning curve, his intelligence more prominent than ever.

'I must admit I never anticipated feeling like this. I can't ever recall a time when my body and mind have been on higher alert, or more stimulated, or aroused, I suppose you could say. I am literally buzzing inside and out, with both fear and pleasure.'

'Fascinating, that's great. It means it's all working.' He sounds lost in his thoughts.

'What's working, Jeremy? Where are you going with this, anyway?'

'That is another two questions, Alexa.'

I am completely exasperated. He completely ignores my exasperation.

'I want to play harder, I want to push the boundaries further between you and I.'

'Push the boundaries. How much more could you push?' My voice sounding instantly high-pitched, staccato. More questions! 'Oh, sorry, I didn't mean to ask …' I trail off, not knowing what to say. He is turning me into a submissive, blind mute.

Oh, dear god. Another 'aha' moment ... and now it comes full circle. Of course there is more to it; when is there not with Jeremy? How could I have been so naive? My thesis! He really does want to take me to a place I have never been, never dared to go. I knew I should never have given him a copy of the damn thing, I knew when I did I might live to regret it. Who would have thought it would come back to haunt me after so many years?

'I'm going to push you, further than we ever have, but I want you to know that I will ensure you are safe, looked after.'

'And you want me to be the experiment for your research, Jeremy, don't you? Just admit it.'

'Yes, I do.' I'm a little shocked that he has admitted this so readily. 'I need your body and brain on both sides of the experience, like I said. I think we are honestly on the cusp of discovering a cure and you are one of the few people who can help us. Your role is critical.'

'Of course I'd love to be involved in discovering a cure for depression, Jeremy. Who wouldn't? But I do have questions, plenty of them, you must understand that.' A few spontaneously erupt in my brain just to prove my point ... to myself, that is.

How do you want to push boundaries?

What does that mean?

What's different this time?

What if I don't want to?

How do I know I will be okay?

Are you crazy?

Am *I* crazy?

What the f**k could I be getting myself into now?

'Of course I understand, sweetheart, and I would tell you if I could, honestly, but in this particular instance it can't work that way. Why do you think I made it a condition of this weekend?'

Oh shit, I have played completely into his hands. His two conditions for this weekend — no vision, no questions. What has been driving my fear and anxiety? Exactly those two things! Maybe my brain is slowing down as it reaches middle age. Why hadn't I come to that realisation sooner? He has carefully constructed the situation I'm in right now where I must ultimately decide whether I'll take this personal risk for the greater human reward. A decision he knows I will, for the first time, honestly consider. Will I continue this journey into exploring my personal darkness with him, a journey I have never been courageous enough to experience until this point in my life? He really is the consummate mastermind.

It scares me. It excites me. Can I take the plunge? How far does he want to go? How far does he want *me* to go? Can I handle it? I have absolutely no idea. I gulp another mouthful of the berry drink to distract me from my rising tension.

'All of your questions will be answered in time, I promise,' he smoothly states, as if reading my mind.

The doorbell rings and he lets someone in.

'If madame would care to accompany me.' The words make me freeze. It's difficult to decipher whether the voice is male or female.

Jeremy senses my reaction and wraps his arms around me. 'You will be fine. I will be with you shortly, I promise. We just need to get changed. Have that shower you wanted.'

'Why can't you come with me? Or I stay with you?' My neediness shocks even me.

'It's just not how it works around here. I promise I'll be with you again in ten minutes or so.'

'Please, Jeremy, don't make me go.' I feel like a child on the first day of school, being coaxed away from my parents by the teacher. He lifts me from the couch, holding my hands. He replaces his hand with the stranger's soft one and I am led away.

'I'll be with you shortly.' I sense him staring after me as I stumble along uncertainly. I cannot honestly say whether I believe he is concerned or amused by throwing me into what feels like the lion's den, once again. I surmise it is probably a mix of both, which is totally disconcerting.

I needn't have been so apprehensive. The stranger takes me through a long corridor and into a warm room. My clothes are carefully, considerately and silently removed. I'm led to a toilet and I am relieved to be relieved. I hear a shower turn on and feel the steam near my skin. My nakedness is complete but no longer significant. I take a step forward to the steaming water and let out a sigh as I allow my body and hair to run wet. I stay this way for some time until a hand stretches out my arm and proceeds to scrub. Unlike the soft, gliding hands from this morning, the scrubbing is vigorous and shocking. My other arm receives the same treatment, as does my back, my chest, my stomach, my butt, each leg and foot. Layers of skin are removed from my body and, although the motion is rough and hard, it feels good. Like it is serving a purpose. I consider yelling 'stop, it hurts' or 'I am not that dirty', but I don't. I allow the firm hands to continue scrubbing until their mission is complete. It's almost like I'm happy for the dirty layers of my skin to be scrubbed clean. Will this make me clean? Physically, yes. Emotionally, it barely touches the surface.

The shower shuts off and a luxuriously soft, warm robe is placed around me. I stand still, momentarily lost in the unknown world I have allowed myself to enter. I'm guided away, barely conscious of my situation.

'Wasn't so bad, was it?'

It takes me a moment to realise that, true to his word, I am reunited with Jeremy.

'No, not too bad. Where on earth are we?'

'Alexa, please, I implore you, no more questions — not here!' His voice echoes around the room, sounding more anxious and concerned with each word.

'Okay, okay, I'll try.'

'Thank you. Can you guess where we are?'

'Not really. It sounds very echo-y, but muffled somehow. I can hear water dripping in the background.' I hope we are alone.

'Here, come, feel this.' He guides me along a few steps and places my hand on what feels like cold marble. I place my other hand on it and start to slide it a little further downwards.

'It feels like a torso.' I slide a little lower.

'Now it feels like a butt.' I laugh. 'Please don't tell me we are in a museum in bathrobes, Jeremy.'

'No, not quite, but we are surrounded by statues.' It feels very odd caressing a sculpture. You'd never be allowed to do this in a museum or gallery; imagine sliding your hands over the statue of David in Florence. 'Move around to the front.'

I shift my hands carefully around the torso and feel a very large erection. Jeez, obviously not David, then. I feel quite naughty as I fondle its length and girth.

'Do you like it?'

'I'd prefer you.'

'I'm very pleased to have that confirmed. What about this one?' He guides me along another few steps and places my hands on another marble torso.

'This one is female.' I quickly remove my hands. Jeremy

guides them back toward the breasts, his hands cupping mine to keep them there.

'Is this difficult for you?

'I have only ever felt my own.'

'They're just marble, Alex. Feel them, for me.' I allow my fingers and palm to linger around them, as he stands close behind me.

'Roll the nipples between your thumb and forefinger.' I wonder why this is so erotic. 'That is what I do to you, sweetheart, with merely my words.' His hands twine through my robe to cup my breasts and confirm the truth in his statement. My lower belly grinds in agreement.

'Come.' He takes my hand and guides me away from the sexy statues.

'Lie down. I need to reapply your eye drops.' I'm lowered to a hard bench; it feels like a narrow, marble plank. I lie down in the full knowledge that I am accepting his conditions of this weekend, without the resistance that has been causing me so much nervous tension and anxiety.

'Thank you.' His words are heartfelt.

Once again, he methodically goes through the procedure of ensuring my continued blindness. This time, I accept my fate calmly, but instinctively, I can't help but try to open my eyes. They are so heavily weighted, my lids won't separate at all.

I lie still awaiting the full effect of the drops and ointment for the second time. Jeremy slides my robe to either side of my body letting it fall off my shoulders and encourages my arms to rest above my head. I know he likes me in this position, with unfettered access to my body. He slowly and methodically shifts my legs either side of the bench, leaving me open to him. It is as if his softness and intensity are attempting to compensate for his act of ensuring my continued blindness. My pulse quickens in anticipation. He lightly kisses my nipples and gently takes them in his teeth and rolls his tongue around their tip until I imagine they look like the statue's. Oh, he is good at this. My brain clouds over. Goosebumps take over my body at his touch. His mouth continues painstakingly along my belly, his focus thoughtful, intense. My body ripples in response to his delicate caress ... my skin is highly sensitive, alive and tingling due to the harsh scrubbing a short time ago. My desire for him is so acute it is as though it has been years, not hours, since we last connected sexually. I'm aware of his closeness as he lowers himself between my thighs. I am so highly aroused I could be floating on the ceiling. He blows lightly, gently and silently into me. The sensation is exquisite. Nothing touching me but his breath, until his lips join in slowly, considerately, then eventually his tongue joins the rhythm he is creating through my body. It is excruciatingly divine. I feel the rush of blood flowing and pumping through my body, swelling in anticipation as if I have never desired him more.

And then, just like that, he stops. I'm left in torment, unfulfilled, unreleased. I sense his face close to mine so I reach out and pull him toward me, kissing his lips, desperate for him. 'What are you doing to me? Please, don't leave me like this. I need you, I want you, please.' My mind is spinning, my heart pumping.

'All in good time, sweetheart. I need you more wanton than you have ever been.'

'Wanton? God, that is so not fair.' I actually think I'm pouting; how childish.

'I know it's not fair, GG, but it will be worth the wait, I promise.'

How the hell does he have the strength to impose this sort of control? And why don't I?

His arms lift me to a standing position. My legs are quivering like jelly against the unreleased constriction of my swollen sex, and he takes both my hands and slowly, slowly edges us a few steps forward until I regain my balance. I feel warm water dancing around my feet as his forefinger crosses my lips, cautioning me to silence and preventing any more questions escaping from my mouth.

I'm now naked before him, and hopefully only him, not even a blindfold or sunglasses to hide behind, just my closed eyelids, sealed shut. He guides me down a ramp and silky liquid encompasses more of my body with each step we take. His arms lift me up and further deposit me into the liquid, which saturates my skin; I feel like a baby being given a warm and loving bath. Something about it feels serenely relaxing, yet there is an undercurrent of apprehension, foreboding. I push the latter feeling away.

'Let's just take some time to relax, unwind and soak up the experience.'

I don't argue.

His hand slides down to the small of my back, gently pushing me forward until I am fully immersed, floating in the water. It feels amazing. For some reason, I have the sense that he is cleansing my body, preparing it for a greater purpose. Images flood my mind of the baptisms and christenings I have attended and the symbolism that embodies the ritual of purifying water. The silence surrounding us combined with the buoyancy of the liquid in which I'm floating, solidify these images in my brain. The water lapping at the edges is the only sound amplified. It is as if we have been placed in some form of magical aqua cocoon. Once again, I can't help but wonder where we could possibly be.

It feels wonderful to be floating. I try to soak up the experience as I feel Jeremy floating serenely beside me in this strange pool. I envision him from above, a floating circular version of da Vinci's Vitruvian man. Beautiful. The temperature of the water seems to be in perfect unison with the temperature of the room, creating a surreal womb-like effect. We alternate between different pools: a very hot one, which is shocking to enter and initially makes me feel light-headed, but feels sublime when my body adjusts to the heat, and a cold one, which invigorates and cleanses, making my heartbeat faster and pump blood rapidly through my veins, letting me know I'm well and truly alive. My circulation is pounding with the fluctuating temperatures and my skin greedily soaks up the minerals. I feel like I'm somehow restoring my vital balance. I'm quietly pleased we aren't talking as the silence helps replenish my peace of mind and facilitates calm after the wild ride I have been on since meeting Jeremy for an 'innocent' drink.

It feels like an eternity ago. My intuition slyly suggests that that version of myself withered away when I accepted my blindness and I should acknowledge I am in the process of being ritualistically reborn. I don't allow myself to dwell on it further.

On leaving the pools I am wrapped in a towel. What skin I have left is alive and sensitive, and this becomes even more apparent as I am laid face down on my belly. I am adjusted a little as is the towelled bench I am lying on. As strong hands begin to knead my shoulder blades and various parts of my back, I am thrilled to verify I'm on a massage table. Jeremy has certainly planned the last few hours to perfection — aside from the 'missing in action' orgasm.

The towel is whisked away from my body, as the strong scent of orange and honey penetrates my nostrils. I raise my head slightly from its position to confirm the sweet citrus odour. My head is eased back as my hair is scooped up from the nape of my neck and bunched up away from my body. A sticky substance is dolloped on the small of my back before the hands return and the massage begins in earnest. The gooey ointment smoothly discovers my extremities as the skilful hands ensure I'm thoroughly embalmed in the intoxicating yet sticky combination.

I allow my mind to wander, not wanting to focus on anything in particular. I know in myself that the more I consider my situation, the more stressed my body will become — not a good thing when strong hands such as these are dissolving tense muscle tissue upon contact. I try to focus on my breathing ... it works for a while. My mind seeks to further unravel the need for Jeremy to have me blind and questionless this weekend. His logic makes partial sense, and I can't deny that I have certainly experienced sensory overload. As for emotions, I don't know whether I am coming or going ... I should be relaxing and letting go, I love a good massage and this is glorious. This feels so good, I am becoming as soft and gooey as the ointment as it sinks into the pores of my skin. What is holding me back? I can't help but sense there is still something more to all this that Jeremy isn't telling me. It's not normal to put relationships at risk like this for a bit of frivolous and, at times, terrifying fantasy, is it? Even if it is with Jeremy ... even if I feel more sexually alive and sensual than I have in my entire life ... Is our relationship about more than this weekend?

My thoughts are suddenly interrupted by reality as a number of arms lift me up, turn me over and place me back on the towelled bench. More orange and honey arrives on my belly as smaller hands work my stomach, chest and breasts. I jolt when they slide over my nipples and instantly attempt to normalise my breathing. *It's only a massage*, I convince myself. The hands establish their rhythm with my breath and the kneading continues, as do my thoughts.

Jeremy was right. I have too many questions; they seem to be multiplying exponentially in my brain like a viral disease. My body relinquishes all pretence of flesh and bone as the insistent palms morph me into soft clay. What could I do now, anyway? Would I once again be prevented from leaving? I don't even know where I am. My breath becomes shallow as I consider both the consequences of being here and the reality of trying to escape. Is that what I really want? Deep down I know I don't want to leave, I'm just scared of exploring what he has planned for me, as I always am — at first. Damn him for doing this to me; for forcing me to reach for a conclusion that seems impossible. Am I honestly this weak? All the values I have clung to so desperately in life, those that have given me stability and meaning and worth. And I am throwing them out the window for one careless, fanciful weekend? Is that all it will be? Or is this truly valuable research?

My mind implodes with the weight of my moral dilemmas until only numbness remains. My body becomes limp, there is no resistance left. I am a mere jellyfish awaiting the next current to reveal my future path. Exhausted mentally and emotionally, and now physically pliable, just as he wants me to be, I'm sure, I allow the blackness to surround my mind and let the futile desperation in my thoughts dissipate.

Flashes of memories flitter within my dreamlike state. Happy memories: my babies, birthday parties, smiling faces, my son telling me he loves me eight hundred million, billion, zillion times more than the universe, and my daughter explaining why she will live with me forever and ever and that is why she must marry me and only me. The memories of my children flood through my subconscious one after the other. Simple times, uncomplicated times, but why does Robert appear somewhat forlorn, disengaged, in these visions of our family unit? I hadn't noticed before. These pictures make up so much of who I am, minute by minute, day by day. Yet, why does it feel like there is still something missing? Why does his body language reflect that something is also missing for him?

My internal arguments and debates are spiralling out of control. Jeremy has talked before about the possibility of me exploring my secret, dark fantasy, the one that provided the basis for my thesis all those years ago, the one I have never truly acknowledged as my own, except very briefly to him. Am I brave enough? I could never go there with anyone but Jeremy, and he is handing this experience to me on a personal and professional platter. What if I say no when it is exactly what I have always longed to experience, just to know and understand once and for all? Is fantasy just fantasy and should it be left that way, or is there a need and desire to act on it, to experience it first-hand? My mind seems a little fuzzy, meandering, and no longer able to accommodate the complexity of my thoughts as I surrender to the masseur's magic hands.

The sound of rolling wheels restores me to full consciousness and it is only then that I realise I am moving; lying down, but moving nonetheless. I struggle and attempt to raise my jelly-like limbs off the table. They are so relaxed and heavy from the massage it's almost impossible. I try again.

'Please lie still, we won't be long.'

'What? Where are we going?' My voice sounds raspy and the words can barely leave my mouth.

I realise I must have dozed off … for minutes? hours? Surely not? We come to a stop.

'Madame. You are awake, may I help you?' A female voice speaks to me.

'Ah … yes, thank you.' My natural politeness kicks in.

'Can you tell me how long have I been asleep?' Hands raise me gently to a sitting position. A robe, not the same one as before — this is more velvety and feels heavier — is placed over my shoulders. I notice it has no arms, or at least my arms are not threaded through any sleeves. It feels smooth against the silkiness of my skin, with no remnants of the massage oil's stickiness.

No answer. Has everyone I encounter been told not to answer my questions?

'Would madame like some tea?'

Oh, tea, that's a surprise.

'Yes, madame would.' The words pop out of my mouth a little too harshly. 'That would be lovely, thank you.' I remember my manners.

'Could you please tell me where Jeremy — I mean, Dr Quinn, is?' Nothing. I have no idea if he is with me or not, but I don't sense that he is, if that makes any sense.

'Jeremy?' I try again.

'Please answer me if you are here. We need to talk. Please?' My voice sounding more anguished with each word.

Typical, just when I need to speak to him, he has vanished.

Hot tea is carefully placed in my hand and smells delicious. It calms me and distracts me from my rising nerves. I embrace the infusion in the air, scenting camomile, with a hint of vanilla perhaps. I taste a little at a time so I don't burn my lips. Perfect. The tiny cup feels like a heavy weight in my hands given the relaxed state of my muscles. As I finish the remainder, I feel bands around my wrists. The cup is taken away from me, giving me the opportunity to explore further. It feels like leather with a small jingly thing rattling above and below. They are a couple of inches long and fit quite snugly around each wrist. Shit!

'Jeremy!'

Silence surrounds me.

I try to find where they are buckled, but can't seem to locate an opening. Don't tell me these, too, have been tailor-made. I feel my pulse quicken. I scan my body mentally to locate any other foreign objects and sure enough, there are also two, slightly larger versions around my ankles. Oh god, I go weak at the knees. In sheer defiance I quickly attempt to find an opening or buckle to remove. There is nothing. This happened when I was asleep?

I'm startled to feel that another band is being swiftly placed around my neck; there is a strange sound as it is tightened into position. I'm momentarily stunned, finding it difficult to breathe as I adjust to the constricted feeling. It too, has a jingly metal component, one on the front and one on the back. I freeze. This is it. This is what Jeremy was talking about. Wanting to play harder, push the boundaries.

What does he want to experience with me like this? More importantly, what does he want me to experience like this? *Okay*, I think to try and calm myself down, *it is not as if I didn't know this was coming in some way and here it is.* It is apparently going to happen very soon. Oh, dear. The adrenaline pounding through my heart and pumping through my veins is more pronounced now than it was when I jumped out of the plane. The physicality of my emotions is as fascinating as it is astounding. So real, so intense, so vital. Am I prepared to stop now, when my response is this intriguing?

What are the alternatives? I could speak. I could scream. Perhaps that is what I should do, right here, right now ... but I don't. I remind myself that I did exactly that at the dinner to no purpose whatsoever, and thank goodness he completely ignored me then because the sexual tension was exceptionally gratifying in the longer term. I literally feel carnal energy shooting through my body at the memories. Ah yes, it was definitely worth fighting through my own fear to achieve such phenomenal rewards.

This must be part of his master plan. He has certainly succeeded in sending me into hyperventilating overdrive and nothing has even happened except for an exquisite massage and leather straps bound to my body. I love and hate that he can do this to me, make me feel and experience things I never believed possible. It makes me feel as if every beat of my heart is meaningful to my life. I will do this for him, for myself and for his research. I will be strong for him and maybe, just maybe, it may help set me free. From whom, from what I wonder ... possibly, from myself ...

Am I willing to discover the truth first-hand rather than watch from the sidelines of life?

I stand silently as my wrists are bound behind my back.

Still silent, as a velvet hood encircles my face.

Remain mute, as I am ushered along a corridor, my bare feet shuffling on the plush carpet. Demurely being led to a destination without force, by unknown, faceless strangers, without resisting. How many people surround me? I have no idea. I sense their energy, not their quantity.

I am forced to confront the stark reality of asking myself once and for all, if I do, in all honesty, trust Jeremy. Imagine my life without the seductive, beguiling, enticing and challenging Jeremy in it. Of course I trust him, when have I not? He brings my otherwise black and white life into brilliant technicolour. Although I'd be remiss if I didn't also acknowledge his expertise in creating phenomenal psychological dramas, such as the one I am currently in. My thoughts are suddenly interrupted by a deep baritone voice.

'Bring her to me.'

I am brought.

Strong male hands lightly grip my upper arms.

'Remove her robe.'

It is removed.

My legs are stationed apart.

Life is strange, you know. We spend our whole lives building up self-esteem, learning to love ourselves, educate ourselves, 'better' ourselves, and then it comes to this? How incredibly quickly the confidence we build for ourselves, built carefully layer upon layer over the years, the decades, can dissolve into insignificance in mere seconds.

The way people look and dress and act, what you do, what you earn, how well educated you are, means nothing when you are stripped bare, desperately naked, vision violated, symbols of slavery strapped to your ankles, wrists and neck.

Two fingers deftly penetrate my vagina so efficiently that my mind is instantly silenced and reality slices through me. I stagger forward with the shock of the intrusion but am held securely in place. My breathing quickens in response.

What power is left? What ounce of human dignity?

How is it then, that if I had a penis, I'd have a massive erection?

I have a sense of slipping into a psychological void, a place I have never dared enter within my own psyche, somewhat like I imagine Alice felt sliding down the rabbit hole in her mind. I am compelled to continue the journey.

'Note that,' says the baritone.

Noting ... I really am on the other side of the experiment now. Who would have thought that I would be standing here accepting the violation that has just occurred to my body? Not me, not in a million years.

'Place her in position.'

Outwardly, no voice, no sight. Complete acquiescence as I am lowered into a kneeling position.

Something long, thin, smooth and cold slides under my breasts. I inhale sharply at the touch. Like the bow of a violin, it moves back and forward across my chest, sliding slowly below my breasts, then above, then carefully and accurately past the tips of my nipples as if tuning itself to my body. The sensation is slow and rhythmic and I'm grateful I'm already on my knees. My nipples harden in anticipation as illicit shivers cascade through my shoulders and back. The bow then moves seamlessly and elegantly between my thighs, creating such a heightened sensual tension it causes me to cry out in anticipation of what is to come. It is preparing my body for imminent play.

'Hmm. She does react instantaneously, J, just as you said. This is excellent news.'

J — Jeremy? He has been discussing me with others? *Of course he has, I'm here aren't I?* I answer my own question.

'Jeremy! Please talk to me.' My voice escapes more softly than I expect; apparently it has been buried too long.

Finally, his voice comes from behind me, I'm relieved to

know he is so close. 'Yes, Alexa. I am right here.' His words whisper comfortingly against my ear.

'Oh, thank god, there you are.' I nestle my face towards him. 'Is this honestly what you want from me, want me to experience?'

'I have never wanted anything more in my life,' he states quietly, sensually.

'Really?' Okay, this is it. Can I do this for him, for myself, for us?

'I want you to embrace every emotion you encounter and accept it, knowing that it is part of you, part of your sexuality. I will never leave you and I will look after you. All you must do is trust me enough to give yourself wholly over to the process. Surrender yourself to me, to this experience, knowing that the fear is worth the pleasure. Only you can decide whether we continue or not, right here, right now. Just tell me, yes or no.' How is it that he may as well be having this conversation with my clitoris, instead of my brain?

Tears well up in my blind eyes. I can't control the intensity of my emotions any more. Do I surrender to this innate longing that has haunted me for years and simply say, *yes*? Our shared memories dance in my mind. The tension. The game playing. The teasing, the tormenting. His dominance. My submission. And our combined love of these roles. So he wants to push the boundaries. Deep down I acknowledge that I, too, want to know how far they can be pushed, knowing I would only ever allow them to be pushed by him.

'Yes.' My decision relieves me beyond belief and I let out an almighty sigh as I finally succumb to my destiny, the destiny Jeremy has created.

'Thank you. You won't regret this. I promise.' He removes the hood and softly kisses my lips.

'I am going to silence you now so you are unable to speak. Is there anything else you would like to say before I do this?'

I shake my head. The reality that I'm willing to allow myself to enter such uncharted territory scares the living daylights out of me, yet arouses me so ferociously it's intoxicating. He opens my mouth and squirts a citrus-tasting spray onto my tongue and the back of my throat. It produces a strange numbing sensation and I can't help but test its effectiveness. No sound whatsoever — I am now mute as well as blind.

'Please place her in position.'

The strong arms raise my body off the floor, like a rag doll, as I am lifted to some higher place. A platform? It's almost as if gravity is inconsequential and I am weightless. Once again, I am placed on my knees and, still in this position, my legs are separated with both knees and ankles anchored to the firm spongy floor, thanks to the added convenience of my leather binds. Given my wrists are still bound behind me, I am well and truly stationed in position.

I want this. I need to understand where it leads me. I don't struggle. I'm strapped to the floor. I am not free to see; I am not free to speak; I am not free to move. I am free to experience the complete and utter fear, excitement, shame and arousal penetrating each and every cell as anxiety trembles physically through my body. How peculiar and fascinating that these emotions can exist in unison.

'There are a few items requiring clarification before we progress further.' The baritone voice again.

I have been remiss. I should add to my list, I am free to hear.

'Please examine her again.'

Once again, two fingers manoeuvre deeply into my vagina. They probe a little longer this time and are promptly removed.

My body responds to the intrusion, but the impact is less obvious given my captured position.

'Good, let us proceed.'

I feel a strange sense of having travelled through time and participating in some ancient sexual rite of passage.

'There is no requirement for the subject to acknowledge anything I say. It can be verified on her behalf by J. It is, however, important that she hears the words before we remove that sense as well.'

I feel my breasts rising and falling with each breath; the anticipation as to what is coming next is so distinct.

'It is our understanding, Dr Quinn, that the subject gave you permission to effectively render her blind for forty-eight hours?'

The subject. I am truly a nonentity.

Pause.

'True.'

'It is our understanding that you made her aware, on a number of occasions, that there were implications for her behaviour over this period.'

'True.'

'And that for each question she asked, there would be consequences?'

'Yes.'

'Is it your belief that she understood these requirements?'

'Yes.'

'Finally, you have discussed our research program and she agreed to be involved?'

'That's correct.'

This is it, it is actually happening. I have handed myself over to him, to them. Although I do wonder why are they going through this mentally tortuous process.

'This is truly excellent work. We can say categorically that she is perfect for our program. I am very much looking forward to analysing the results.'

Wow, positive feedback. Jeremy must be very pleased with himself. I wonder whether all of this is turning him on.

'We must address the consequences of her actions. How many questions has she asked in total?'

Before I am given the privilege of hearing the answer, earplugs are inserted into my ears. Oh god, this is full on. Complete silence, complete blindness, completely mute and completely exposed. I have never gone into a state of shock before; I can only imagine that this is what I am feeling now. Completely devoid of ... well ... everything! Completely 100 per cent numb, frozen in time. There is now absolutely no sensory way to predict what will happen to me and absolutely no way of preventing it. Touch is my one and only remaining sense.

Something helmet-like is placed over my head. It feels weird, a little onerous at first, and it takes me a moment to register that, of course, they will be monitoring the neural activity in my brain. This is the missing link in their research and I am their human experiment. Instinctively, I attempt to control my thoughts, then scream silently; I want to test the device and its tracking mechanisms to see if it will make any difference when they analyse the results. This situation is almost too bizarre to comprehend.

My wrists are released from behind me and rebound together in front of me. My arms are stretched way beyond my head. No further please, I pray silently. My hips are steadied as the stretching continues and my body is then forced to bend over a spongy bar until I reach the floor where my bound wrists are attached and secured, along with my neck. This position ensures my chest is now lower than my now-protruding arse. I can only imagine my breasts dangling free as my breathing escalates, ensuring I understand this is all very real and not a dream at all. All hands are removed from my body. My restraints are now entirely non-human.

The sound of my racing heart consumes me. It pumps so hard and fast I wonder if this is it. Is this what a heart attack feels like? Am I having a heart attack right this second? What a position to die in. Before I fully assimilate the possibility of heart failure, my body bucks against the intrusion of yet more probing fingers. I feel my nipples harden and my butt jolts at the invasion. I hold my breath as they stay longer this time, apply more pressure, test and stretch the confines of their now slippery surrounds. Warmth emanates from within me as my vagina moistens in anticipation of their touch. The sound of my heart racing threatens to explode in my ears. I exhale sharply as they retract; shocked at the emptiness they leave behind.

Then nothing but my beating heart.

I am stung so hard and fast on my arse I freeze, completely rigid.

It happens again. It stops.

There is no breath going into or out of my lungs.

And again. It stops.

I need to inhale.

In quick succession, I am struck again and again and again and again. I inhale with each thwack of the strap landing across my arse, unable to exhale from the sheer shock of it. The oxygen intake is in stark conflict to the silent scream frantically attempting to leave my throat, rendering it impossible. I spasm as my head spins in turmoil.

The stinging sensation is like nothing I've experienced before; not too painful but not un-painful. Just enough to feel the bite on the surface of my flesh for a second or two, then just as quickly the sensation begins to recede. It starts and it stops. I am left panting, overwhelmed. Cooling ointment is being caressed into my buttocks, so smoothly, so seductively I could weep at the miraculous change in intensity. I'm already emotionally spent. Can I really take this? Perhaps my thesis would have proved a very different piece of work had I experienced this first-hand.

Then again thwack, thwack, and again higher, lower, within and around ... and I lose count ...

My world slides into slow motion. I'm splitting in two.

My body arches and retracts in both desperation and desire as it attempts to avoid the impact of the relentless lashes on my buttocks. I'm writhing and squirming internally as my arse maintains its rigid position as if it is begging for more. Is it, I wonder?

My hips are held firm as yet again the probing fingers effortlessly slide in to reacquaint themselves with my vagina. I feel the deep vibration in my lower body that releases a seed of invitation to this entire experience. I feel my vulva swell in anticipation as if my vagina is welcoming a long-lost friend and I am throbbing, aching and wet. I have no doubt the owner of the fingers is ensuring this information is 'noted', given its extended stay within me.

They leave. Cooling ointment arrives, applied with hands stroking softly, gently, my arse attempting to replicate the rhythm of the caress. Once again tears flow with the relief and tenderness of it. What is happening to me?

I'm left alone. I breathe. I sob.

Blackness and silence encompass me.

It is only now that I register I want more.

The straps under my knees and binding my ankles are released. My legs tremble and shake in response. Knees are repositioned further apart, spread wide, re-strapped and ankles realigned and anchored accordingly. Oh, dear god. Abstractly, I wonder why I use the term 'god' in such highly sexualised moments. The bar is shifted into a higher position, resulting in my arse becoming an even more obvious spread-eagled target, if that were possible. The essence of my womanhood, the physical entrances to my inner sanctum being showcased, spotlighted, publicly stage managed for examination by however many people are present in this sadistic audience. This can't possibly be who I am, can it?

My heart cannot beat fast enough to accommodate the power my anticipatory arousal cascades over my entire body.

Thwack. Pause. Then a smooth, cold, sliding sensation over the sting.

Then again. Thwack. Pause. Slide.

Thwack. Pause. Slide … It establishes a rhythm my body starts to anticipate and desire, shifting itself like a ladder across my arse. I try to prepare for the collision, but am left with only the sensation of the exquisite pain before the reassuring slide and relief of the more caressing touch. I throb in anticipation of this effect. The focus shifts to my inner thighs, not as forceful, but so enormously arousing.

I want more.

I need more.

I receive more.

The combination of pleasure and pain is blowing my mind and my body has no choice but to revel in this carnal ambush.

It stops. I gasp. Given the concentration on my behind and thighs, it takes me a moment to acknowledge someone is fiddling with my nipples, tweaking them before clamping them. The sensation shoots straight to my groin. Something is belted around my waist that forces my body closer to the floor, my arse maintaining its position over the bar. All restraints are checked again and tightened, and their security is tested by my own body as a low current emits from whatever is attached to my nipples, the warm shock of it ensuring my entire body bucks against the restraints. I silently shriek at the tantalising impact. As I adjust to the sensation, it's as if the current from my nipples is directly attached to my clitoris like a sexually charged triangular wire. The tingling warms my entire body and the pain becomes a teasing, pleasurable vibration. God, what are they doing to me? I have become a sexual exhibit, something you might see depicted in the future of MONA's darkest hours.

The striking continues, bringing the intruding pain to the forefront of my body and mind. Then the pleasure returns, albeit briefly. Then the pain. My body allows them complete control in alternating between these extreme sensations with the flick of a switch. I am Pavlov's dog.

It is as if my body has acclimatised to the sensation of such pleasurable pain as it takes me a moment to realise it has been replaced once again by a low vibration flowing through my nipples. The fingers reassert themselves beyond my vulva, and attach something that emits an intense vibration close to my clitoris. Too close! I freeze with panic and desire; my vulnerability is absolute. The intensity of the vibration increases, slowly and steadily. I feel myself break into a sweat of sexual anxiety. The fingers bypass my buzzing clit and spend time probing and exploring my vagina, my perineum. If I could move, I'd have collapsed in a heap on the floor by now. As it is, my body is like melting wax hardening in time against the mould the restraints provide. I notice that my body temperature is rising, along with my rapturous arousal.

The fingers are now warm, experienced, pleasure-seeking fingers and I feel my opening welcoming them in further, deeper. My mute throat groans with both shame and desire as I beseech my mind to stay alert. The fingers locate dimensions I have never found before, never explored myself. My perineum, my anus, nothing is ignored in this process. Oh god! Jeez, there's that word again. They play and push and press and probe, as if monitoring and assessing the impact their every touch has on my body. I desperately try to control my responses, to rein these intensely sexual feelings in, but they are free spirits, they won't be tempered. The fingers settle, positioning themselves carefully, then insistently, then rhythmically, then intensely as they set off rippled explosions through my muscles. I absently wonder if an orgasm can be forced upon you. Do I want to have an orgasm in front of others? Will I have the choice?

Oh god ...

Vibrations soar through my nipples and clitoris as my mind becomes awash with pleasure and desire. My ability to control the ambush of pleasure penetrating my body is a receding black hole in my mind's eye. Although entirely bound and anchored to the earth, my grip on reality is being diluted by the second. I sense the ominous waves building momentum over the horizon, threatening to annihilate my mind and enable my body's ultimate surrender.

I focus.

They probe.

I resist.

They vibrate.

I freeze.

They target.

I relinquish.

They pleasure.

I release.

They win.

The next second introduces me to the most amazingly intense, shooting, powerful sensation I have ever felt in my life. It enters at the tip of my nipples and surges through my body at lightning speed, coinciding with the very lubricated penetration of both my vagina and my anus. I reel against the total ambush of my body so completely I now feel as if I have torn free from my restraints and physically crashed into the ceiling.

All concept of time is suspended; my rational brain officially closes down, enabling my sensory mind to take full control and allow direct passage to every feeling and sensation colliding with my body. I am launched into another stratosphere.

Surrender!

Freedom!

Pure ... sensual ... ecstasy ...

Warm, throbbing vibrations emanating from the core of my being.

It is all-encompassing, wave after endless wave of bliss.

The rhythm, the waves of rapture moving through me.

I'm throbbing, pulsing ... is this too much?

Can I take any more?

I certainly hope so ...

Vibrations regain their intense focus in my very being, pounding deep within my core, but the ride has become smoother, not as wild and overwhelming as before. I'm not going to fall off the edge like a log over a roaring waterfall.

Eventually, my mind re-establishes itself in my brain. My earplugs are removed and the strong arms release me from my binds; I'm lifted away, no longer anchored to the floor.

I'm now lying down on something large and soft and warm and I feel like my entire body is melting like a giant marshmallow into toasty fire, the cushioning is so perfectly accommodating my every movement. It feels good to stretch and be free again.

I detect a delightful flickering across my breasts arousing me from my liquid state.

God, that feels so good.

Now it's on both sides. I feel blood flowing to the tips of my nipples.

How erotic. I let out a deep sigh …

The flickering turns into gentle pulling and kneading.

Each nipple has a slightly different tension, different rhythm …

It becomes more intense. Moist warmth arrives on my lips.

It is difficult to know where to focus.

My mouth is pried open softly by a warm tongue. It feels familiar but odd somehow, like it might be upside down. I squirm slightly under the soft pressure but allow the sensations of the kneading, sucking and licking to continue unabated … So many tongues accessing my body — oh yes, Jeremy, this is absolutely worth it! No fantasy in my mind could ever match this reality. I find it impossible to imagine what it looks like from the outside, as the touching and feeling are all-encompassing.

All of this attention feels so incredible on my body.

As my mouth and breasts are being consumed, my attention is drawn to light flutters moving steadily up each thigh. My legs open automatically to ensure their progress isn't hindered in any way. Oh, yes, please come in. This is truly divine.

Flicking, tugging, kneading, biting — not too much, not too little. It is so perfect, I could cry. There is too much to focus on so I just let go, let my body absorb the intensity of desire and longing within me.

The tongue below reaches my entrance. It explores my inner depths ever so carefully, yet so purposefully and intensely.

Like it is sifting through precious jewels, probing to locate something rare and valuable. It takes my breath away. Tongue and lips suck and nibble and are never distracted from their mission until the tongue finally locates the gem it is searching for. It focuses like a missile penetrating deeply and wholly and relentlessly on its target. The tongues from the other mouths intensify their response to replicate its energy and penetration.

Desire threatens to devour my entire body as the tongues multiply exponentially, frantically searching for a place to penetrate, deeper, further, harder, faster. My ears, mouth, neck, breast, bellybutton, vulva, fingers, toes, wrists, ankles, knees, underarms — it feels like no part of my body is left untouched.

My body arches violently with the magnitude of my desire. The tongues and lips and teeth don't skip a beat with my movement, instantaneously igniting their insatiable quest for more. I need them to slow down, ease up, though I desperately hope they don't. They quicken to the pulse of my heartbeat, like a drum beating to a tribal rhythm of life. Wild passion ignites deep within my soul and integrates with the essence of my body; we pulse and beat mindlessly as one heart sends blood flow and orgasmic lust to the farthest reaches of my being and spins itself into a crashing hiatus, like the eye of a tornado.

No heartbeat.

No pulse.

No thought.

No mind.

I plunge into the profound abyss of euphoria.

And then it ignites and roars into a violent and awesome flow of sheer energy exploding, crashing and pumping through my body as though the centre of my being is Mount Vesuvius erupting over Pompeii.

The entirety of my world bursts so fast it takes everything away ... away ... away ...

And my body convulses as it reacts to an electrifying series of erotic explosions over and over and over and over again ...

Like it has never experienced before ... like I never believed possible ...

Pumping, pumping, pumping through every orifice of my body, setting my skin alight with liquid lava.

Wave after wave after wave of intense sublime pleasure ...

Creating orgasmic flows of energy ...

As if my body has never before reached true orgasm ...

How long can this last?

I release a silent guttural scream, long and hard though it can't be heard.

And immediately inhale deeply and desperately as though I'm a sexual newborn drawing its first breath, urgently seeking oxygen for survival.

My arched back finally releases from its rigid, captive state as I gasp for more air and allow the oncoming bliss to encompass me entirely. I groan with joy and heat and freedom and ecstasy and leave this earthly world to experience heavenly bliss ... I am the sex goddess of the universe ...

* * *

'Oh, Alexandra. You are exquisite. You have blown our minds.'

'And our analysis.'

'Absolutely. Beyond all projections.'

Is someone talking? Don't know, don't care …

I'm so very far away …

All I know is that the vibrations pounding through my body are truly, fucking unbelievable!

And I am absolutely, comprehensively shattered.

'Alexa! Can you hear me? Are you okay? Here, please drink this.'

I can smell delicious hot chocolate. Someone helps me sit up. I am on a firm bed of some sort, with soft cotton sheets.

'Be careful. It's hot.'

Something touches me and brings a cup to my lips.

It tastes like heaven and its heat cascades through to my chest.

'Jeremy …' My voice is barely a whisper.

'Don't strain, this will help your voice. Here, have some more.'

I finish the drink.

'That's it, now snuggle in. Understandably, you're exhausted, it's time for you to rest.'

He lays me down again, covers me up with a feather quilt and seems to secure me in place. It's warm and cosy and he's right, I've never felt more exhausted.

'Go to sleep, sweetheart, we'll talk later. You were beyond my wildest dreams.' He kisses me gently on the lips and smoothes my forehead. I begin to waft into a subconscious state … dreams … sounds like a good idea.

'All good here. Our work is done, for the time being at least. Great job, Dr Quinn.'

'We'll just pack up the rest of our things and leave you both to continue on your journey.'

'Remember, J, the next twenty-four hours are critical, and the situation will need to be closely monitored for the next three or four days. Confidentiality is paramount. She must not see or speak to anyone other than you. Our competitors would kill for these kinds of results.'

'Of course, not a problem, I have it completely under control.'

'Well done, gentlemen. Until next time. This has certainly exceeded our expectations. We shall look forward to the complete results. Keep us posted in the meantime.'

'Will do.'

Doors slam shut.

I'm not sure what the distant voices are talking about as they swirl around me. I feel so mellow. I vaguely hear engines vibrate beneath me ...

And I drift into a totally unconscious state.

Part VI

'The magnitude of a sensation is proportional to the logarithm of the intensity of the stimulus causing it.'

— Fechner's Law, 1860

[Part V]

My fingers greedily feel for their surroundings.

Luxurious, soft delights. They explore a silky mound and discover its pinnacle.

I curl up in delight. What is this I have discovered? A breast?

I cup it and feel its suppleness against the palm of my hand. I play with its mountain peak until it hardens, and then have the good fortune to discover another.

I tease it to life so it matches its twin.

These are the softest pillow breasts imaginable. Oh so reactive, so full, so very changeable under my touch.

I continue my playing, my teasing … they just feel too good to pry myself away.

Another hand gently touches the breast.

'They do feel amazing don't they?' says Jeremy's voice softly.

I pull my hands away, embarrassed. I thought I was alone. 'Oh, I didn't realise you were here. I'm sorry.'

'Nothing to apologise for, Alex. They are yours to touch.' I can hear the smile in his voice, which reminds me I'm still blind.

Strong arms wrap around me, cradle me.

'And of course I'm still here. I said I'd look after you.'

My thoughts feel vague and scattered.

'Have I been dreaming?' I smile to myself ... Ah yes, amazing dreams and fantasies, like nothing I've ever experienced before in my life. My body reacts instantly to the memory, the intensity of feelings trembling through me.

'Are you okay?' Jeremy asks urgently, his voice concerned.

'Oh, yes ... but I'm not sure ... what happened, Jeremy ... where are we?'

I suddenly feel a dull pain across my buttocks as I ask these questions and instinctively stop myself from asking more.

'Shh, just relax. You have been through so much.' He gently strokes my hair.

Still in a fog, I decide this is the best option. As I snuggle into his perfect, firm chest I raise my hand to my eyes, confirming the presence of the silky blindfold.

'Yes, it is still there, sweetheart. It will be for just a little longer.' He kisses my hands, keeping them away from my face. He places a warm duvet over me.

I hear his voice from within his chest, but not his words. It lulls and soothes my thoughts like fluffy clouds floating across a blue sky. I'm in a blissful state, so very content just to be warm and safe and close to him. He could be reading me a story, a poem, a newspaper article for all I comprehend. I am unable to decipher his words ... I hear his heartbeating with one ear and perhaps rain pounding against a window with the other and I concentrate on both sounds rather than what Jeremy is saying. I zone back in to his voice in time to hear, 'Are you thirsty, hungry?'

Wonderful idea. 'Is there any more hot chocolate? It warms me up from the inside out.'

'Sure, I'll make some more.'

The mattress moves as he shifts his weight and I feel like I'm falling. I grab his arm anxiously.

'It's alright, sweetheart, I'm not leaving you. I'm just getting your drink. Try not to move around too much.'

'It feels so weird to move, like I'm really heavy.'

I hear him making noises. It sounds like he is in a kitchen which seems odd in a hotel room.

He returns and places my fingers around the mug. I can't quite grip it firmly enough.

'Let me do this for you.' He brings the warm liquid to my lips.

'Ahhh, thank you, you do make a great hot chocolate, Jeremy.'

I picture myself sitting here blindfolded, with Jeremy and a hot chocolate, after all I have just been through. It is as if we are completely ignoring the elephant in the room. For some reason this thought sets me off into a fit of the giggles. I can't contain the laughter that erupts from within me at this thought, as if releasing all my nervous tension.

'What's so funny?' Jeremy grabs the mug from me before I drop it.

I am gasping for air and my stomach starts to ache from the spasms as I try to explain to Jeremy what is so funny. I can't get the words out because I'm laughing so much, which sets me off again. I hear Jeremy chuckling now too, probably at me. I don't care, I haven't laughed this hard in years; it hurts but it feels good. My eyes are streaming. I try to contain the spasms overtaking me, to get some breath into my lungs. I'm going to wet myself. I move to the edge of the bed and collapse straight onto the floor, still paralysed with convulsions.

Jeremy is instantly at my side. 'Oh, my god, Alexa! Are you hurt?' His words come out in a rush.

'Ba— ba— bath— bath ro—om,' I frantically utter between gasps.

Jeremy scoops me up off the floor and places me on the toilet just in the nick of time. My bladder explodes in relief and appreciation. I take the opportunity to calm my stomach muscles and inhale much-needed air as the release of my bladder continues. I look directly into his concerned eyes and wonder why he looks so worried. It takes me a moment to register that I am, in fact, looking at a vague image of Jeremy's face. Excitement flushes through me.

'I can see! It's still very dark and you are extremely fuzzy, but here you are, in front of me,' I blurt out rather obviously. 'When ... How ... Has it been forty-eight hours?'

'More or less. The final effect of the drops will have diluted more quickly given that fit of hysterics and the blindfold came loose when you fell off the bed. So, yes, you will have complete vision back in a few hours or so.'

His words bring me instant relief, but also a strange sadness knowing our time together is coming to a close. It is weird, like opening my eyes in the middle of a cave, where I can't see anything but what's directly in front of me.

With my vision not restored enough to absorb much more than his blurry face, I feel quite unsteady and rather self-conscious that I'm sitting on the toilet staring at him as he holds me in position. Embarrassed that he is seeing me like this, I quickly wipe and get up to wash my hands, exceptionally grateful for my new-found independence. I take a step forward but my legs immediately go limp and I crumple into a heap. So much for independence.

'That's why I'm holding you, sweetheart, you're not quite with it yet.' Jeremy anchors his arms around me and I'm manoeuvred to the basin. Something about his face makes me smirk at him in the mirror.

'I'll be fine, really, you don't need to fuss. I just need a moment.'

He holds his hands up in mock surrender, which I take as a positive sign. With a concentrated effort, I lean against the basin and wash my hands and face. As I turn around to face him, my legs fail beneath me again and this time he scoops me up before I hit the floor.

'What on earth? I just don't understand ...'

'That's enough. You are not capable of looking after yourself at this point in time. That's exactly what I'm here to do,' he adds sternly.

With these words, I am whisked out of the bathroom back into the bedroom and placed carefully in the centre of a large bed.

For some reason, my uselessness sets me off once again into a series of giggles and I can't even raise my head in protest. I realise then that I won't be able to trust my legs for a little while yet. The look on Jeremy's face registers with my brain that I'm staying put, regardless.

'What am I going to do with you?' At least he has a small smile.

'What have you done to me? Don't you think that is the important question here?' I say to him, recognising my mind is starting to clear from the fog.

'Fair point. There is a lot to explain, I suppose.'

'Yes, I suppose there is,' I agree.

'Why don't you start with what you remember?'

I raise an eyebrow at him. Oh, here we go ... his clever trickery to get me to go first. He quickly adds, as if reading my thoughts, 'Alex, sweetheart, you know I've always been honest with you.'

'Yes, that's true, even too honest at times.' I can't muster the energy to argue with him so I let my mind flick back to the memories of the weekend. I notice the strangeness of my memories as feelings come flooding back to me instead of clear images. In some cases I have a perception of what I believe my memories are but they aren't represented visually, I just get an extraordinary rush of sensations through my body as I remember certain aspects. It's really weird. I shake my head … my brain isn't ready for this sort of overload.

'I remember fear, excitement, shame, then exhilarating pain and pleasure bundled up so comprehensively it seems impossible to distinguish which was more overwhelming. Then sexual tension and arousal and all-encompassing energy; like the force of life itself was whisking through my veins, but it all seems somewhat muffled now.' I know my cheeks flush as these words flow out in a jumbled mess. He strokes my hair in understanding and pulls the covers up to keep me warm. He is being very attentive.

'What's wrong with my head, Jeremy? I can't think straight.'

'It's the sedative. It should be completely out of your system within twenty-four hours.'

'What, you gave me a sedative?'

'Yes, just to allow your body some time to recover. It was in the first hot chocolate I gave you before we came here. I should have remembered how much anything like that affects you so it may take a while longer for the impact to wear off.'

My head swirls with his words, as a distant memory comes flooding to mind.

222

I had gone to a bar in Kings Cross for a girls' night out and ended up talking to some guys we didn't know. One drink later, I felt strange and woozy so my friends called Jeremy, as they were really worried about me. Apparently, the guys took off quickly once they realised we had male friends arriving, so we assumed they must have spiked my drink. I was totally out of it, couldn't stand up and don't remember another thing. It was scary how quickly something like that could take effect.

I wake up at Jeremy's place some time the next day to him prodding and poking my body and mumbling to himself. Feeling way less than average, I roll over in a daze and continue my slumber. The next time I wake up, Jeremy delivers a cup of tea, which I think is really sweet. I reach my arm out from the covers to take the cup and notice my arms are covered in blue, red and green markers. I try to remember what happened last night but my mind draws a complete blank, not a good sign. I place the teacup down carefully and peek under the sheets to find my body entirely naked, covered with the same markings: lines, arrows, circles — all colour coded. I groan in disbelief, not really wanting to see if the other side was the same, but know it will be as I catch the cheeky grin on Jeremy's face.

'Well?' I raise my eyebrows to him, awaiting his explanation.

He's like an excited puppy as he jumps on to the bed beside me.

'Well ... Alex ... I was bored while you were out of it for so long, but I didn't want to leave you by yourself.

I needed to ensure you were okay. So I decided not to waste my time and do some study.'

My eyes bore into his as he continues.

*'And, well, as you can see, it was really worthwhile.'
He whips the covers off the bed. I lie beside him looking like an ugly roadmap.*

'I mean, good learning for me. I missed a couple of things but nailed muscles, organs, arteries ...' He looks at my face and continues hastily as he shifts my body to illustrate his point. 'I'm pissed off that I missed your appendix by half an inch but everything else was pretty accurate. Nervous system was all good — brachial plexus, lumbar plexus, principal arteries of the circulatory system, the organs of the digestive system, although I think I was slightly out with the duodenum which is annoying. Principal components of the lymphatic system — all okay. Female reproductive system was a lot of fun to do. Obviously I took care not to specifically mark the vagina, labium minus and clitoris, but I did manage to highlight the labium majus and the anus for example ...' His hand floats elegantly yet deliberately over each of these parts as he speaks, 'which didn't seem to disturb you too much before moving onto—'

'Okay, okay. I get it,' I interrupt and try to flick him away from me. 'This better come off.'

He starts kissing the parts he refers to. 'And then there's my favourite, more intimate places that not everyone knows about ...' My body feels leaden against his light, fluffy, erotic kisses that are gently, but persistently, stirring me back to life. I don't resist

224

him. Anger dissipates as my medical student, studying
anatomy, transforms into my lover, studying me. I
allow him to play with my body as if he is my master
puppeteer. His magic touch deftly transforms my wooden
frame into a sexually awakened being. As has always
been the way between us.

I'm brought back to the present with the thudding realisation that absolutely nothing whatsoever has changed between us from that time to this, given the state I'm in at this precise moment and his desire to utilise my body for his studies. However, first things first.

'How long will I feel like this? I have my next lecture … What's the time?' I look anxiously around the hazy room for a clock, but realise we are almost in complete darkness — or at least I am thanks to my still incomplete vision. I don't even know if it is day or night.

'It's okay. It's only eight p.m. now.'

'Oh god, Jeremy, how could you? You don't understand. I can't even stand up and I have to give a presentation to the Board of the Australian Medical Association in twelve hours. I can't even think straight. Do you understand how important this is to me, to my research? They are my biggest critics and you put me in state like this? How could you? You're meant to be a responsible doctor, for goodness' sake!'

'Alexa, please calm down. You don't have to worry.'

I interrupt him vehemently. 'Easy for you to say, Dr Quinn. Your career doesn't depend on it; you obviously don't need any more funding for your work as you seem to be doing quite well for yourself.' I flop my hand around the room to indicate the suite, my lack of muscle control making my gesture look ridiculous to both of us. I continue, undeterred by my complete absence of coordination. 'You're not the one who has to stand up in front of the AMA to pitch your case to critical and highly qualified professionals, most of whom would prefer to discredit my work, not endorse it. You wouldn't even know what it feels like, they think you're the medical messiah!' I'm shaking with emotion as I try to struggle over to the side of the bed. I need some water, coffee, anything to help sober me up quickly. I'm fumbling around as effectively as a beached sea lion trying to target a quick-moving penguin.

'Will you please lie still before I have to restrain you again? You will do yourself damage.'

I'm precariously close to the edge of the bed again but I'm determined not to let him put me in a position that risks the future of my career. He must understand that. He moves to the side of the bed, either to prevent me falling out or to prevent me getting out, I'm not sure which at this stage. I carry on with my sea lion movements to the other side.

'Where are my clothes anyway? I hope they are still in the walk-in robe.'

'Will you just stop for a moment? Please!' His voice is sounding as exasperated as I feel with my sluggish movements.

'No, Jeremy, I can't actually.'

Resigning myself to the fact that he will not assist me, I eventually make it to my destination and attempt to haul my log of a leg over the side of the bed with both hands.

'Ahhh. Why do you persist when you know it's just not going to happen!'

He grabs hold of my ankle before it hits the floor and quickly fastens the connecter to my wrist. It is only at this point I realise I still have leather straps fastened to each limb. Oh, lucky me.

He deftly does the same with my left side, attaching my wrist and ankle together and heaves my whole body into the centre of the bed, rendering it virtually impossible for me to move, let alone walk. He surrounds me with pillows so I'm sitting in an upright position, which is the only slight relief because lying down in this position would have been rather precarious to say the least. Thank goodness I practise yoga.

'Damn you. You can't keep me captive here, I'm not your bloody puppet. Why are these restraints still on me?' I explode at him.

'They're great, aren't they? Save so much time and energy … If only I had had these at uni, imagine the fun I could have had with you …' His voice trails off as his mind wanders.

'JEREMY! I have no time for trips down memory lane right now.' My throat feels hoarse from yelling at him.

'Oh, yes,' he says, coming back to me. 'Now, can you just lie still and let me explain?'

'I'm assuming that is a statement, not a question,' I say acerbically. 'It's not like I have a lot of choice!'

'No, you don't.' Even though he sounds bothered, he looks pleased with himself as he nestles in close to me.

I can only roll my eyes and hope his explanation is short.

'Let me say, first of all, you are not going anywhere.' His hand puts up a stop sign to pre-empt my protest. I ignore it.

'I have to, Jeremy. You don't understand, do you?' I'm getting desperate now and try to explain the importance of this meeting, how much it means to me. I struggle futilely against the restraints in sheer exasperation and break into a hot sweat.

'Jeremy, this is my career we are talking about, the one I have worked and studied so hard for. You, of all people, must understand …' He straddles his long legs either side of me, trapping me further with his body as his hand nimbly covers my mouth.

'Let me make myself perfectly clear. You are not leaving this room until I authorise your release — medically or otherwise.' This time his hand blankets my mouth *before* any expletives escape. Am I that predictable to him? I think I must be if ... the room starts to spin around me ... everything suddenly feels very strange ... loses focus ... spins ... feels very fuzzy ...

* * *

Next thing I know a bright light is shining in my eye and someone is taking my pulse and blood pressure.

I try to lift up my head. I can't.

'Have you got a vein yet? That IV needs to go in *now*!'

'Not yet, her veins seem to be collapsing.' A woman's voice.

'Here, give it to me.'

I feel a sting in my hand.

'Done. Tape it up. Sweetheart. Can you hear me? Look at me, it's Jeremy.'

'Wh— what happened? What is all this?' I look around and notice a drip, monitoring equipment, a nurse.

'Oh thank god. You must take it easy. Do you hear me? *Do you understand?*'

'No ... I don't think I understand, Jeremy. I ... don't think ... I understand at all.'

'No, of you course you don't, sweetheart, because you never allow me time to explain.'

'This is my fault?' I say confused.

'No, no that's not what I meant. God, you just had me so worried. You fainted.'

228

I must drift off again as next time I open my eyes the room seems really bright, which reminds me what we were talking about before all this medical business interfered with our conversation.

'Is it morning? Jeremy! Have I missed —'

'There's nothing to miss.' He attempts to calm his voice. 'There is no presentation to the AMA.' The light diminishes.

'You cancelled me? My one chance to present?' I ask, incredulous.

'No, sweetheart, please lie still. Try to keep calm. You are exhausted. God, I've pushed you too hard ... too far.' He pauses. 'There never was a presentation to the AMA. It was all organised to ensure we had enough time together.'

'What? No meeting?'

'You have no more lectures for the rest of the week. The only lecture you had to present was the one you did last Friday.'

'What? ... How? ... I don't understand ...' I'm so tired I can't get my head around his words.

'There is too much for you to understand right now and nothing you need to worry about except rest, which is the most important thing you need.'

'No lectures? ... All cancelled ... Was it that bad, my first lecture? ... you said it was good.' Strangely, insecurity sweeps through me. I feel really weak.

'It was great, you know it was. Now, just close your eyes and rest.' He places his palm on my cheek and nods to somebody positioned behind me.

'No, I can't rest Jeremy. What happened? Why am I like this? I might be okay ... in a while ... to present, you know ... could be ... and ... why do I have an IV? ...'

Reality vanishes.

* * *

I wake up with my eyes acclimatising to their restored state, which puts a smile on my face. A fleeting thought wonders where I am and my foggy head takes a moment to register that Jeremy is staring at me with an anxious expression from the armchair in the corner of the room. Seconds later, he is by my side.

'Just checking your vitals,' he says before I have the opportunity to utter a word.

'How do you feel?' Light penetrates my eyeball. I try to shift my head away to no avail.

'Foggy, but better than before, I think.' I notice the IV still in my hand. 'Is this necessary?' My voice is croaky.

'I'll let you know in the next hour or so. There are a few more things we need to check first.' He pumps the band around my arm and concentrates on my blood pressure; it feels sensitive and I twinge a little.

'So, definitely no lecture today?'

'No!' His expression is anxious as he continues his doctor business. I sense that now is not the right time to venture into 'why the hell not?'.

It was always near impossible to distract Jeremy mid-task so I don't bother now. His eyebrows are furrowed as he determinedly checks over my body.

He lifts up the sheet and for the first time I notice a tube coming from between my legs.

'Oh god, please no!' I cringe in disbelief.

'What? Oh, it's just the catheter,' he says nonchalantly and covers my legs with the sheet so I'm protected from the view. 'That can come out when I remove the drip,' he says in his matter-of-fact voice. I suddenly wish the drip would whisk me away into blankness again.

'Right. Not great yet, but not too bad,' he says to himself as much as me. 'Are you thirsty?'

'Mmm.' I nod as I notice how dry my mouth is.

'Nurse!'

Nurse? Could this be more embarrassing? I mean, honestly.

He raises my upper body slowly off the bed and brings the water to my lips so carefully, it is as if he thinks I will break. I assure him I won't … break, that is.

'Frankly, I will be the judge of that.' Great, still in doctor mode. I decide it's safer not to argue and 'frankly' I don't have the energy to debate him, so I let out a long sigh instead.

'I don't like all of these tubes, Jeremy. You know I can't handle anything hospital-like.'

'I know, sweetheart, just a little longer. I need to know you are getting the right fluids and we only have one more test to complete, then it's precautionary. I can't afford to risk anything when it comes to you.'

My head spins with his words.

'Test? Risk? From fainting?' I wonder if I am sounding as confused as I feel.

'Nothing you need to worry about. I will take complete care of you, I promise.'

'Jeremy, you're scaring me *and* treating me like a child. What are you talking about?'

He lowers his forehead to mine and kisses my lips lightly. 'You were amazing, perfect. The results of our experiment, your neural connectivity, well, let's just say they opened a whole new pathway of research relating to the limbic system.' He slides his fingers slowly between my breasts, delicately circles my belly button. He continues lower and slides his hand gently between my legs, so as not to disturb the tube, and lightly and magically massages my secret parts.

His touch, his words, ignite a deep rumbling from within my core. The pleasure is intense, as he targets his approach, the waves unrelenting as my mind struggles to stay present with him and I drift off as delightful tremors overtake my body. It's as if he has a remote control button for my clitoris. I can't understand why I am so instantly reactive to his touch. It completely distracts me from asking him what is going on here. The drip, catheter, nurse … it all surrounds me, but makes no sense at all.

Reality returns as he removes his hands and passes the nurse a small sample of something before she hastily disappears from the room. I suddenly feel like giving in to it all. I don't want to fight any more; Jeremy can do what he likes. The relief of my surrender is almost overwhelming. I try to look away from the intensity of his stare and eventually close my eyes as I feel big, wet tears sliding down my cheeks.

'You're emotional. Alex, I'm so sorry. You have been through so much. Too much in some ways. It has taken its toll on you. I promise I will explain everything properly. You just need to rest for a while. Let me look after you.'

I can't say anything. As I close my eyes, embracing again the blindness I had railed against only hours ago, tears continue to fall soundlessly, mindlessly. I sense Jeremy's eyes continually seeking understanding, trying to discover the vulnerabilities that lie beneath the surface of my body and mind. I have nowhere to go, no further layers to hide behind and I know I don't want to hide from him any more, ever. I love the idea of him intimately understanding my secret places, even more so because they are now so raw, so exposed. I want to be available to him to explore, to experiment, as he wishes, whenever he desires. I have never felt more powerful yet so in need of his power over me. I feel astonishingly proud that for whatever reason, he has chosen me to take on this journey as I lay here naked, truly bare beside him.

Jeremy wraps his arms around my shoulders, carefully avoiding the drip in my hand, and cradles me close into his chest. There is nowhere I want to be except in his arms. I feel like a small, dependent child as he encircles my body. I am helplessly paralysed as the tears continue to fall. He lovingly wipes the hair away from my face, slowly and softly kissing my eyelids until the tears subside.

It is at this moment I feel utter exhaustion, even more so than from a long childbirth. I never thought that seeing his eyes, his face, would prove to be so emotional for me. He said he wanted to open me up like the layers of a blossoming rose, ensure I experienced more than I ever had, and he has done exactly that. He has seen parts of me — both physically and emotionally — that perhaps I have never seen or explored myself. There is nothing left, no desire to go against him, no need to seek further understanding, no need to fear. I know and understand that, although he has pushed me far beyond any boundaries I created for myself, he will look after me wholeheartedly while I am in his care. He always has and always will. I give myself over to him entirely. Because for some reason, deep within my psyche, I know that whatever has happened and whatever will happen is now entirely beyond my control, and for some strange reason, I feel a powerful sense of freedom in that knowledge, just as he said I would.

I can't say how many times I doze in and out of sleep or for how long. I vaguely remember Jeremy coming and going, checking and rechecking. I don't remember the drip or the catheter being removed, for which I am grateful. I have no idea if it is night or day and therefore no clue as to the time. I still feel incredibly fatigued, but with each return to consciousness, my head seems to be in a clearer space, which is a great relief.

* * *

I open my eyes to smile at him lying next to me.

'You're awake, welcome back!' He smiles down at me. 'I just need to roll you over, sweetheart, to tend to your beautiful behind.' He turns a single light on in an otherwise darkened room.

'Oh, not doctor mode again, please.' I groan in protest.

'Lay still. This may still be a little sore, but it will heal in no time.'

'Do I have a choice?' I say, raising my eyebrows.

'None whatsoever. I'm so pleased you finally understand.'

It is not sore as much as tender and I can't help but think he is overreacting a little. As I lay there, getting my arse tended to, I hear my stomach growl beneath me. I realise I'm absolutely famished, which can only be a positive sign.

'Hold still. I just need to do one more blood test and then you can eat.'

'One last? How many have you taken?'

'This will be the fourth.'

He reaches towards his bench of medical paraphernalia and prepares things before harnessing my upper arm and inspecting my veins with his fingers. I barely feel the slight sting in my vein, but look away as he chatters on. 'You know you have special blood, Alexa. AB is the most biologically complex of all the blood types. It is less than a thousand years old and is more or less an evolutionary mystery. Only around three per cent of the global population have type AB blood, making you incredibly unique, but of course, I always knew that about you. And treasure you all the more for it,' he adds with a wink before continuing. 'I recently attended a lecture on its characteristics and it has both medics and scientists intrigued, given its complex and perplexing nature. It's an enigma really.' He looks lost in thought.

'Hmmm, lucky me, an enigma *and* having a name that matches my blood type, what a coincidence.' Thankfully, the needle is removed before I can be too concerned, his monologue about my blood type providing appropriate distraction from his actions. He swiftly places cotton wool on the entry point and bends my arm for me. I shake my head in defeat.

'So, are you now bottling my blood, due to its "uniqueness"?' I ask as I notice how many tubes he has filled. No wonder I have been feeling weak. The nurse efficiently removes the vials and herself from the room.

'Some of the research Ed and I have been involved in investigates the "newness" of the AB blood type to the human race and its particular characteristics and we've developed some interesting hypotheses. Your involvement in the experiment enabled us to confirm that AB blood has fascinating results when the female is Anglo-Saxon — reflecting the societies where depression is endemic — and these results are even more pronounced if she has completed a full birthing cycle and is pre-menopausal, as you are. That is why we need to monitor your hormone levels and correlate them to the fluids sourced from your orgasms.'

Just when I think it's impossible for him to provide any more shock value, here we go again. Is this science fiction or reality?

'So that is what you just handed the nurse before?'

'Exactly. Our results over the weekend have been more conclusive than we were expecting, so we're a tangible step closer to finalising the formula we aspire to. We've been analysing the release of hormones into your bloodstream and correlating them to the secretions of your prostate gland during orgasm. This has confirmed the production of naturally-induced serotonin which stimulates your nervous system. Even more so than we anticipated. Now that we can continue to monitor your hormone levels and sexual activity as it occurs, we can test and finalise the formula that's been eluding us until this point.'

This discovery is both intriguing and somewhat disturbing, given my direct involvement. No one does cutting-edge medical research quite like Jeremy! He gives me a moment to absorb his words, and then it dawns on me.

'I have granted you your greatest wish, Jeremy. I am officially your human guinea pig.' I don't know why I am stunned by this realisation after so many years. In hindsight, it is so blatantly obvious.

'Sweetheart, you know you are so much more than that.'

'Since we met, I have been your guinea pig, your practice patient … blood tests, injections, bandages, and casts. What has changed? Nothing. You're still doing it, except we are older, have more responsibilities and you very clearly have far more money, power and access to resources than we ever had back at uni. Which just ups the ante on the risks you are willing to take and, heaven help me, I'm considering coming along for the ride. I'm a mother for god's sake!' Strange that all of this is just dawning on me now.

'Oh, come on, Alex, you love it, you always have.' He snuggles into me with his puppy dog eyes and kisses and canoodles. I try to nudge him away without moving my arm just in case we end up with blood dripping over the white linen sheets. 'And besides, since when did motherhood give you permission to deny your sexuality?'

Jeremy and his killer questions — how, pray tell, do I respond to that? I try to think of a stinging response as my stomach launches a tumultuous cry. The perfect excuse to change the subject.

'I could really devour a burger with the works and some super-chunky fries. Can you magic that up for me?'

'I've no doubt that could be arranged, but you are having a delicious spring vegetable soup, it's almost ready.'

'No, you don't understand. I really *need* fat-saturated food, seriously.'

He starts packing up his medical bits and pieces. 'However, it's a great sign that you have your appetite back. It has been a while.'

'Jeremy, it's not fair, after all you have put me through.'

My eyes search for a phone but I can't see one so I try to shift towards the edge of the bed. He pulls me back by the ankles.

'No way, AB, you need to stay right here. I mean it; I don't want you off this bed. If you move, I swear I'll attach you to it.' I realise I still have the bands around my wrists and ankles; therefore his threat is a distinct possibility, just as he did before.

'You can't tell me you have the legal right to keep me bound to the bed?'

The look on his face reminds me of one of those psycho movies where the unstable psychiatrist is able to lock up innocent patients, all presumably for their own benefit. God, that can't be possible, can it? Do we honestly give doctors that much power? He grins to show me he's joking, in this instance at least.

'Okay, okay, I'll stay put, but when are you going to take these off?'

'After you have eaten all the soup.'

'I am not a child, Jeremy!'

'I can assure you I'm very well aware of that fact, Alexandra. Your body needs good nutrition to fully recover.'

I dutifully eat all of the soup he insists on feeding me, until every last drop is consumed.

'Well?' I ask, when finished.

'I'll see what I can organise.'

* * *

Content, full, and more clear-minded than I have been since my arrival on Friday evening. I rest my head against Jeremy's chest. He also seems calmer, more at ease than he has been. Automatically, he strokes my hair and face. He has always been exceptionally tactile and I love this about him.

'I'm so relieved I didn't have to present to the AMA. There is no way I could have done it.'

'Hmmm, you do have a lot to thank me for I have to admit,' he says teasingly. 'Seriously, Alex, you had me worried for a while there. It will take you more than a few days to recover, so you won't be going anywhere until the end of the week.'

'You know I can't stay here, as much as you appear to be delighting in my entrapment. I have other commitments, regardless of your plans.'

'Sweetheart, you have no commitments this week except for me looking after you. And you know how seriously I take my work.'

I raise my chin to look up into his eyes, to help me decipher his words and assess their truthfulness. 'You're not joking.'

'Not at all. You are my one and only responsibility until I chaperone you to your plane back to Hobart.'

'But you can't! You have nothing to do with my lectures. Fair enough the AMA but there are others …'

'I do and I have. You are mine for the week. Period. I promise it will not impact on your work in any way, shape or form and besides, part of your work is for me now, anyway.' He looks very pleased with himself as he adds these words. 'This whole event has been carefully orchestrated at so many levels, with limitless funding. Do you understand what I'm trying to say to you? Our meeting on Friday night didn't occur by chance, Alex. The entire plan has been in place for months. We provided the funding for the Tassie tiger trip for your children when it almost fell through, and sponsored your recent research and supposed series of lectures this week.'

I am beginning to realise that this whole weekend is about much more than it first appeared to be. I am a pawn in Jeremy's greater game of life.

'But why?'

'My world is no longer complete without you in it.'

His words shoot like Cupid's arrow into my heart, leaving me speechless.

'Here, I think these can come off now. They have served their purpose.' He picks up some kind of magnetic rod from the bedside table and carefully slides it along the seam of the leather bindings, releasing them. No wonder I couldn't remove them. I must look shocked as he offers me further explanation.

'They were magnetically locked, you need this instrument to remove them and they've also been serving the purpose of continually monitoring your pulse.' He really does look smug now.

'Your invention?' I question.

'Unfortunately not, but as you know, I do work with some very clever people.' What hope did I ever have? Strangely, their absence from my wrists and ankles makes me feel disconnected, as if something meaningful is missing.

'I'm really pleased you are starting to feel better, but it's important that you stay in bed and rest now. There will be plenty of time to discuss all this later.' Although his words sound gentle, I sense they are steadfastly non-negotiable. He ensures I'm snuggled in tight beneath the duvet, kisses my forehead and leaves the room in darkness once again, closing the door behind him. I am asleep in minutes.

Part VII

'Our eyes are holden that we cannot see things that stare us in the face, until the hour arrives when the mind is ripened; then we behold them, and the time when we saw them is not like a dream.'

— Ralph Waldo Emerson

Jeremy isn't in the room when I open my eyes again but to my great relief, the bedroom door is open. I don't appear to have any clothes in this room, so I gather up the sheet and wrap it around my body. The light streaming through the doorway temporarily blinds me so I take a moment to allow my eyes to adjust to the brightness they have been denied for some time. Walking through the doorway makes me feel suddenly uneasy, as if I'm crossing over a threshold to another world. It then dawns on me that this room is not the same as the second room at the hotel. For some reason, I had just assumed we were back at the Hotel InterContinental and Jeremy had sensibly wanted to set up hospital in a room other than the master suite.

Startled by this realisation, I instinctively tighten the sheet around my body and tentatively step out into a whole new world.

'Oh, you're up. I've just made some green tea.'

He takes one look at me and places the cups immediately back on the bench. The look of astonishment on my face isn't subdued by the sunglasses he quickly retrieves and hastily hooks around my ears, presumably to lessen the extraordinary intensity of light on my eyes. I stare at him, utterly speechless as I step into the expansive space, sheet trailing behind me.

The colours ambush my vision as I am assaulted by the blueness of the cloudless sky, the greenness of vast, lush forest and the complete and utter absence of any civilisation. The sheer cliffs of the mountain peaks provide a stunning backdrop for the crystal waters that sparkle beneath a shimmer of white sand. I take a few moments to blink and comprehend this vista, before continuing my silent exploration, unable to form words. My eyes cruise past an enormous deck and fall upon a sunken spa bath as if it's embedded within the horizon. A huge modern kitchen opens into a quasi-formal dining room and lounge room, complete with ultra-modern fireplace suspended in the middle of the room which is surrounded by the largest lounge suite I have ever laid eyes on. My sea legs slowly zigzag my body across the split-level room as I try to absorb this vast, remote environment.

How? When? Where?

Everything appears round or circular — truly unique to my eyes. Jeremy remains still as he allows my continued investigation. I move further along a corridor and open up a double set of doors into what is clearly the master bedroom. The room itself is round and surrounded by glass panels and is built within the canopy of the forest. A luxurious, sophisticated treehouse. In the centre of the room is an enormous bed, also circular, with the round pillowing on its outer edges, obviously made to measure and decorated with the finest of gold thread. The décor and colours of the room blend in perfect sympathy with the environment — except for the stark contrast of a mass of deep red blooming roses, with all but a few fully opened. Just as Jeremy promised when we met. Their beauty takes my breath away. I sense the tears in my eyes as emotions swell in my heart at the enormity of everything I have experienced with him since then. I have honestly never felt like this in my life. I quietly walk around the entire room, examining the view from every aspect. Again I search for any sign of humankind. Nothing. Just us and nature. Although the beauty surrounding me is close to overwhelming; I can't help but wonder — where on Google Earth are we?

I feel a little light-headed with this being up and about business. I sit on the edge of a gorgeously soft, sandy-coloured marshmallow lounge chair, completely overcome by this totally new environment. Jeremy enters the room with a grin on his face and walks over to me, hugging me from behind.

'See, I said you were mine for the week.'

My words take a little while to be spoken aloud. 'Jeremy, where are we?'

'Avalon,' he answers smoothly. 'A place where we won't be disturbed by anyone and I can look after you completely.'

'But, where is Avalon?'

'That, unfortunately, I am not at liberty to say, but as you can see, you won't be going anywhere until I know you have completely recovered.'

I don't know what to say or how I'm feeling. If I thought him taking my phone away from me left me feeling disconnected, it was a drop in the ocean compared to this!

Jeremy suggests that now I'm feeling better, we should move into this room and excuses himself to organise the transition. Utterly perplexed, I flop into the middle of the peculiar round bed, once again overwhelmed by the surreal reality in which I have landed. When he returns, he is bare-chested with a towel loosely hanging around his hips. A very encouraging sign, I think to myself as he smiles and cups my face in his hand. One look at his toned torso and I pray this isn't a dream.

'Why don't you replace your sheet with this towel and join me in the hot tub?' He hands me a towel and I wrap it under my arms. He scoops me up and carries me out through the lounge room, out through the massive glass doors and onto the balcony.

This place is unbelievable. I think I'm in shock as I just stand staring transfixed toward the magnificent views. Jeremy unravels my towel and discards his own, our naked bodies descending into the awaiting water together. It's wonderfully warm, although I notice my butt stings slightly as it hits the water. I wince at the sensation. He notices immediately.

'Is it bad? I feel awful that you are in pain. I can give you something for it.'

'No, no, it's okay. I'm fine, honestly, no drugs required.' I allow myself to become fully submerged in the water.

'It's only a shock because I still haven't quite got my head around everything that has happened, and the intensity comes flooding back as I feel it in my body or down there ... which is all just too strange.'

I breathe deeply and close my eyes as the thoughts and feelings come flooding through my mind, too many, too fast. I quickly reopen them to disrupt the flow. I can't help but wonder if it feels this intense because of my lack of vision when I went through the experiences.

'Why, Jeremy? Why choose me? Was it just because of my blood type and female profile?' I return his stare, wanting to question his soul, but I allow my eyes to drift away before I become lost in their depths. He remains silent for a while strokes my body very gently, carefully, as though I'm a delicate peach.

'It could never have been anyone other than you,' he states simply and meaningfully. I attempt to interpret the intensity behind his words.

'But the whipping … or whatever it was …?' I find it difficult to articulate the words out loud, but the thought alone stirs some deep carnal spring as heat rises within my core. God, what hope do I have if the mere memory does this to me?

'You looked sensational, Alexa, I had to muster all my strength to not take you then and there.'

'I have never been more scared in my entire life, Jeremy. I didn't have a clue what was going on, what was coming next and god, I can't believe I'm saying this, but the whole experience was literally mind-blowing — even though I was being punished for asking questions. I mean, what was that about?'

'It was important that you believed the consequences were real and measurable, so the fear was genuine and released the relevant hormones, without going to the extreme.'

'If that wasn't extreme … I've never experienced more extreme emotions, volatile emotions, unbelievable feelings …' I feel my blood pressure rising and raw energy pulsating through my veins.

'I had to push the boundaries with you, you know that. I knew you could take it, knew that deep down you wanted this more than you'd let yourself believe. So tell me, was the pain worth the pleasure?'

Again, just his words trigger the waves from deep within. These sensations are the most bizarre thing I've experienced. As if they are a trigger to immediately extinguish any regret or anger or hurt. Soft, warm, orgasmic waves penetrate through me, causing what feels like my whole body to flush with a glow of pure sexuality.

'Oh ... Alex, this is truly incredible. Clearly, I have my answer.'

He glides me through the water so I'm resting between his legs. There is no use pretending to argue with him, pretending this isn't happening, so I close my eyes and allow the rhythms dancing within my loins to overtake me again.

'You were wet, moist, engorged, more so each time you were struck. It was as if your body craved it. Honestly, sweetheart, you were dripping with desire. I was checking, monitoring, making sure you were physically sound every step of the way. The data we collected from a fear and pleasure perspective had a greater correlation than we'd ever imagined ...' My body's reaction distracts him. The feeling of the memory is as instant as it is vivid. Probing fingers deep within me, never knowing when it would happen next or for how long, then desperately hoping they wouldn't leave.

'God, Alex, this is incredible; I can literally feel the reaction you are having as we talk about it. I can't wait to take you through the detailed results; such unexpected insights. Having you on both sides of the experimentation process was sheer genius and I am completely in awe of how you surrendered to the process. I have so much to thank you for. I know it wasn't an easy decision for you to make.'

It means a lot to me to hear him acknowledge this truth out loud.

'I'm still coming to terms with it all. I had no idea that I'd take to it so much.'

'I'm pleased you are finally getting to know the woman I love.' How did he know this about me before I did? 'A letter is being drafted as we speak to invite you to become an exclusive member of our core research team because of your skills and expertise. Your involvement is essential to our success, now more than ever, as our research progresses to the next phase.'

I have no idea how to respond. I agreed to be involved in this research and take an active part in the experimentation process. I have now experienced what I never thought I was capable of and survived, yet I have never been so physically debased and pleasured simultaneously. How does this work in our brains? How was I capable of experiencing such sheer, unadulterated pleasure under such extreme circumstances?

I more than survived — I loved it. Would I do it again? Under certain situations, absolutely. Do I want to learn the answers to all of these questions? More than ever! He massages my shoulders as if to rub away any potential concerns I may have and I take solace in our quiet time together. Eventually he lifts me, with such delicacy, out of the hot tub and painstakingly dries my limbs before we snuggle together on the lounges, soaking up the warmth of the sun.

'Did you ever believe your body was capable of experiencing what it did over that forty-eight hours — even in your wildest dreams?' The memory of multiple euphoric orgasms is still palpable and Jeremy holds me tight as the pleasure of it threatens to collapse my body, again. Thankfully, I'm already lying down. It is impossible to be anything but pleased with him when my body experiences such waves of pleasure, in perfect recollection. 'Tell me, describe to me what is happening to you.'

I try to explain the bizarre sensation to him when my breathing has returned to its normal rhythm.

'The memories are so strong and so unbelievably intense, it overwhelms me physically. You mention it and my body reacts, immediately.' He waits silently, patiently for me to continue. I guess he knows everything anyway so I decide to continue.

'I had this amazing … well … very real fantasy, I suppose you'd call it. Truly incredible. I was so in the moment, and the moment was so powerful, like I was at one with the world, and then it felt like there were tongues everywhere … I couldn't focus …' I'm embarrassed saying it out loud; even after all we have been through.

'They were everywhere, penetrating, probing my inner depths. I just don't know how to describe it fully, it was so immense, intense …' I look at him nervously as he studies my face and analyses my words. 'I have no visual memory of it, just the complete force and concentration of the sensations. It takes over my mind and consciousness for a moment. I don't understand how a memory can trigger such a response, Jeremy. Is it even possible? If not, what is happening to me?' I look toward him, seeking his answers. He pauses momentarily.

'There was no fantasy about it, Alexa. It was all very real.' My body aches with primal lust at his words. My blush is long and deep, as is the throbbing below. 'Having blocked your other senses, you were only left with touch, until we eventually added sound. Your cognitive processes are connecting the intensity of your feelings to your physical being. That is, they have become neurologically linked, which is why your body and mind are reacting so strongly to that specific memory or anything that triggers the memory. This is exactly what we were hoping for, actually, more than we'd hoped for. This is the critical part of our research, our uncharted waters, so to speak. With your knowledge in psychology coupled with having experienced it personally, we will end up learning more about female sexuality than has ever been researched, let alone published.'

I am dumbfounded at his words; the conversation with Samuel and his 'elite researchers' comes floating back into my consciousness. No doubt he will be thrilled with the results. I become suddenly anxious at the thought.

'Jeremy, Sam wasn't there, was he?'

'No, Alex, he wasn't. I'd never do that to you. Just two of my colleagues and some people we organised for your "real fantasy".'

'Thank god.' That's a relief. My arse could only deal with being on display if it were anonymous.

'But I have copied him in on the results and can't wait to discuss them with him. All going to plan, we will be able to develop a drug for depression that the market has never seen before, without the sometimes horrific side effects of what is currently offered, achieving far greater success and reliability for the patient.'

'Honestly, you're really that much closer because of what I went through?'

'You are fundamental to our success, my love. You are at the very heart of what we are hoping to achieve.'

'I can't believe we will be working together after all these years, Jeremy. Who would have thought? Tell me, what is the exact nature of the role you want me to play in the future?'

'All of that will need to be explained later, Dr Blake. You need to have signed a multitude of documents for legal purposes first.'

* * *

As twilight descends, Jeremy lights a fire in the suspended fireplace and ensures I am nestled cosily into the lounge. He won't let me do anything — at all — as he buzzes around getting things organised for dinner. To my surprise and delight, he delivers a perfectly chilled glass of Pouilly Fumé, my favourite French wine. I'm still awestruck by my environment and can only presume that we are somewhere in the southern hemisphere, judging by the stars which are just coming out. I don't know how I arrived here, I don't know the date or the time, he hasn't mentioned my phone or its whereabouts and I haven't bothered to ask. I sense the answers to my many questions would be deemed irrelevant by Dr Quinn, so I let them float away with the rapidly disappearing light of the day.

After a scrumptious dinner of grilled salmon with Asian greens, we snuggle together on the lounge by the light of the fire and have what becomes one of our many conversations over the course of the next few days.

The whole question thing still makes me hesitate but I ask nevertheless.

'Can I ask you something?'

'Of course.' I'm relieved it is no longer an issue.

'What would have happened if I had said no to you on Friday night?'

'No to staying, or no to being blind?'

'Both, I suppose.'

'I would have persuaded you. I always have.'

'Why can't I ever say no to you, Jeremy?'

'Do you wish you could?'

'I'm honestly not sure, it's weird. Parts of me do and parts of me don't. I can't help but think about my marriage, so I doubt I'll feel great about it when I return home and reality bites, but then again, it has been years since Robert and I have been together in a sexual sense.'

'Really? What's going on there? I can't manage to keep my hands off you for more than a few hours at a time.' His previously resting hand slides smoothly up my leg towards my thigh.

'I'm not sure … but after all of this, I'm not sure I can return to my asexual life. It never bothered me before, but now … well, let's say I feel like a dormant volcano that has well and truly erupted due to significant seismic activity.'

'Are you calling me seismic, Dr Blake?' He manoeuvres himself between my legs.

'And then some, Dr Quinn. Seriously, what do you think?' I impede his progress.

'It never feels wrong when we are together, Alex, no matter what the circumstances and now it's even more important than ever.

'Really? Please don't tell me you can justify being here with me purely in the name of research?'

'No, not that exactly.' I raise my eyebrows, waiting for him to continue his explanation. 'It is just that our relationship with each other goes much further back than it does with anyone else. In reality, we have been with each other on and off for almost half our lives. It feels like I am meant to be with you, like we've always been connected somehow and just needed to find our way back to each other. We've shared so much that I don't feel like it's wrong or bad. It's difficult for me to feel guilty about it because I don't care how "society" views our relationship. And with what you have told me about Robert, he is wasting you, and I want you, very, very badly. As I said before, I can't imagine my life without you in it, and being in it like this is just icing on the cake.' He tweaks my nipples playfully to coincide with his last point and continues, 'It is pure dynamite when we are together, and I'm coming to understand that I have been an idiot for allowing you to be out of my life for so long. You have your children, which you have always wanted, and not much of a marriage by the sounds of it. I have my career, which has been my focus to this point and my focus is now you. I love you, Alexandra. I always have and I'm not prepared to share you for too much longer. That is something that you will need to work out in the very near future.'

He loves me and he's not prepared to share me? His last statement sounds like a command I need to action. I'm astounded by his articulate, almost rehearsed response and his words resonate with me in an unexpected way. Before I can respond, he takes my hands.

'Let me ask you this. Did you want to be with me this weekend? Had you considered it before you arrived at the hotel on Friday afternoon?' My glance shifts nervously towards my trembling hands before I eventually meet his eyes. He need only search my eyes for a flicker of a second to confirm the answer to his question. 'Right. Same for me. Do you have any regrets?'

'That is a very big question, Jeremy.'

'Oh come on, sweetheart. You have come so far this week, don't go all shy on me now.' He pushes for an answer, pinning my arms beneath me so he has free access to keep teasing my nipples, which instantly swell and harden under his touch, and then proceeds to massage my breasts when I continue to procrastinate.

'Perhaps I should have worn a bra tonight.'

'Perhaps you shouldn't be wearing anything tonight.'

My dress is suddenly sliding onto the floor beside us.

'Now stop changing the topic and answer the question.'

'Okay, okay, no, no regrets. It is very difficult to regret anything when you are under the masterful spell of Dr Quinn ...' Near impossible would be more accurate as my body begins to writhe under his touch.

'Seismic activity, masterful spell … what's all this about?' he asks with a cheeky innocence.

The massage continues as his light kisses on my neck become more insistent. My legs spread further under the weight of his and I feel his desire for me against my groin.

'It's about my body betraying me at every opportunity when I'm with you, regardless of my thought processes. And it is something I am going to have to get under control very soon, particularly if we are going to be working together.'

'Please promise me, sweetheart, that it isn't high on your busy to-do list.' He nibbles my ear lobe as he scoops me off the lounge and carries me to the circular canopy that is the master suite, throwing me gently into the middle of the giant round bed. 'Do not move an inch, I'll be right back.'

I submit to his request as my mind swishes around the edges of a salacious whirlpool. I'm just thankful I'm lying down. He returns with a sneaky grin on his face, no doubt up to more mischief. There's no time for words as his caresses explore further, deeper. Oh good lord, here we go again!

'When is enough, enough?' I sigh.

'With you, sweetheart, never, but you can always say no to me.' His low husky words in my ear send me into overdrive, as he is fully aware that for me, it is never an option.

'What, so you can strap me down and have me whipped until I change my mind?'

'Hmm, something like that …' He laughs and turns me over to position my fully naked body on all fours, as he continues to fondle and tease.

'Try to stay still, I want to try something.' I can feel him insert something coolish into my vagina, not too big, but not small either, and then the vibrations begin, slow at first but steadily increasing. I can't focus on anything apart from the spasms cascading through my body. I am wet with desire in seconds. My body instantly responds to the memory of the warmth and vibrations that took place when I was strapped in place on the platform. Such sensations so soon. How is this happening?

Jeremy reaches down, slides his thumb into my anus and I tense my muscles waiting for the tightness to reject him. To my surprise, his entry feels anticipated and delightful. Oh good grief, what has he done to me to achieve this? He gently wiggles his thumb around and finds a particular pressure point and massages gently at first, then more persistently, pushing the sensation toward the buzzing in my vagina. I gasp as my mind begins to spin and my body convulses with the memory of previous euphoric waves. He is more than pleased with the result, registering the surprise on my face with a crooked smile.

'Is it comfortable?'

'Yes,' is all I can sigh as the rhythms pulse through my body and his fingers continue to explore and create new sensations. I feel a rush of heat rampage through my vagina and arsehole, as he slowly withdraws his thumb and grabs a condom packet, ripping it open. He positions himself behind me ensuring the condom is secured over his length. I can't help but send a questioning look over my shoulder, though his beauty is rather distracting.

'Relax, sweetheart, I promise, I'll take it slow.'

His lubricated penis penetrates the tip of my arsehole, teasing the entry before carefully, gradually moving forward, allowing me to adjust to his thick presence in such a confined space, every step of the way. Each time he penetrates a little further and deeper, asserting his position over me without losing the intensity he is creating. Seamlessly, this continues until he fills me as if his member was made to measure and I groan in exhilaration. It has never felt so good back there. His possession of me is perfect, all encompassing and totally complete. His other hand playfully massages my clitoris, becoming firmer, more insistent and I begin to lose any sense of focus.

He flattens my chest toward the bed, causing friction between my nipples and the crispness of the sheet. His elevated body gives him complete control of the desire he is stirring within me, cleverly replicating the position of my previous experience, without the constraints. His fingers carefully tease me to the edge of orgasm, but refuse to thrust further and ignite what is ready to explode. Oh god! My anus is stuffed to the brim as his member shoots electric pulses through my body and to my astonishment, I feel my hole open wider to take him deeper and deeper into my nether regions. I yell, not from the pain of it, but from the depth of my love for this man and the sheer, exquisite pleasure he can incite from deep within my core. I am literally drenched in desire as his fingers complete their final play and I can't hold back my voice as I am thrust over the edges of mind and body. My screaming continues unabated and I climax over and over, wave after wave, from both my physical reality and my neurological memories. Completely out of control, only animal instinct powering my guttural cries. He adjusts slightly and it happens all over again. And again. I moan and groan with each equally penetrating wave as once again I lose all sense of self. Spinning and toppling into a world I hadn't known existed before this weekend, I ascend to my newly discovered unconscious orgasmic universe, absolutely saturated in sex. I would do anything, go anywhere, for this man and the things he can do with my body.

What has happened to me? Am I a sex maniac, an addict? I can't even think of the correct term. I have never in my life imagined so much sexual pleasure. How is it even possible? Of course, like most people, I have read about some people's ability to have multiple orgasms, but this, what I have experienced, is out of this world. The intensity is so overpowering I remain lost in sensation for quite some time.

'Is this normal, natural? It is so sudden, so full on ...' I ask as my consciousness returns and I reacquaint myself with my surroundings. I find Jeremy's face equally as amazed and fascinated as I feel. He gently removes the vibrator and carefully seals it in a plastic bag. 'More tests?'

'More results, more discoveries, greater good, you know ...'

'From mind-blowingly awesome sex, who would have thought?'

'Even I never believed it would be like this.'

'Well, I'm very happy to partake in these experiments, Dr Quinn.'

'Right back at you, sweetheart!'

We don't say much else for a while, lost in our own little worlds and too satiated, just comfortable with each other's bodies, touching, caressing, arousing. Words aren't necessary as we happily prolong our experience and the infectious waves of pleasure and aftershocks.

'While I have you here, it's time for more ointment.'

'You have to be joking? You did it not long ago,' I complain.

'And how effective do you think that will be after our recent activity?' he questions, raising his eyebrows.

I just shake my head.

'I promised to look after you, and you know how dedicated I am to my work!'

He holds my buttocks in position while tenderly applying the ointment. As I look back up at him over my shoulder, he gives me a cheeky wink and blows me a kiss.

* * *

True to his word, Jeremy spends the rest of the week looking after me. He feeds me, bathes me, monitors me, medicates me, stimulates me physically, stimulates me intellectually, exhausts me emotionally, ensures I sleep, brushes my hair, massages my body, heals my wounds and my bruises. I don't make a single decision or liaise with the outside world. It is as if there is no world outside Avalon. I am securely wrapped in the carefully constructed cocoon of Dr Quinn. I have never felt like this in my life. So utterly cared for, so utterly fragile, almost as if I had always needed him to take care of me. How had I ever survived without him?

We continue to talk, laugh, play and reminisce; it's as if we are on our own little version of a honeymoon. It's pure bliss. Except that I miss Jordan and Elizabeth and it's so hard knowing I can't contact them in their wilderness. It has never been this long, but even if I were at home they wouldn't be back yet, so that eases my mind. I push the discussion I know I need to have with Robert on my return to the far outskirts of my mind. Presumably, the world is operating as it always has outside of this place and I, removed from all other reality, exist solely within the isolation of this luxurious treehouse and Jeremy's love and attention.

'Come here and let me check your blood pressure. You appear to have more energy than before.'

'Not again! You've monitored me so much I could well be the most examined case study in history.' He ignores my exaggerated statement.

'If it has returned to normal, we'll go to the beach. Actually, it is really good. No wonder you have more energy. Why don't you get yourself ready and I'll pack a picnic lunch? There is a box in the walk-in robe with everything you need.'

I stand staring at him dubiously, firstly wondering if he is serious and secondly, what he is up to this time.

'Go and get ready before I change my mind.' His words trigger me into action.

I breathe a sigh of relief to find normal clothes in the box, thankful that I am no longer required to play 'dress ups'. I put on a swimming costume under a sundress, just in case the water is warm enough for a quick dip. I grab sunglasses, hat and sunscreen and feel more energised and fabulous than I can remember. Jeremy has a backpack ready to go and we finally embark out the giant double doors of the treehouse. A driveway heads up behind the house towards the ridge of the mountain. I notice a large man standing outside a checkpoint-type hut. He is in uniform and has a rifle slung over his shoulder. Jeremy acknowledges his wave as I am swiftly guided in the opposite direction, down toward the beach. Shivers scale down my spine as an eerie feeling flows through me.

'I thought we were completely alone. Is that necessary?'

'I'll explain everything when we get to the beach.'

For the first time in days, I notice a perilous undertone in Jeremy's words, but I don't want to think about it.

We settle ourselves down on the blanket with a beautifully laid out picnic feast before our eyes. The expansive view is as endless as it is breathtaking with the sky crystal clear. 'Wow, this place is incredible. I hope we're in no rush to leave.'

'We have plenty of time. It's great to be outdoors with you again.'

'It's even better being able to see the outdoors this time.'

He affectionately smooths some loose strands of my hair away from my face and tucks them behind my ear.

'How are you, really?' he asks gently.

'I feel so much better now, thank you. How could I not? I have had your undivided physical, emotional, mental and medical attention. What about you? You look like you have much on your mind.'

'I do. There's quite a bit I need to explain to you and I couldn't risk it up there.'

His hand motions behind us.

'How come?'

'Truthfully? I'm not sure whether it's bugged or not. I know we will be safer out here.'

'Bugged? By whom? What's this about, Jeremy?' I look at him nervously. 'Or do I not want to know?'

'I would love not to involve you in any more of this, Alex, but you need to know some of it, as you are right in the middle of it now.'

I have a foreboding that the cocoon Jeremy has so meticulously orchestrated during our time together is slowly but surely about to unravel. He holds my hand and caresses my fingers, as if lost in thought for a while.

'I think you had better tell what you need to, Dr Quinn.' He nods and begins.

'I don't need to enlighten you on the statistics for depression; the market for an effective drug is massive and is only looking to grow over the next decade, particularly in western economies. Antidepressants are a billion dollar industry and every large pharmaceutical company around the world is currently undergoing a frantic search for more effective medications, researching many different avenues and spreading their seed funding nets far and wide. This has become even more urgent given the recent studies conducted by the FDA, which concluded that some antidepressant drugs can be linked to an increase in suicidal tendencies compared to a placebo. All hell has broken loose for companies to develop a new drug. Competition is fierce and desperate and although I hate to admit it, not always above the line. Which is why we need to have this conversation.'

He sounds a little on edge, which is unusual for him and it's why he has my undivided attention.

'Someone hacked into Sam's computer in the last twenty-four hours and will have access to the results I sent him. This is the reason for the added security. We haven't been able to determine who it was and it may take some time. I don't mean to scare you more than necessary, Alexa, but if our competitors stumble upon the potential of the formula we're developing as a result of last weekend, and your involvement in it, well, let's just say it may put you in undue danger. And that is a risk I'm not willing to take. I have organised a qualified bodyguard who will pose as your full-time research assistant at UTAS to ensure your security at work when you return.'

'You're serious?'

'I put you into this situation and I'll take full responsibility for ensuring your safety. I don't know what I would do if anything were to happen to you.'

'What could happen, Jeremy? What are you so worried about?'

'All pharmaceuticals are concerned with protecting their existing and potential patents and the major companies spare no expense in doing so. They have special departments for their investigative work and they aren't staffed by the average person, if you know what I mean. They recruit ex-SEALs, computer hackers, scientists and neurosurgeons, and ex-judges who are or were at the top of their field. Some of the most highly trained and skilled people on the planet are retained on exorbitant sums of money to fulfil certain requirements of the firms they work for.'

'And are you one of those people?'

'No, not necessarily. I have a specific arrangement with a pharmaceutical company in relation to the development of a drug for depression. These special departments are all about ensuring the intellectual property of the company is protected at all stages of development — and at all costs. In essence, they protect the security of our research results. As we get closer to developing a formula or product and embark on the process of preparing for a legal patent, which can be a long-winded process, they become more engaged. Intellectual espionage is rife in the pharmaceutical industry and for some organisations the human cost of achieving patent rights is of no consequence. It's part of the way they conduct business. My concern is that if one of our competitors is involved in the hacking, which hasn't been confirmed at this stage, they may well want to verify our results for themselves.'

'You mean with me?' To say that I'm shell-shocked would be an understatement.

'It's unlikely, but not totally out of the question. I don't want to alarm you, Alex, and I won't let anything happen to you, but you must accept the extra security that will be coming your way. I won't be taking no for an answer.'

'Do you honestly think something could happen?'

'We hope not, but we will certainly be taking extra precautions, just in case. In the meantime, I'd like to give you something, Alexandra, both as a memory of our time together and in the hope that it will help to keep you safe.' His expression is serious. He pulls a small box from his backpack, opens it carefully, and places a solid silver or platinum bracelet into my hand. I study it closely. It appears to be encrusted with what looks like pink diamond chips and illustrated with ancient Gaelic inscriptions, their intricate and delicate design a stark contrast to the bracelet's robust weight.

'Jeremy —' I start.

'Alexandra, since you're not in a position for me to be putting a ring on your finger just yet, I'm hoping that you can promise me you will wear this and not remove it.' He looks deeply into my eyes. 'Will you do it for me?'

I return his gaze. I have been through so much this past week. He has asked me and pushed me to do many things I'd never even imagined, let alone dreamt I would do ... am I going to argue with him about wearing this precious piece of jewellery? I can sense how important this is to him.

'Yes, of course.' As if I'd ever say anything else. 'It's so beautiful. What do these symbols represent?'

'The Gaelic letters for *anam cara*. It means "friend of your soul" or "soul companion".'

My heart swells and I quickly swallow to suppress the deep emotion threatening to swamp me. Our eyes lock and for a long moment we exist in a place full of energy, yet serenely peaceful. I know I belong to him and him to me. Without further words, I extend my arm to him.

'Thank you, Alex. May our souls smile in the embrace of our *anam cara*.'

He places it around my wrist and as he seals the clasp shut, I hear a strange computerised noise. Once again a perfect fit. Not too loose, not too tight, but unable to be slipped over my hand should I want to remove it. I feel undeniably connected to him in every way and am delighted with this physical symbol of our love.

'What was that noise?' I can't help but ask.

'It is digitally encoded, sealed around your wrist both physically and electronically and will enable both Sam's and my teams to access your location 24/7 should anything unforeseen occur. It was important to me that you were happy to wear it willingly before that happened.'

Well, I hadn't considered being connected to him quite as pragmatically as this.

For quite some time, I sit contemplating this precious piece of new 'techno' jewellery, embracing — or perhaps entrapping — my wrist. My mind flicks back to when I did some work for Argyle pink diamond mines in Western Australia and the precautions the company took to ensure the safe delivery of these precious gems from the mine to Perth. Several dummy flights per week occurred so no one knew which flight would carry the actual diamonds — the most rare and expensive diamonds in the world. Now I sit staring at their chips embedded in the bracelet. It really is incredible to consider the lengths and expense companies go to in securing their assets. Just when I thought this *Alice in Wonderland* adventure was coming to a close, now this. My stomach tumbles with emotions. Strangely, no questions flood my mind, just a quiet acquiescence. I sit before him consciously breathing and unconsciously stroking the silver bracelet.

We return to the treehouse many hours later after attempting to wash away the more sinister 'what-if' scenarios of our future in the ocean. It appears to be just the tonic we both needed.

Our last night is significantly more subdued than our previous evenings. We sit comfortably in silence, embracing each other for a long time, absorbing the impact of the path we have finally chosen together. Our conversation is limited, yet our connection is thick with emotion. Our lovemaking has heightened to an intensity that takes on an almost spiritual meaning, as we bask in the awareness that our lives have been irrevocably altered as a result of this experience. We both understand the significance of not knowing what life may become when we leave Avalon. There is an irresistible edge to our unknown fate. Sleep lasts for a mere few hours, as we lay lovingly entwined in each other's bodies.

* * *

As luck would have it, the morning is heavily overcast. When we take off in a private plane, I am given no clue to the terrain below as it is blanketed with clouds and mist until we rise above it into stark sunshine. I'm aware Jeremy is an exceptionally resourceful man when he wants something; I had no idea that resourcefulness extended to the weather. I don't know if we are flying above water or land and he won't budge on telling me the whereabouts of Avalon. He assures me that the less I know, the safer I'll be and that must be his priority. We hold hands the entire flight. At some stage, I doze off, resting my head on his shoulder only to wake up as we commence our descent and our imminent separation.

We hug with deep passion and I shed a few silent tears before I disembark from the aircraft. I don't want to leave his embrace but I know I must. Apparently my luggage will be automatically forwarded and loaded onto my flight to Hobart. Jeremy is continuing on the plane, eventually making his way back toward Boston.

As if on autopilot, I settle in for the flight home, grateful for the empty seats beside me. I attempt to assimilate everything that has happened in the last week, the potential risk of my involvement, and the future of my family life. It is almost too much for my brain. I bend down to place my boarding pass in my handbag and notice a thick envelope in there. I open it up and find a note in Jeremy's handwriting.

> *To my gorgeous Alexandra,*
>
> *I thought you might like to look at these now so you can see more clearly the woman I am in love with. Don't forget her when you return home, she means the world to me.*
>
> *Take care, my love, until we meet again.*
> *Safe travels.*
> *J xo*

To say that I'm shocked to see the photos in front of my eyes would be the understatement of the decade. Could this person really be me? I leaf through them slowly.

* Lecturing on Friday afternoon at the Great Hall
* At lunch with Samuel and his research team
* Arriving at the hotel lobby, hair up, looking businesslike
* In the red dress, blindfold on
* Sitting on the rooftop, blindfolded and cuffed
* Singing and playing the guitar

- Another in a leather jumpsuit and boots
- Two leathered bodies, riding on a motorbike
- Skydiving, freefalling
- Driving, happy with sunglasses in a black convertible
- Floating naked in blackened waters
- Hooded, cloaked body with leather straps
- On the beach, swimming with Jeremy
- Dressed, as I am now, for the plane journey home

It is amazing to see these images compared to the ones I have in my mind. The blindfold seems to mask my nervous tension and my body looks like this undeniably sensuous creature soaking up every experience. The prints have a warming effect on my physiology; I hug them close to my chest. Who would have thought I was this person?

I reflect on the question I couldn't answer Jeremy during our time together: 'Since when does motherhood give you permission to deny your sexuality?'

Who would have thought I had been denying myself all these years? Who would have thought it would take something as extreme as being blind, questionless and open to psychological, physical and neurological experimentation on the limbic system for a weekend to reignite the sexual passion within me? Only Jeremy, of course.

* * *

I enter my home and greet my gorgeous children as though nothing has changed in the world, but secretly knowing everything has. I hug them long and tight and love them more than I ever believed possible.

I decide it is now or never. My week with Jeremy has sealed my fate and I am committed to having the discussion with Robert that I've been putting off for years. I organise for my sister to look after the kids so we can go out to dinner together. I don't want to have this discussion at home, but equally I question whether we should be out in public. I have been running through scenarios in my head about the best way to begin such a sensitive discussion.

I needn't have worried so much. It seems that he has wanted to talk about our marriage as much as I have. I tell him about being with Jeremy and how it has impacted me. How I can't deny his presence in my life any longer. I don't mention my role in the experiment. Robert sits silently across the table as I wait for an emotional response to provide a clue to his thoughts. I am shocked when I see relief. Not anger, not tears, but relief. He eventually explains how he has been struggling with his own sexuality for years, always trying to talk himself around. Not wanting to have the conversation with me because I'm a psychologist and he didn't want his wife analysing him before he had worked things out for himself. And he didn't want to hurt me, or our children. He tells me he too, can no longer deny this part of himself, that he needs to explore and investigate, to discover whether or not he is gay. He believes he is.

I am sitting across from him wondering how my news is going to impact on him and he responds with this! It certainly explains our lack of a sex life. How could I have missed this? I can't help but deliberate on how I would have accepted this revelation had I not had my time with Jeremy. It would have been crushing, I imagine ... but now, well, somehow it makes everything potentially possible where it was impossible just a week or so ago.

We open up to each other more in these hours over dinner than we have for the past five years. Our conversation flows and we engage with each other on a level that stems from respect and friendship. I can understand why I was attracted to this man who sits before me, the father of my children. He is a good man with a good heart. It's just that we don't share each other's hearts any more.

We resolve to make this work for our children and to continue to support each other. It feels like a giant weight has been lifted off our burdened relationship and we are free to engage in the lightness of life again. We smile. We hug. We move into separate rooms under the same roof. We are happy with this arrangement in the short term. The kids notice our change in spirit and we all laugh more than we have in years.

* * *

A few days later, just as Jeremy had promised, I receive a letter inviting me to become a member of his global research forum.

Dear Dr Blake,

I hope this letter finds you in good health. I would like to formally invite you to become a member of our private research team specialising in developing a cure for depression. Your specific skills and expertise are required for the role of psychology lead for Project Zodiac, working closely with a number of accredited medical researchers and practitioners.

As you are aware, this project is highly confidential and will remain so for at least the next twelve months. You will find attached a comprehensive confidentiality

agreement, which must be signed before further
information and background can be released to you.
As our research progresses we may be in a position to
publish our results over the next two to three years,
when your significant contribution to our studies will be
formally recognised.

The research is predominantly part-time at this stage
and accordingly, we are hoping you can accommodate it
with your existing university workload. I have personally
taken the liberty of speaking with your dean, who has
pledged his support in this regard. You will also be
required to attend several international conferences, the
first one being held in London next month, details of
which are outlined in the attached documents. Payment
for your services will be considerable and agreed upon, in
person, in the next fortnight.

Your academic credentials, professional background
and recent research experience are of paramount
importance to the success of this project moving forward
and we truly value your unique contribution. Thank you
for taking the time to meet with us and we look forward
to a fruitful, amiable and productive relationship over the
coming years. We very much look forward to welcoming
you to the team.

Yours sincerely,
Lionel McKinnon
Chairman

My stomach flips as I finish reading the letter; waves of
excitement and apprehension are competing for attention in
the lower part of my body. Colour instantly floods my cheeks.

The letter in my hand looks so official, so noble, its sexual undertones cleverly disguised. I unconsciously caress the bracelet around my wrist.

'Everything okay?' Robert looks up from reading the paper.

I notice my hand trembling as I pass him the letter to read.

'This is about the research you discussed with Jeremy?'

I nod.

'Fantastic news, congratulations! You have worked so hard, you deserve this.' He kisses my cheek. 'This calls for champagne.'

I can't help but wonder what I have done to deserve the men in my life.

Epilogue

Here I am, sitting in first class, which is another thrilling new experience, waiting on the tarmac for take off. I would never have thought in a million years this could be happening to me. I feel like I am steadily becoming the person I was always meant to be. I am so excited about seeing Jeremy again. The butterflies in my stomach are still there, just like before I met him in Sydney, but this time they are big and colourful and I welcome their presence as they let me know I'm vital and alive.

My mind wanders off to the other day when I was working around the city at lunch time. I was walking past a store selling saddles and stirrups, when out of the corner of my eye I noticed a riding crop. Intense emotions ricocheted with such ferocity through my entire body, I was momentarily blinded and breathless as I leaned against the cool glass pane of the shop window. I had been erotically winded! The continual internal low-key buzzing I had acclimatised myself to since my return immediately ramped up to electrifying vibrations from my clitoris to my nipples. I was eternally grateful for padded bras as I found myself gasping for air as heat, like liquid gold, seared my private parts. One of my students, who just happened to be passing by, stopped to ask if everything is alright and whether

I needed any assistance. Even though I nodded that all was well, she stood before me for a full minute, wide-eyed, before I regained enough composure to assure her I was perfectly fine and send her on her way. God, if she only knew. I'm desperate to talk to Jeremy about having these psychophysical ambushes occurring at a single sight, sound or memory of the weekend. One part of me is mortified by these happening in public, but I'm fascinated as to what could trigger another episode and eagerly anticipate the next experience.

My flights are seamless; no delays at Singapore and finally I arrive in London as scheduled.

I walk through the swinging doors at Heathrow and notice a chauffeur standing with my name on a placard. What a pleasure it is to travel like this. We exchange greetings as he takes my luggage.

When we arrive at the black sedan with the door open, there is another man standing beside it dressed in similar attire.

'Good morning, Dr Blake. Welcome to London.'

'Good morning. Thank you, it's great to be here.'

I smile as he opens the door for me and the first man takes care of my luggage. As I settle myself in the back seat ensuring I have everything, I hear my name being called from somewhere in the distance behind me. As I look over my shoulder I am stunned to see Jeremy and Samuel running toward the car. What on earth are they doing here? I didn't think they were due in until late tonight. I wave my hand in surprised recognition as the driver's assistant suddenly shoves the door closed and bolts into the front seat. I see the panic in Jeremy's and Samuel's faces as they run toward me. Just as I am about to ask the driver to wait for them, the car surges forward and I am flung across the seat. I ask them to stop, telling the driver that I know them. Jeremy is now running after the car, banging on the back windows. I try to open my window to speak to him, but there is no button. The window tint turns black and I can't see his face any more. The door is locked and as I turn around to look at the driver, a blackened barrier rises between the back and front seats. I scream and bash on the door and the glass. We are speeding up. I start to tremble as the memory of Jeremy's agonised face is etched on my brain. I fumble for my phone in my handbag, only to find there is no service indicated. I don't understand any of this. I am in a blacked-out car with no phone reception. Who are these drivers? I bang on the windows screaming at the men, trying to make sense of what is happening. I try to open the doors, check both of them, bang my palms against the black tint of the windows. What is this about? Suddenly I feel woozy, faint. Then I don't feel anything at all ...

Author's note

I doubt there are too many people today, in Western societies, who haven't been touched by depression in some way, shape or form. Depression affects around 120 million people worldwide and causes over 850,000 deaths a year. A frightening and staggering statistic that makes it one of the most serious conditions impacting humans.

In the United States, prescriptions for antidepressants have risen nearly 400% since 1988, with more than 1 in 10 Americans over age 12 taking an antidepressant. More than 21 million prescriptions are written each year for stimulant drugs to enhance attention, primarily for children aged between six and fourteen. Antidepressant use in children has risen 333% in the past decade.

Interesting, isn't it?